Heroes of the Third Age:
Merilanna

Shadows
of the Light

A World of Narianna Novel

H. Shane Alford

Cover Photographs by
Khaleesi-26 © Cathleen Tarawhiti / DeviantArt
The Witcher-Geralt © GreatQueenLina / DeviantArt
The Witcher-Geralt © Shihouart (Photographer) / DeviantArt

Cover Design by H. Shane Alford

Edited by Cheri A. Bernard-Alford

Maps and Art by H. Shane Alford

Published by Mystic Merlin's LLC
www.mysticmerlins.com

ISBN-13: 978-0-9890730-97

Printed in the United States of America

DEDICATION

This book is dedicated to Dee Hayden who poured so much love into the creation of Merilanna, the character spotlighted through the eyes of Lyri, the Child of Shadows, in this work. In part, this novel is to say thank you. In part, it is to bring the wonderful persona you imagined to life for the enjoyment of the readers. Truly, I appreciated all you did with her at the game table through the years; and, though, this is my rendition of her, I hope that I have, in some small way, done her justice. Through her – and, of course, through you – the World of Narianna has been made a richer place. She will always be yours. Thank you for sharing her with me.

AUTHOR'S NOTE

It has been said that writing a book is a labor of love. Birthing the characters and the world in which they dwell takes a commitment of time, energy, and patience, so, as a father of four, I can appreciate that adage – though, I confess, more credit is due my wife than me for our wonderful kids. When I set out to write *Shadows of the Light,* I did so with every expectation that it would be a long, arduous, and often frustrating process. I had completed my trilogy, *The Waystone Saga,* and had muscled through the first *Heroes of the Third Age* novel over the past decade and, over a million words later, was still trying to figure out how to be a good author. The job does not really have a defined job description, so the measure of that effort remained undefined in my mind. I, at least – and this may be true for every writer – was never satisfied with what I had written. I knew only that I felt more comfortable with the process and considered my later works superior to my first. Still, I asked myself more than once if this "book thing" was just a flight of fancy or something that I earnestly wished to pursue. Ever, I leaned towards the latter, but the self-reflection was still there.

Three things happened in 2019 and early 2020 that pushed me along and helped me reach this point again: writing an Author's Note at the beginning of another, my fifth, completed book.

First, I took the year off. I did not write, other than my constant scenario spinning for my Saturday *Dungeons & Dragons* group. Instead, I spent the year traveling to conventions and readying much of the marketing and branding materials I felt I needed to move forward with this "book thing" as something more than a dalliance and diversion. Of course, I realized that the blade of my art was in danger of growing dull by doing so, but I both needed the break and I needed to step back far enough to regain my perspective. Some hone was lost, I suppose, but my view of my work, my passion, was renewed.

The second thing that happened may seem small; but, sometimes, it is the small things that matter. Specifically, I had traveled to Charleston, a couple hours from my home in Columbia, South Carolina, to attend the AtomaCon sci-fi and fantasy convention. I had heard through chatting with other authors that there would be a number of panels held that were geared towards new, aspiring writers and that it would be well-worth me going. So, I did. Now, I have been to many conventions in my time, so I was accustomed to the zaniness and fun of fandom. In years long passed, I would have been clad in my best medieval chainmail and hobnobbing with the rest of the crowd. This time, though, I was more focused and purposeful; and, thanks to some sound advice, reaped a great deal from the trip. It was there that I met James Nettles with Author Essentials. He took the time to peruse my last book, *Lightbringer*, and we chatted for well over an hour sitting in the hotel lobby. I am sure that Jim has done this with countless others. Helping authors become successful – by whatever measure they use – is what he does when not crafting books of his own. Nonetheless, it was good counsel he offered and I appreciated it very much.

One of his suggestions was that I write a novella, a bite-sized piece – not the three to four-hundred thousand word behemoths that I was accustomed to doing. A work of that scope would be more manageable to produce and would provide me a new, attainable opportunity to introduce myself to my intended audience. I agreed; it made sense. After that conversation, I knew what I needed to do next: write this book. Thus, I set out to spin this tale in late December of 2019 and finished the manuscript draft at the end of April, 2020. I had intended to have it done before my next convention date in May at ConCarolinas and had succeeded. Unfortunately, the coronavirus pandemic tossed out my hope of catching up with Jim at the convention to show what I had done. Steinbeck was right: "The best-laid plans of mice and men often go awry."

Third was SAGA, a convention geared specifically to aspiring authors, this one held in Charlotte, North Carolina. I remember well arriving at the hotel around midmorning Friday. The wind was absolutely howling. I am not likely to forget that because I ended up chasing my fedora halfway across the parking lot. After a two hour drive, I guess the Fates had decided that I could use the exercise. Luckily, my prize hat was saved from becoming roadkill.

Once I got checked in, I went downstairs to the conference room level and oriented myself to the lay of the land. There would be seminars over the next three days and I wanted to be sure I knew where everything was. Jim was there along with John Hartness of Falstaff Books, with whom I had chatted on several occasions. Too, I mingled with other familiar authors and enjoyed good tales and light banter.

Saturday, between a couple of sessions, I decide to pick up a book from the bountiful offering. As it turned out, I bought a trilogy: David Coe's *The Lon Tobyn Chronicle* and, during the break, started reading the preface material for *Children of Amarid.* As I read, I was struck by something that I had, for whatever reason, not considered. In the foreword, David explained that the book was the author's edit and that he had felt compelled to go back and revisit his earlier works, knowing that his skills as a writer had improved and wanting very much to sharpen his prose in this trilogy. To more veteran writers, this may have seemed unremarkable. I learned by querying some other authors that weekend that they, too, had revisited their prior projects. It was far from an irregular practice. To me, though, newbie that I am, it validated the desire that I had long held to go back to my first book in the Waystone Saga, *Shadows of the Past,* and do better. After all, if the first book in a series is its weakest link, it does not matter how good the second and third books are. Readers will never get there because the first was the least illustrious. Of course, this revelation did not pertain directly to this book, but it did help me gain a better sense of where I was in my career as an author. It was heartening to know that what I was thinking and feeling was not uncommon. It was a little thing; but, again, sometimes it is the little things that matter most.

So, here I sit on the evening of the 28th of April, 2020, and muse and reminisce about what has brought me to this point, the Author's Note for my fifth book, and I think to myself: Maybe this is what I am meant to do. Maybe, I can be a good author. It is still a maybe, but I am giving it my best effort. You, my readers, will be the judge.

Thank you for picking up this book. I hope you enjoy it as much as I enjoyed writing it. Admittedly, Lyri is one of my favorite characters, and I knew she would do a good job introducing you to Narianna, my world, again, and to Merilanna, whom I think you will like as well.

Shadows of the Light
Heroes of the Third Age: Merilanna

Chapter 1: Hunting Demons

I stood in the darkness amidst the wintry wind of night and listened to the screams of men dying. Everywhere, all around me, their cries filled the chill air. Ringing steel sounded through the chorus of voices, cutting them with clamor and sending their wails into the snow-strewn sky. Above, great grey trees arched and ached, crackled and groaned as the elements howled back, thrashing their proud limbs and suffocating the chthonic roar beneath their boughs. Wood against wood. Steel against steel. No silvery moon stood guard in the sky as lives were lost. No stars shined down with pity or judgment or remorse. The gods gave no heed to the carnage. All above was empty, a monotonous void of cold impassivity.

The rawhide seams of my boots wept, unable to withhold the insidious seeping that wormed within. The ground beneath me was a gelid, churned mix of befouled snow and mud that sucked at my feet. Water and blood oozed betwixt my toes.

Though the tempest raged, the smell of burning homes and those dead and dying, charred within them, yet reached my nose. Snow and smoke rode the same whirling winds. Both stung my eyes and skin. I could taste the bitterness; I could taste the horror.

Fire warred with ice as lives burned before me.

Where I stood, a green field of wheat would be born in the spring. I wondered if its farmer would survive this night to tend it again. As I looked about in all directions and surveyed the diffused, orange glows, I knew that hope was small indeed.

My innocence had died on a night like this. In the mud and in the blood, I had lost my world also. But I remembered everything.

In the hoary gale, in the darkness, in the nightmare, my heart held a beat. I closed my eyes, focusing upon all around me, seeking a breath of calm just as an old friend had once taught me to do. In that instant, the whole of it – every bloodcurdling scene – invaded my mind in gruesome detail.

I shook as rage overtook me once more.

As always, the moment of inner balance was fleeting and quickly exhaled, fogging the wind as resolve ignited in my soul. Then my anger flared and my glare snapped upon the shadows shifting through the flames. My enmity would soon be theirs.

My sword, Wind-Song, caught the light as snow kissed her edge, shattering the sanguine glow. I heard her sing as she split the shrieking wind. The flickering flakes shimmered as they trembled in fear.

It was time for demons to die.

Between the world of the living and realms of the dead, there is a thin Veil. For most, it is a barrier that only in death may be slipped. Only by dying can their souls cross over. For me, death came cruelly; it was neither kind nor everlasting. I was denied my mortal rest. I knew no such peace. I was cast back, never to reach Urrel's great hall to sing with my ancestors. A goddess had woven my fate so. No choice was I given.

You may wonder: What evil had I done that I should be so condemned? What transgression or blasphemy had earned me my sentence? After all, to behold me, to envision that I deserved such a judgment defies your senses. How, you would ask, how could a child, a girl of ten years, have provoked the heavens so? Why would the gods hate her – she, who to all appearances, offends none.

Your question and your confoundment were my own, once. Why death had favored me was a mystery which seared my soul and fueled my hate. I hated the gods. I despised their wanton persecution. I had done nothing to deserve their curses. They had made me into this monster: neither alive nor dead; not of this world – though born of it – nor any next. How could I do anything other than revile them?

In the end, none of it mattered. No measure of scorn, defiance, or contempt alleviated my suffering. I was cast into the fire and tempered by a destiny threaded into the Tapestry of Creation. It was of no consequence what my dreams might have been. That innocence was taken and ripped apart. Mercy was not an option. The heavens needed a weapon, and that weapon was me.

Along the Cusp of the Veil, where the shining laws of the gods are dimmed, where Twilight begins, I moved towards the fires. Around me, the world was cast in a bluish sheen. The ghosts of the newly dead staggered, staring at their fallen forms, bewildered by the shock of death. Them, I ignored. There was nothing I could do to guide them, to show them to salvation. That was not my part to play in all of this. My role was darker.

Pyres rose up around me: a barn, a circle of small houses, fences wherein animals would roam in warmer times. Everything was burning. Many were corpses.

In the middle of it all, I slipped from the Veil and felt the biting wind again. In the Cusp, everything moved with watery indolence. Time abated. An instant seemed an hour; an hour, an eternity. In the carnal world, however, I snapped into the present like a silent thunderclap, felt but not heard.

My cloak had barely lifted into the blasting gusts before every wicked eye turned my way.

Thus, is my greatest charm and the black blessing I bear. So deep is the well of my darkness that every vile wind succumbs and is drawn into its maelstrom.

From the Cusp I stepped and all the demons whipped to me. A howling, they rushed.

For the besieged souls of this small village, ironically, through me, some mercy was granted. Not all of them would die this night. Perhaps, the farmer might yet live to tend his field.

The first demon to find me tore into view, sprinting from around the corner of the burning barn. Like so many I had hunted of late, the fiend rode the soul of a Dyard warrior. Clad in furs, the tribesman hefted a wicked war club. Shards of black crystal festooned its surface in long rows. The weapon's length matched my height. Given my slight form, I guessed its mass did my weight as well. Blood gleamed upon the brutal thing.

Paint traced the berserker's snarling visage. Bones rattled about his neck as his fetishes danced. More, sharp and fearsome, pierced his nose and ears. Against his pitch-black skin, the trinkets gleamed in contrast. In all, he was bestial – more like a monster than a man, towering, muscular, and terrifying. In his eyes, I saw the fires around me blaze.

More appeared, drawn to me like damned moths. The accursed magic that flowed through my blood brought them on, delirious in their lust to claim it.

I waited as they closed.

Beyond the Veil, tenebrous tendrils stretched out behind the Dyards. Black Arts had bound them to shadows. Their mortal coils where entwined by diabolic rites. I could see their demons in the ethereal light, whipping them to frenzy. Their hunger transcended all reason, all fear, all care.

I stood in the center of the trap.

They came. And I sprang their doom.

The first to meet it was not the charging brute. One of his brothers was given that honor.

Behind me, I heard snowflakes shattering as a javelin pierced the wind and flew towards my heart. Its arc was true, shallow and sure, swift and certain. No chance would an Asgev child have of escaping its barbs. Its sender grinned with assured glee.

How odd it must have seemed to him, then, when the missile's pointy end impaled only the swirling ashes where his quarry had stood. It took a few blinks of his widening eyes before he realized that his own heart would thunder no more.

He looked down at me, confused. I looked up at him along the length of my sword and smirked. He watched as I slowly withdrew my blade from his chest. The furs he wore wiped away his blood.

I turned towards the others. Each studied the air where I had been. To their eyes, I had simply vanished.

The thud of the tribesman upon the snow behind me caught the nearest ear. Its owner cried out, redirecting his fellows. There were six.

I slipped the Veil. The firelight flashed blue and white as the world blurred.

Then there were five.

The man that had screamed watched his own body fall before darkness filled his rolling eyes. His head came to rest at the feet of the warrior with the wicked club before he realized his end.

Four. Three. Two.

The last Dyard looked up from the face of his brother and saw the others drop.

I waited within the Cusp, watching as his ferocity drained away. Terror replaced it drop by drop. Searching, he spun about. His club trembled in his outstretched hands.

I let him suffer. I let his fear build.

He panted, huffing hot breath into the deadly wind.

Ting.

The steel of my sword chimed as I tapped him on his back.

Stung by panic, he leapt and twirled about, his warclub leading the way. His war cry sounded most unmanly.

I watched the weapon's lumbering arc and timed its path impatiently. Shifting into the ether, it passed without consequence.

Overwhelmed by the desperate momentum, the warrior lost his footing. The wet snow betrayed him. He sprawled most ignominiously.

Now I towered and he cowered.

From his back, the demon behind his eyes beheld Oblivion. There was no escape.

I could see my pale face reflected in his black eyes. My countenance was colder than the storm.

He stammered something in his strange tongue.

I cocked my head and read the sound. I am not sure what he said, but the words were awash with terror. Too bad.

"Yes," I said back. "I am Death."

I walked away leaving the Dyard to cough and thrash. His breath and his blood steamed and sprayed from the slash across his throat.

"That wasn't very nice," an annoying voice chided wryly from the shadows.

"I didn't like what he said," I snapped curtly towards my critic. My eyes cut his figure out from the shadows. His own glowed like golden suns in the firelight.

"Hmm," the spectator chuckled, "I'll take care with what I say then."

"Unlikely," I replied. "You're too much the fool for that." My glare became a glower. The attack on the village was far from over. "We're not done here, Fhaed. Where are the others?"

He smirked. "They're coming...riding hard. Not all of us move at the speed of your ire, Lyri. Most of us are mortal."

Knowingly, he surveyed my handiwork. "Step into my web, said the spider to the flies," he murmured, marveling.

The runes upon his eldritch sword hissed and smoldered as he unshouldered his great blade.

"They're all demons," I stated the obvious.

Fhaed nodded. "You didn't claim them," he observed calmly. The mirth had passed; his demeanor grew serious.

"I wanted to," I confessed. Looking to the last Dyard that I had dispatched, my dark hunger gnawed at my will. "I really, really wanted to."

I hungered for the darkness in men's souls just as they lusted for mine. Like a drug, I devoured their wickedness. It satiated the monster within me, if only for a short time. I fed upon their shadows and savored the insidious, damnable power it gave me. With it, I defied even the gods of heaven and mocked their arrogance.

Disgusted, I tore my gaze away and found Fhaed's. He was watching me – as always. His eyes were gentle; they bore me no judgment, only empathy. Fhaed, alone, understood my struggle – better than anyone else could, anyway. He, too, had stared into the yawning, black pit of the Abyss. He grasped something of the depths of my hunger. Still, a vile as I was, he did not forsake me. I was an enigma, cursed and robbed of my innocence; but, inexplicably, I was not alone. For that, though it was hard for me to admit, I was very grateful. Fhaed stood by steadfast. He wouldn't let me fall.

Resolved, the demon-hunter moved to the black hulk and extended his sword. The arcane markings upon it flared with red fire, an incandescent glow like that of a blacksmith's furnace. I could hear the demons bound within the molten sigils shrieking.

The Dyard's body suddenly convulsed. His back arched and his limbs splayed. Had his throat not been cut, no doubt he would have screamed.

Reflexively, I let my vision slip into Twilight. There, in its bluish glow, I watched as the demon trapped in the warrior's body was torn from the man's flesh. Tendrils of shadow streamed to Fhaed's sword like smoke returning to a fire. In a moment, it was over. The corpse collapsed and Fhaed lifted his blade and studied it. One of its arcane marks blazed with satisfaction.

Methodically, the demon hunter repeated the process with each of the remaining members of the war band, incarcerating one fiend after another, imprisoning them within his black sword.

"I'm going after more of them," I announced as he finished.

"I'd argue with you, but what's the point?"

"There isn't one," I answered flatly. "They're going to pay for all of this."

Fhaed looked about at the carnage, sighed, and acceded with a slight bow of his head. "Just be careful," he chastened paternally.

I frowned.

Fhaed lifted his hand cajolingly, "Look, the *Aesyranna* warned us to be on our guard. There's something new driving the Dyards now that their witch-king is dead. She can't see what it was…"

"You be careful, then," I snapped. "I'm going to find out what it is. Then, I'm going to kill it!"

"Lyri, there are a lot of demons in the world – now more than ever. Now that shadows have fallen, there's no telling how many or what sorts."

I listened but I did not relent.

Fhaed did. He smiled thinly. "Just be careful."

"I'm not the one carrying a sword full of demons," I quipped. Before he could sigh, I slipped into the Cusp and vanished. There were still screams to follow.

I did not know by what name this village had been called. Like so many scattered throughout Einhervaldheim, it had probably been redubbed by its conquerors to suit their fancy. The largest settlement of any size, Talvekstad, was a half-day's ride to the east along the same river as this woe-begotten place. It was named for a brutal warlord, a man of whose infamy even I was aware. But, then again, butchers seldom remain anonymous or forgotten. I guess that's why his people acclaimed him so generously. He had served them well.

Einhervaldheim was my homeland, but even that name, so cherished by my people, the Asgevar, had been broken beneath the heels of its new masters, the Turanians, since before my mortal birth. For decades, with their every imperious stomp, they had shattered the sacred forests, plains, and hills and made of them a mosaic of duchies and baronies – haughty terms that meant nothing to my folk. Altogether, they called their grand creation Alli-Turan, the "Land of the Knights," a realm where civilization had beaten back the barbarians – like me.

It was a gilded lie, of course. Our barbarity was daring to hold onto the beliefs of our ancestors, to guard our culture, and to defend our homes.

I never understood by what right they dared to claim us.

No, that's not true. I did. I had learned. I had left my naivete in the mud, snow, blood and ash when my own life was taken and burned by their hands. There was only one right that really mattered: the right of conquest. Now, the whole world was at war, and I was in the middle of it, torn by all sides and allied with my enemies against enemies of us all.

The gods were truly mad!

The irony tonight was deep. I was here saving Turanians from a new invader, a new barbaric horde risen from the south. I might have laughed at this ridiculous twist of fate had it not been so profoundly unfunny.

I didn't let my mordancy linger long – not because I had grown nobler through time, but rather, I suppose, because I had not grown crueler despite it all. There was no greater irony than that.

Oh, I had hate aplenty to go around. Yet, something in my childish heart still survived the insanity and the wickedness. I could not bring myself to see these people, running with their children in their arms, as monsters or invaders or conquerors. I had seen real ones and knew well the difference.

Call that ennobling, if you wish. I do not. I just count their tears no less real than my own.

The Dyards, though? For them, I held far less pity or mercy. Perhaps, they, too, loved their children and prayed for a peaceful life. Who can say? It is easy to hate those you don't know or understand. But, so far as the Dyards were concerned, all I had seen, all I had known were demons clad in flesh. The tribesmen had embraced the darkest shadows. They had surrendered to the fiends that dwelled there. That was their choice. That was their doing. Thus, they were condemned and I was their condemner.

Hundreds fell in my wake through the night. Fhaed had his work cut out for him.

These are heavy, heady thoughts for a young girl, you may believe. Hate, war, slaying hell-spawn – such things are not commonly associated with the life of a child. I would only argue that you know nothing of me. How could you? What little I have scribbled here is not enough for you to decipher my soul. So, I will not begrudge your skepticism or your confusion. My story is too twisted for a short recounting anyway. Suffice it to say, then, that death took me as a child, but my life ever since has been far from childlike. Again, such was not my choice. I was not given one.

As the grey glow of dawn limned the heavy, winter sky, a war horn blared. I had reached the center of the village. Some of the wattle and daub structures still stood, though fire consumed their thatch roofs. Above, upon a high, manmade hill, a fort sat watching them burn. A deep ditch guarded its base. Therein, frosted water blazed, catching the fiery light and casting it back. The river beyond wore the flames also, but it still flowed.

Upon the timber palisade, pennants flew and heralded the lord of these lands, a Turanian duke. Justinian Nighthawk was his name. Between the hewn post tops, I could see the fearful faces of those that ran the fastest and had escaped the Dyard's raid. They stared down at the growing flames, all hope gone from their eyes. Me, they could not see. I remained a ghost to their mortal eyes, a grim specter standing in hell just beyond the Cusp.

In the blue haze of Twilight, I paused, listening to the horn's note ebb. Odd. It was not a plaintive Turanian call begging for aid. The voice of their trumpets had a sharper pitch. No, it was an Asgev horn, deep and throaty. As well, it came not from the keep. Its robust cry sounded from the west, across the river. Too, it was a rallying sound, not a plea but a beckon.

My steps were drawn its way. I reached the riverbank before I shook myself free from its allure.

"Magic," I spat. Oh, how I hate magic.

A shiver ran through me as the horn sounded again. The call transcended the air and rippled the ether. Spirit magic!

Movement caught my eyes. Left. Right.

Beside me, ghosts drifted by. The blizzard could not touch me, but I felt their eerie chill. I saw their shimmering auras. Like wisps of silvery smoke, they passed. Across the river, they went.

Some were Asgevar. Some were Turanian. Some were even Dyards. Curious…all heeded the horn.

The sound of hooves in wet snow and mud returned my face towards the village. I heard horses snorting and heaving from their exertion. In moments, a band of riders caught the firelight. It gleamed upon their steel as they galloped into view. Their leader, a grand knight in plate armor, shined brightest of all.

"About time," I muttered.

From the fort, a joyous shout rose. Salvation had arrived.

I didn't care that none of it would be attributed to me. Glory was other people's business.

My attention went back to the river. On the far shore, the last, pale glow of the spirits was fading into the wood line. I started to follow, then hesitated.

I hate hesitating.

In the Veil, a flowing river in the mortal world is not an obstacle. That shiver of magic though…it still prickled my flesh; it iced my steps. It warranted caution.

"Be careful." Fhaed's voice reached out from my mind and pulled back on my reins.

I snarled and stepped back into the corporeal wind. Reluctantly, I turned and trudged back through the snow towards the village.

Appearing out of thin air from the darkness of night amidst the revelers that were spilling out of the keep's gate might have amused me; but, for the sake of my more diplomatically minded companions, I chose to walk amongst them in a more mundane manner. Enough demons had fallen upon these poor people for one night. So, I was charitable.

Skirting the throng, I found Fhaed quickly enough. He, too, held to the shadows arear of the gathering.

Sir Iaom, the aforementioned knight gallant, had dismounted and was clasping the forearms of the local lords. I detested pleasantries and tried to ignore their flowery salutations.

To Fhaed, I offered my own sort of hello.

"Are you sick?" I said crossly as I shouldered up to the same tree where he leaned, arms folded casually within his cloak.

He regarded me with his golden eyes from beneath its cowl and grinned broadly, knowing well that he was being baited. He took it anyway. "No, why?"

I gestured to the survivors with a jut of my chin. "You just saved a village full of farmers' daughters yet here you are, standing like a scarecrow, all alone in the cold."

The demon hunter eyed the crowd and smiled. A few lovelies merited his notice.

Sourly, I read his countenance as he made a show of considering pleasant options.

"I must be, then," he chuckled at last. "But – if I should dare to correct you – I'm not alone."

He was trying to be charming. But I was not so easily baited or beguiled by his roguish wit.

"Hmm," I scoffed, glancing to the seething sword swung into the baldric on his back. "I guess not. You have lots of new friends to keep you company."

Fhaed snorted and assuaged. "None are as lovely as you, Petunia."

I rolled my eyes up at the grinning devil. They blazed with hellfire. "You're not being careful," I warned.

He laughed and unfolded his arms, his gloved fingers fanning like a shield to guard against my glare. "Alright…alright, I'll join the maidens if that's what you want. It's the least I can do."

I was caught by my own hook. I fumed. "Do what you want," I muttered. "I don't care."

"Oh, that hurts." Fhaed clutched his chest above his heart in feigned agony.

My teeth locked my tongue in my mouth before my juvenile reflexes could shoot it forth. Inwardly, I chided myself with a vicious curse. With Fhaed, I was always reckless. I never felt in control. Basically, he vexed me…a lot…and he basked in stoking my fire.

"Enough," I hissed and changed the subject. "Did you hear the war horn?"

Fhaed nodded. His expression twisted as he mused, struggling to ascribe words to what he had heard. "It was odd," he stated finally.

"Very," I agreed.

"I've only heard one like it, but that was in Armadar. The Morarmadin used it to call the damned to prayer."

My puzzled expression must have alarmed him.

"Are *you* alright?" he asked.

"Armadar? But that was an Asgev horn."

Fhaed's brows lifted. "I'm pretty sure it wasn't."

I looked back to the mass of people. My brow knitted. I frowned. "I hate magic," I whispered.

"Hmm, you heard an Asgev horn and I heard an Armadeshi horn." Fhaed pursed his lips then clucked his tongue. "Odd, indeed."

"It called to the spirits," I explained and guided his gaze back towards the river with my own. "Something's out there."

"Harvesting souls? That's a game we know something about."

"I'm not so sure," I hedged.

Our darkening thoughts were interrupted as one of Iaom's men-at-arms approached. "Lord Chael, My Lady," he ventured respectfully with a slight bow, "the captain would know if the hunt will go on tonight." He faltered, gathering a breath. "If so, the horses will need to rest first."

I studied the man. Clearly, he was faring no better than the horses. None of the cohort were. The cold and the hard ride had battered them towards their graves.

"No," I replied, to his obvious relief. "Rest."

The soldier bowed again and withdrew. Fhaed and I watched him return with the welcome words to his fellows. They would relish warm, safe lodging in the fort for what little remained of the night.

Absently, I brushed the snow from my hair then looked back to my tall companion.

"You're not done with the hunt," he noted offhandedly.

"I want to know who is blowing that horn."

"So do I." His gaze surveyed the icy river. "Too far to jump and no bridge in sight," he joked, resigned to the reality that the hunt would go on without him.

"I'll be careful," I promised then flicked a glance towards the retreating crowd entering the fort.

"Do," came his simple reply. All jesting was done. I knew he meant it.

I nodded once then slipped the Veil.

Within the blue of Twilight, I waited and watched as Fhaed resettled his sword on his shoulder, fogged the air with a long exhale, then jogged to join the others.

"I will," I whispered. My predatory eyes then turned towards the distant shore and narrowed.

Chapter 2: Moth to a Flame

Crossing the river proved harder than I thought. Riding the Cusp, terrestrial forces have little power...usually. I've treaded over water and walked through fire; I've pierced gales and flown through hailstorms; I've scaled sheer cliffs and slipped through the cracks in the earth. So, dashing across this mere tributary should have required nothing extraordinary. But it did. There was a headwind of a different sort opposing me: the will of another soul. It proved a force to be reckoned with.

Oh, I still managed, but the same magic that had summoned the spirits worked hard to repel me. I had scarcely stepped from the near shore before the turbulence hit. The ether, ever so still and calm, exploded without warning into a hurricane. My skin crackled as spectral lightning traced my limbs. Beads of energy washed over me like wind-driven rain across a windowpane. I spun and spiraled, hammered by the fantastic energy. Too late, I recognized its nature. Too late, I realized that the threads of the Tapestry of Creation itself were snarling around me. I was a spider ensnared in another spider's web. And then, just as suddenly, all of the tension snapped. I fell into a void at the eye of the storm and hit the far shore hard. My landing had no measure of grace. I tumbled and I sprawled. Wet ferns enveloped me.

As pealing thunder faded from my eardrums, I shook my dazzled eyes back into focus. All around me there were ferns – thick, green, humid ferns. They covered the shore of the river, basking in the hot sun.

I had begun my crossing of the river in the depths of winter; but, it seemed, I had ended it in the middle of summer.

Despite the aching that filled me head to toe, I forced myself to rise.

Twilight was gone. I had been snatched from it. The world with all of its vibrant colors surrounded me.

I spun back towards the river. It flowed swiftly, silver and green, painted by dancing sunlight. I looked to the far shore. There was no motte. There was no fort. There was no village. Just more ferns and more forest. All was primordial, beautiful, and…terrifying.

My lips mouthed Fhaed's name as I struggled to make sense of what I saw.

Instinctively, I leaped for the Cusp, for the shelter of Twilight.

Nothing happened.

It wasn't there!

"I'm dreaming," I declared, trying to convince myself that my senses were lost in some fabrication in my mind.

When I'm afraid, I have a rather primal response: I get angry.

"What in shadows is going on?" I demanded of my strange and wondrous environ.

Nothing…

No reply save for my own pleading voice. "Wake up, you fool."

I stood there for a ridiculous length of time, exposed and paralyzed. The world seem to grow larger and larger as I did. Or, was it that I felt myself becoming smaller and smaller, diminishing with each pounding beat in my chest?

Anxiously, I let fly my senses, reaching out as far as I could with them. Part of being the monstrosity that I was included having preternaturally keen awareness. Before the crossing, if an earthworm farted, I heard it, felt it, and smelled it. Now, the world was unbearably dulled. I heard the river. I heard the wind in the trees. I heard the voices of the forest. I heard my own frantic heart and the chuffing of my breath. But, beyond that, I heard nothing.

My wits circled in my brain searching for reason.

"Trapped," I muttered. "It was a trap." I always assume the worst. It's a survival thing.

Slowly, I shook myself free from my rigor and surveyed my surroundings. I still wasn't sure if I was inside my own mind. Unfortunately, everything felt real, albeit, less real than I was accustomed to.

After a few more minutes of brooding, I set my glare back in the direction from where the horn had blared. If this was a trap, I mocked its maker. Jaw set, I headed into the forest. Freedom lay that way and the bastard would pay for his audacity.

Wading through wet ferns did not prove overly difficult. Wind-Song's razor-sharp edge made short work of any impeding vegetation. Once beyond the floodplain, the undergrowth thinned anyway, preferring the sunlight to the dappled shade beneath the great Silverwood trees. Game trails appeared also, easing my trek. Still, I was in hill country, so there were no straight paths. Everything that lived here meandered. I was obliged to do so as well.

Soon, I realized that my condition was a bit more perilous than I had imagined. The trap maker was indeed insidious. My demonic prowess was totally gone!

Climbing over hills, even when winding about on ready trails, was tiring – a sensation I had not endured for a very long time. It was unfamiliar and wholly unwelcome. Not only had my transformation muzzled my formidable senses, but also, it had enfeebled my body. My speed, my strength, and my endurance were all taxed. Within a few hours, I was huffing and puffing along, sweat stinging my eyes. Eventually, I was forced to do something I had not needed to do in a very long time. I had to rest.

It didn't get any better after that. The old burdens of thirst and hunger – the mundane sorts – beset me...and irritated me all the more.

A few insolent brambles along the way also reminded me what scratches were like. My flesh did not heal in the following instant. Lingering pain was an unwelcome sign of mortality. I had walked into a nightmare and I was not a bit amused.

By the time evening approached, my whole body was complaining. My stomach protested its neglect. My feet hurt. Everything ached. I needed food, a fire, and a place to sleep – another aspect of mortal life that had grown alien to me.

Thankfully, before my curse took hold, believe it or not, I had lived a normal existence. I had a family; we had a humble farm in a small village. I had been happy – just a child whose days were filled with chores and play. It seems now so strange now.

That was a different life, but it prepared me for today. I was not totally bewildered by my circumstances. My parents had taught me the rudiments of survival. I knew how to build a fire and how to forage. Even if this was some figment of my imagination, it mirrored Einhervaldheim, my homeland. So, I wasn't going to starve.

Reluctantly, I succumbed to the trap's allure in the waning hours before dusk and started gathering wood and sustenance. Both were abundant – a strange trap indeed.

Beneath the overhang of some boulders, I found shelter and struck my steel to stone, sparking a flame. I had forgotten how dark night was. It soon surrounded me and pressed in against my little light. With my back to the rocks, I nibbled on the mushrooms, nuts, and berries I had found. It wasn't much, but it quieted my riotous belly.

After adding some larger pieces of wood to the fire, I gathered my cloak about me and settled into my nook.

Sleep came and took me off-guard. I had thought to deny it, to stubbornly defy my humanity, but it proved the stronger by far; and, within seconds, the darkness became absolute.

In the middle of the night, I startled awake. Nightmares within a nightmare – how annoying.

By the stars, I knew there were several hours to go before dawn. My fire had burned down to a meager red glow. Dutifully, I feed it some more wood and began to resettle, recollecting the fading images that had filled my slumber. Fhaed was among them, laughing the way he always did, smirking at my awkward, taciturn take on the world. As usual, I scowled and growled, if only at his apparition, and tugged my cloak tighter. Still, I wished he were here to receive my exasperation and discontent personally. He would have dismissed it, of course, but…well, at least I wouldn't be alone.

I berated myself for the thought. I needed to be stronger. Being alone hadn't killed me before. I'd spent a long time alone and had survived. Much of it was in places far darker than these woods.

My eyes had only fluttered closed for an instant before my ears pulled them open again. An odd sound drifted through the woods. Someone – a woman – was singing. Her voice was distant, but it drifted to me like a lullaby. The effect, though, was far from soothing. I leapt to my feet, heart pounding, and stood, spinning in place until I had assayed the direction. Once sure of it, I stuck that way at a run.

Nearing the sound, I marveled at the beauty of her aria and quickly recognized the *shi* tongue. The words were undeniably Elven – beautiful but filled with unearthly power.

A few hilltops away, I spied a soft glow and approached her stage cautiously. No matter how pretty the song, I was wary of more enchantments.

From the nearest rise, I peered towards the blue-white nimbus. It looked as though the moon and stars were dancing within the upturned hands of the earth. Great stones crowned the higher hill ahead of me. Fey light swirled gracefully within their encircling fingers.

A Waygate! I knew the structure instantly – not specifically. I mean, I did not know the name of this particular ring of trilithons, but I definitely knew what it was.

Waygates are holy sites. The threads of the Tapestry are woven where they cross. Circles of stones mark these places. Those that know their secrets can open doors that span the world. Some transcend farther. Some reach all the way into the shadows, into Morthalin, the realm of demons.

Given my current predicament, this latter possibility was the first one I considered.

I could not see the singer yet. In truth, I could make out nothing distinctly within the twirling helixes of light.

I had to get closer.

I hated being a moth.

Nevertheless, I fluttered to the edge of the tree line and alit behind a cluster of boulders. Flickering light splashed wildly across their lichen-painted surfaces. The woman's voice sent shivers through the air. I could feel the breath of the north on my face as I peered from my hiding place. The rocks were frosty and numbingly cold. Around me, it was summer; but, before me, the scene between the standing stones whirled with winter. The moonlight and stars that danced within were cloaked in snow that caught every silvery beam and showered it a thousand times across the landscape.

Mesmerized, I could only watch and listen like a good little moth.

Slowly, my imagination began to sculpt figures from the scintillating light. It made ghosts in the air. From the twirling helixes, apparitions formed. Squinting through my memories, I refined them. Some were Asgevar; some were Turanian; some were Dyards.

I had found the summoned spirits, but where was the sorceress – for now I had no doubt but that it was a woman behind all of this. Witches had been troublesome for me as of late, but that's a different story.

Nevertheless, it was a woman singing, and it was her voice that had woven me into this scene and, somehow, maybe, had unwoven my immortality. I had not quite made it to the question of why. I was still affixed on the trail of the diabolical. Simply, something evil was at work, and that was all I could conceive or perceive.

Everyone knows what happens when a moth reaches a flame. Yet, here I was, ready to hurl myself into the light. I had lost my common sense along with my other senses, apparently. Maybe this trap maker was rather good at it after all.

Brashly, I stalked from my cover, Wind-Song gleaming so brightly that she seemed made of moonbeams.

"Who are you?" I demanded of the spectacle.

Perhaps the woman did not hear. The song and dance went on.

I treaded closer. Damn, it was cold and getting colder. My lungs ached with each breath.

"Show yourself," I croaked at the vortex, brandishing my sword as if I would bat away the obfuscating glare.

The energy within the Circlestone ignored me. It was wild and wondrous, but the icy wind it cast was oddly gentle – not the turbulence that had resisted me when I crossed the river. It came is short puffs, nipping at my nose, teasing me.

Baited by my own annoyance, I stepped to the verge of the towering stone ring and searched the spinning galaxy of light inside. My free hand shielded my eyes against its dazzle, but it could do little to adjure the cold.

The siren sang on.

Damned, harpy!

Oh, well, I was a moth with a sharp stinger and the attitude of a hornet. You can guess what I did next.

Funny, it didn't burn…

My senses had been dulled before. As I dashed between the trilithon's legs, though, they abandoned me entirely. The frosty flames engulfed my fervor. It was like falling through ice into a frozen lake – shocking then instantly numbing. Everything went white. The song became silence so thick that I could not even hear my own scream.

Breathing: that was the next thing I remembered. A slow draw of air into my lungs awakened me. It was warm and carried a faint aura – honeysuckle, perhaps. There was a sound, too: windchimes?

I opened my eyes and beheld a simple bedchamber. Four stone walls, skillfully spanned by the ribs of a low, barrel arch defined the space. A small, shuttered window – not wide enough for me to squeeze through – and a single, wooden door marked opposite sides. A wardrobe, a table, a chair, and, of course, the small bed on which I was nested in soft fur blankets accoutered the room. A brass censer burned in one corner. From it, the heat and the sweet scent came. It was a draft at the window that stirred the windchime. A curtain of tiny, silver rods and crystals dangled in the fenestration and tinkled merrily. On the table, a clay lamp sat and burned with a yellow flame, giving me its light. None crept through the shutters. Beyond, it seemed, it was night. A colorful rug of tightly rolled fabric covered most of the tiled floor. I had seen ones similar, but never in the northern lands.

I studied my surroundings, stealing clues as to my whereabouts. Everything within the chamber – except the rug – bore the marks of Asgev hands. The wood was worked artfully with carvings: *Kaelvrot*, the entwining knotwork sacred to my people covered every surface. Princely dragons festooned the wardrobe's paired doors. Their claws clutched at the hardware. Their wings flowed across the dark, reddish panels. It was master's work.

I sat up. I was clad in a linen nightshirt. Beside the bed were furry slippers.

Someone was trying to make me feel welcome and comfortable. I wasn't. I would have been more so in my leathers and with my sword in hand. Neither were in sight.

I had awoken from one nightmare into another; and, still, my dark senses and powers were wanting.

Ignoring the slippers, I slipped from the covers and tiptoed to the door. It, too, was a piece of art. Metal banding reinforced its heavy, oaken slab. Its handle was wrought of iron by a smith who knew his forge well.

I listened. Nothing stirred beyond. I looked. No light slipped across the threshold. I sniffed. The incense in the smoke beguiled my nose. I tried the handle. Of course, it was locked. I was in a cozy prison.

With a sigh, I moved to the wardrobe and found my assigned uniform. The clothes, like the room, were simple. Grey, woolen trousers, soft, doeskin boots, a long, black and blue tunic trimmed with a golden brocade of knotwork, a wide, braided sash for a belt of similar design, and a soft, furred cloak – all of Asgev styling were assembled therein. I examined these articles and noted something unexpected: they showed signs of wear. That's not to say they were in poor condition. Actually, they were perfectly fine. But, they had been mended and patched. The threads, especially the rawhide cordage binding the leather, wore their age. Apparently, my warden had not conjured new attire for me. These were handed down from someone else.

Given the option of the nightshirt or the offered outfit, I chose to be practical and got dressed.

Once attired, I focused on the only thing that mattered: my escape.

There wasn't much oil in the lamp, so fire was a weapon of limited value unless I intended to burn the bed or the rug. The furniture was solid and well-constructed, so breaking off a chair leg to use as a club seemed a futile and unduly noisy choice. The windchimes and crystals might serve as shanks, but they were small and delicate and not likely to be instantly lethal. That left only the censer. It had ample coals that might effectively sear a foe, but I doubted it would prove effective unless luck was on my side. I considered using it to pummel someone over the head, but...well, admittedly, I'm kind of short. They would need to bow down for me to land a good blow, and I doubted I warranted that sort of courtesy.

Aggravated, I sat upon the bed and waited for my captor's return. There wasn't much else I could do. Time passed and, despite my ire, I dozed.

My captor treaded lightly.

Damn it, Lyri!

Off my guard, I jumped at the clack of the latch of my door. It opened slowly as I coiled. Crouched, I readied to spring.

The flame of a candle led the way for my visitor, limning her fair features. She offered its glow into the room's dimness, pushing it back with a slender hand. Her other clutched at the tails of her silken headscarf and held them demurely at her chin. A hint of snow-white hair escaped the fringe. Gentle, motherly eyes, shimmering and blue, sought me out from the doorway. A smile – far too sweet for a witch – greeted me. She was an odd jailer to be certain. Her dress was that of an Asgev maiden, not an interrogator. Surprisingly, despite her frosty locks, she was quite young – well, a lot older than me – twenty summers, perhaps, but still younger than I expected.

"Hello," she said softly, daring to venture into the room only with her greeting.

Like a cornered animal, my glare locked upon her and burned. She shied from its heat.

"I'm glad you're awake," she continued, mustering her courage while seeking some rapport with me. "I was afraid –"

"You should be afraid," I hissed. I moved like a predator and stalked her, stepping fiercely from the bed into her flickering candlelight.

Reflexively, the maiden gulped the remnants of her sentence and stilled, a flash of fear in her eyes.

"Who are you?" I pressed. Behind her I could see a long corridor. A single lantern marked its end where another passageway intersected. "Where am I?"

Another step forward, another step back. Maybe I didn't need a club to best my captor...

"You fell from the Tear-Stone," she stammered. Her candle had become a feeble shield between us. Another step. She retreated. "I brought you here. Your clothes...you were covered in blood and dirt."

I grinned devilishly and quirked one brow. "Other people's blood," I appended.

The young witch's lips twitched, her eyes darting away, but not before I saw the flash of fear grow.

I had backed her fully into the corridor now. The door opened inward into my cell. She could not close it without chancing my bite; still, if she screamed, my advantage could be lost. So, against my nature, I refrained.

"Where am I?"

"A holy place," she stammered, "a temple...Kyrileshar."

"Kyrileshar? Never heard of it. What land is this?"

She hesitated as if seeking words to explain some enigma and eyed me cautiously.

"What land?" I growled.

"A forgotten one," she blurted. Reading my dissatisfaction, she quickly added, "near the crown of Bearslayer."

Bearslayer?

I knew that name. Shetra, the Seer, had spoken of him in passing. When this war with shadows began, she had gone to him seeking aid but had been refused. He was a king, a *Jhar* of the northern clans: Reaversfolk most called them, worshippers of Kyr-Tur, god of war. I didn't know much more than that. The people of my village sometimes told stories of our wild cousins living beyond the Fellenrev, surviving in places the Turanians dared not go. They were raiders and, to some, heroes that embodied the fire and the fury of our race, defiant and resolved against the western invaders. I suppose I respected that.

"Do you have a name or is that forgotten as well?"

Embarrassment flushed the white witch's cheeks. "Merilanna," she replied. "Daughter of Relgheran."

"Nice. Where's my sword, Merilanna?"

More hesitation. I was growing very tired of this game. She sensed it. But I could tell that I was something very different than she had expected.

"Safe. I cleaned your things and put them away. You won't need them here."

I frowned.

"Obviously, you've been through a lot," she continued, "but this is a safe place. The spirits here will protect you. I promise."

Again, that sweet smile flickered disarmingly. I wished I could see the shadows in her soul, but my eyes were still blurred by whatever magic had stolen my own.

"Are you hungry?"

Kibble to soothe the savage beast.

"I'm fine," I snapped. My stomach heard her, though, and grumbled. "I just want to get my things and get back to the war."

Merilanna glanced down towards the growling and smiled. She apparently liked smiling. "Let me get you something to eat first."

I sneered. "Should I wait in my cell?" I was better at sneering.

She laughed. My advantage was gone, betrayed by my traitorous guts. "No, of course not. You're not a prisoner here."

Could have fooled me.

I glanced at the lock on my door accusingly.

"To keep you safe," she assuaged. "There are guardians here."

"Yes, spirits you said. I don't think a locked door is much good against such things."

"No, I suppose not. But I didn't want you wandering where…" She paused and seemed to consider her words for a moment. "…trouble might find you."

"Then, you did a good job of protecting trouble from me."

Her smile brightened. "You're very clever," she commented as we began to walk down the long corridor. "May I know your name as well?"

I glanced up at her. Fhaed's voice poked me. He grinned a lot, too.
Not Petunia.
"Lyri," I answered curtly.
"Lyri," she echoed. "It's a lovely name."
It means death to some.
"Thanks."

A corner or two and we entered a grand hall. Two great doors contained the wonders of this place. The side passage from which we emerged brought us into an architrave then into an aisle that ran the hall's length. Another paralleled beyond the columns on the other side. The wide space between vaulted to the heavens. The soaring arches and fluted columns magnified and attenuated its splendor. Tall, peaked windows filled with stained glass made a cathedral of the place. Were the sky filled with daylight, it would surely glow with divine majesty. As it was, lanterns burning with bluish flames painted the architecture with cerulean hues. Tile mosaics covered the floor with wintry geometry. Such was befitting for the chamber glistened with icicles and drifts of snow.

Our soft footfalls echoed as awe silenced our banter. In the center of the hall, I stopped and absorbed the grandeur.

At the end opposite the great doors was a raised sanctuary. A fantastic, circular window overlooked the area below. Its design was stunning: a snowflake with a thousand facets. Beneath it, standing with arms raised to welcome her worshippers, was a sculpted goddess seemingly made of ice. A lace of snowflakes spread across her bosom. Her head was crowned and the jewels she wore glittered brightly even in the subdued light from the lanterns. Her face was tranquil and beyond beautiful. Her hair flowed to her shoulders. From there, her dress cascaded to her feet. One slender leg slipped from its folds, accentuating her feminine sensuality.

Before the looming divinity, my escort offered her obeisance. She genuflected, crossing her palms upon her chest as she bowed. "My Lady," she said simply as she did.

I withheld comment until we had crossed the temple and exited to another secondary corridor. I did give a smug, little salute to the ice queen when my guide was not looking. This "Lady" and I were well-acquainted.

"You worship Death," I stated evenly.

Merilanna's steps remained steady. Her smile did not waver. In fact, it brightened. "No, I serve she who guides those that have passed the Veil to their due heavens."

Same thing...

"Do you sing when you do it?"

Her brow seemed tickled by the question. "Always. Though I prefer to dance as well – when I'm allowed."

"When you're allowed?"

Her smile shied. "Death is seldom a happy occasion, but the dead come from all lands and from all cultures; and, in some, it is proper to dance, to celebrate the life that was. When I cannot, when it is improper to do so, I dance in stillness."

"You dance in stillness? And that works how, exactly?"

Her head tilted for a moment, considering. "Well...just as a song is made of sound and silence, a dance is made of motion and stillness. So I dance, but only in the quiet parts of the song. The moving stays inside me, for all of it is My Lady's work, and it is my joy to do."

"Sure," I mumbled cynically.

Merilanna giggled. "I know it sounds ridiculous, but My Lady's gifts are wonderful. Before her, the dead were left to wander. Through her, they are blessed and the heavens can rejoice. So, you see, even in the stillness, my soul forever dances."

I shrugged. "Guess that's why you're a priestess and I'm not. When I dance, things die. When you dance, the dead are give an afterlife."

Merilanna's smile held me gently. She seemed to accept my words.

Soon, our steps brought us to our destination. I could smell the lingering aroma of baked bread long before we entered the kitchen.

"You could feed an army from this place," I noted, scanning its immense size.

Three great, masonry ovens lined one entire wall. Enormous, iron pots, easily large enough to stew a hundred guineas each, hung over wide hearths along the opposite. Well-equipped work areas assigned to specific culinary tasks ringed the room. Spits and skewers, cleavers and ladles, pots and pans, and every sort of utensil – some I had no idea what they were for – were arrayed. A large door led from the chamber, undoubtedly to a feasting hall. Four smaller ones entered a buttery, a bottlery, a pantry, and a storeroom. Clearly, despite the goddess' fit form, her devotees liked to eat heartily. Thus far, however, Merilanna seemed the only soul about. No one was guarding the larder, at least.

As my captor turned hostess began busying herself, preparing what I presumed would be an early breakfast for me, I commented on our privacy, teasing a question. "I guess everyone else is still asleep."

Merilanna's bustling paused then resumed quickly. "There hasn't been anyone else here for a very long time," she said offhandedly with a certain feigned nonchalance.

"Why is that?" I asked, sidling up to one of the thick, wooden tables, mounting a stool, and eying her expectantly. Of course, I had already noted the sharp cutlery also, but I maintained my own disarming air of indifference towards it. Despite my suspicious nature, I did not feel threatened by her.

"Do you like honey?" she asked, evading my question as she brought forth a warmed loaf of bread and cut a thick slice to distract me.

"Sure," I replied, still waiting and still watching. Time for another game, I supposed. "So no one else comes here? Who brings your flour?"

Again, she paused. Her smile remained playful. "Very clever, indeed," she said.

"Let me guess: It's all magic."

The priestess' smile demurred. "My Lady provides," she replied, then turned around to fetch a pot of golden nectar from a nearby shelf.

I left the knife where she had laid it, well within my reach. She was either naïve or trusting. I wasn't sure which. But, if it was a test, I apparently passed. Her smile warmed again as she returned with her treasure.

"So, you live here alone?" I rejoined and surveyed the vastness of the kitchen, letting my eyes and tone convey my dubiousness.

Merilanna set the honeypot in front of me. "No. I'm never alone."

Just crazy?

I sucked some drippling honey from my fingertips. "Other than your goddess, I mean."

Her shining, blue eyes drifted dreamily about the chamber looking for how to answer.

"Or ghosts," I added preemptively.

She laughed. "Well, other than those, I serve two mistresses."

"Ah, two mistresses. Are they priestesses as well?"

"Yes, of course, and much beloved by Our Lady."

I smacked, enjoying the sweet treat, and fussed with my sticky fingers, licking away the dribbles. If it was magic, it was tasty magic. Every demon has her weaknesses and, I admit, sweets are mine.

Before I could press farther in our little chat, a flash of alarm suddenly crossed my hostess' pretty face, scattering her smile. "Milk," she blurted in distress and hopped up as if some great transgression of etiquette had been committed. "I forgot the milk!"

I watched her bemusedly as she scampered through one of the little doors and half-wondered if her mistresses beat her over such small matters. She returned quickly, a generous mug in hand. "I'm so sorry. I'm not used to serving anyone."

"Not even your mistresses?"

Again, she smiled flickered back to life. Every time I cornered her, it did. She seemed to genuinely enjoy this game. Apparently, having someone to talk to was a great indulgence. "Their needs are not so...mundane," she explained. Noting my skeptical countenance, she added, laughing, "No, they aren't spirits."

"They're elves aren't they? Of course, they're spirits," I declared simply.

"Uh..."

Blank. That's the best way to describe her sudden expression. It quickly changed to amazement again; but, to my satisfaction, it started as blank.

"How did you...?"

I shrugged. "Just a guess, but it looks like I'm right."

Merilanna settled on her stool across from me and folded her hands in her lap. She watched me quietly for a moment. I supposed she was dancing in stillness. After this brief interlude, she said, "Yes, the sisters are Shining Folk. They raised me."

"That was nice of them." I sucked some more honey from my fingertips, savoring it. Then, her guard down once more, I caught her eyes with my own and froze her stare across the table. "Why?" I asked pointedly.

She hadn't expected so sharp a question.

"Why did they raise me? I'm not sure," she answered, her voice trailed off and became strangely distant, as though she too, had wondered the same thing many times.

"Pity?" I suggested.

She guarded her reply, and her expression sombered. "Perhaps."

I was close to the mark, I surmised. I may have lost my demonic senses, but I could still sense when my prey was on the run. There was something else in her eyes, too: pain. I recognized it instantly for I knew it well. She had known great loss in her life. I relented and didn't press farther. Call it mercy. I guess the honey was sweetening my sour disposition. So, I changed the subject. "You said I fell from some sort of stone. What did you mean?"

Merilanna's gaze lifted from her melancholy. "Yes, you did," she said. "It's called the Tear-Stone. It's a holy jewel held in the goddess' hands."

A flicked a curious glance back towards the temple's sanctuary. "I don't remember her holding a jewel," I countered, reflecting on the statue in the temple.

Merilanna's grin spread once more. "No, not that statue. There is a different one – one far larger. It stands in the old temple courtyard farther down the mountain. Its guardians brought you to me."

"Guardians again. You mentioned them before. Who are they?"

"There not people – not like you and me."

There's no one like me. I chose not to argue the point.

"They aren't spirits either," she explained. "They're sort of a…combination of both. They live on the mountain and protect its sacred secrets."

Sadly, I had finished my honeyed bread. "Ghost people that aren't people," I mused as the contradications continued to mount, licking the last of the milk from my lip as I gulped it down. "I've met worse," I said. "So, what happened?"

Merilanna shook her head and shrugged. "I'm not sure. Since the southern sky burned and thunder filled the world, unusual things have been happening quite a lot."

"Unusual things like me, you mean."

The young priestess' cheeks flushed. "Um…yes. Like you," she confessed.

I already knew why the sky had burned and why the thunder had rolled. I was there when it happened; but, again, that's another story, so I moved on. "Did you summon me here?" I asked directly.

"No. I swear, Lyri, I don't know how you came to be here. I would never take someone from their home." Her countenance grew very solemn, touched with remorse. "At least, not on purpose," she added. "I'm deeply sorry if I've done something dark to you."

Earnest…true…I believed her words, but we both knew that I wouldn't be here except for her – for something *she* had done.

"Dark is what I do," I joked grimly, easing the weight of my unspoken accusation. She regarded me curiously, expectantly. I had opened this door, so I relented and said, "I guess it's time for my tale now."

Merilanna leaned in and rested her forearms upon the table, her hands overlapping quiescently before her and waited.

I began matteroffactly. "I was hunting demons until something – a horn – called to the spirits of those that had fallen in the battle and pulled them away." The priestess, I noted, held her breath for a second at the mention of the horn. I continued. "They answered and I followed after them and found a Circlestone filled with light." I watched her closely, reading her. "You know what that is, too, don't you?"

Merilanna's expression remained empty, like a hollow mask. She stared at me for a long moment before, at last, she nodded. Once, slowly.

"I heard *someone* singing," I said, the note of accusation returning and punctuating the statement. "So, I entered the circle of light and then I woke up here: in my cozy little cell." I thumbed the tunic I wore. "Yours?"

Another nod.

"Well, that's my story; and, as much fun as this has been, if you don't mind – or even if you do – I'll take my things now and be on my way." I stood up sharply. "Send me back."

Merilanna's mask crumbled as her face conveyed her hidden truth instantly.

I exhaled my exasperation and rolled my eyes. "You don't know how, do you?"

Her countenance drooped. "No, I'm sorry, I don't. I don't know how any of this happened. The horn calls only those souls that have passed beyond the Veil. Only the dead heed it. I can't explain."

"Well, I guess it's time I met your mistresses then."

Her eyes widened and she grimaced.

"Who were you singing to?" I asked. "Who were you trying to call?"

Merilanna fidgeted and looked at her hands. That shot had hit the mark squarely. She hadn't just been doing some priestly business. Someone had been very naughty and, at least this time, it wasn't me.

Stiff and still, the young priestess sat for several moments before her expression softened. Her eyes glistened. "My parents," she whispered.

There was such deep longing and loss in her words. I knew that pain firsthand. "Was it a forbidden spell?"

Contrition is easy to read. Guilt is a close second. Merilanna wore both flagrantly as she nodded.

"I just wanted to say, 'I love you' one more time and...'goodbye.' I never got the chance to do that." Merilanna straightened her spine and leveled her chin. "It was supposed to reach back to them – the spell – back to before they died." Tears slipped down her cheeks. She wiped them away as she composed herself. There was strength in her. I admired that. "I never meant for any of this to happen, Lyri. You must believe me."

"I do," I said. I had a confession of my own. "The world is turned inside out and upside down. A lot of that is my fault. So, no, I don't blame you for this. I believe what you've said, but that doesn't really change anything, does it? Your song reached out and ignited a Waygate – maybe more than one. I don't know. The dead – they answered your call." I considered carefully what to say next, mostly because I had no idea how to explain it. "But something else happened, too. Something that makes no sense to me." Puzzlement spread over Merilanna's face. I knew that I was the one babbling now. "I'm not a sorceress or a priestess. But, before you brought me here, before your song – that spell – ripped me from the world, I was someone very different than I am now." I hesitated, not wanting to reveal my own vulnerability. "Something happened to me," I ventured. "I can't explain to you what, but it needs to un-happen, and it needs to un-happen fast. I need to get back to where I came from; but, more importantly, I need to get back to who I was. You have to fix this."

Remorse consumed the young woman seated before me. "I will," she assured, but I could tell that her confidence had completely faltered. There was pleading in her eyes. "I just don't know how."

I fixed her with my glare. "Well, you're going to have to figure it out."

Chapter 3: Lady Light, Lady Dark

Footsteps are always slower when you're going somewhere you don't want to go. Despite my guide's earnest desire to right what she had done, hers crept down the maze of halls no faster. When we reached the processional ascent to where her mistresses apparently dwelled, they languished terribly.

Exiting from what she called the Middle Temple, we stepped beneath the open sky and were instantly blasted by the arctic wind. Thoughts of warm bread and a toasty fire became cherished but distant.

Dawn was near, but it seemed to dawdle as well. The stars, by contrast, blazed across the heavens, dominating the black firmament and painting it with sparkling rivers of light. Far to the south, an eerie crimson nebula burned marking another range of mountains that I knew was there but could not see; those familiar peaks lay beyond the curve of the world. I had friends there. I wondered how long they would search from me.

A steep stairway carved from the mountainside on which I currently stood led upslope. The path switched back and forth as it climbed. At each turn, stone pillars had been erected. Each was festooned with silvery streamers that flapped and snapped in the icy gale. I was very glad for the fur cloak Merilanna have given me and buried my hands inside it. Its hood wrapped my face and gave some shelter to my ears and cheeks. My little nose, though, felt the wind's bite.

For her part, the young priestess I followed seemed unfazed by the frigid blow. She gathered her thin shawl and clutched it to her breast but only to restrain its billowing. A reassuring smile was given – I think more for herself than me – then we began our climb.

Upon reaching the first turn, we stopped. The ridgeline was precipitous and I was already struggling to breathe. The air was thin, but what little there was of it stabbed into my lungs like icy daggers. A dozen or more flights remained to climb. At the top, a gleaming palace, like a star enthroned on the mountaintop, awaited and beckoned.

Why, I wondered, did the Elves always seem to favor these inaccessible heights. Plopping a palace or shrine at the apex of a mountain must have been a glorious pastime for them. At the moment, though, I considered it quite sadistic. Of course, if you don't want to be bothered by the trifles of mortals, what better place was there to put one?

Below – only a few thousand feet – probably more – I'm not a good judge of distances when my eyes are frozen – sat the ruins of another temple complex. I could just make out its jagged walls and a few crumbling towers.

"Let me guess," I chuffed, "Lower Temple." I looked back to the shining star. "Upper Temple."

Merilanna regarded me and smiled mildly then nodded. Her mind was clearly on something else: the audience we would soon have with her mistresses. The wind had liberated strands of her white hair from their braids and was tossing them wildly.

Squinting through the dim light, I spotted a shimmering star near the center of the Lower Temple also. A colossal, feminine statue – you know who – held it aloft in its hands.

The Tear-Stone.

All the world below the Lower Temple was covered in a blanket of clouds. Here, I was on an island of rock and snow, part of an archipelago that stretched away to the south and east: mountain tops in a sea of billowing white. Its majesty would have been much more inspiring if I hadn't been freezing to death.

Stubbornly, I trudged on.

About half-way to the summit, my guide began to chatter. I guess the inevitability of facing her mistresses finally cracked through her trepidation. She glanced back, fear riding her expression. I was still there. So, yes, she was still in a lot of trouble.

I caught only bits of what she was saying. I could barely hear her through the buffeting wind. "When—get there, I will go in first—make your introduct—n. The ladies—not accustomed to visitors, but I'm sure—see you."

She said a lot more: stuff about bowing and how to address her mistresses properly; how very important it was, and that my life depending on it; and other such nonsense that I ignored. To be honest, I was rather fixated upon setting one foot in front of the other at the time. Lessons in etiquette weren't much on my mind. It is not so easy to walk when your vision is haloing and your brain is struggling to remember where you're going and why. It's pretty damned disconcerting, actually, when you forget which way is up. Nausea just added to my misery. Bread and honey don't taste as good on the way out.

I'm pretty sure that Merilanna carried me to the Upper Temple's doors. I don't really recall much after I figured out where the ground was again and collapsed. Being hauled inside like a sack of potatoes does seem faintly familiar, though.

"I didn't know what else to do," Merilanna was saying as my ears reawakened. Her voice was downtrodden, without inflection. My eyes were a bit more sluggish, but they, too, gradually got back to work.

I was, I discovered, reposed on another bed – well, a cot really – in yet another small room. The door was closed – probably locked – but that was just my cynicism reawakening as well – and Merilanna was outside pleading her case.

"Then I will tell you what to do," a sharper but still melodic voice replied. "Cast her beyond the clouds and let her kin see to her there. She does not belong here and cannot remain."

"But Mistress –"

"She's awake."

I rolled my feet to the ground as the door opened and white light spilled in. My head was exploding and the glare didn't help. It's hard to be awed when your skull is splitting between your eyes.

"I was just leaving anyway," I grumbled under my breath. It seemed the air was fuller here. Muttering curses might again be an option.

Merilanna moved to tend to me and knelt at my side. "It's my fault she's here," she protested over her shoulder to the dark angel limned gloriously in the doorway.

"Quite. But that changes nothing. Our Lady Ilé forbids the unworthy from entering these halls."

I guffawed. It would have been louder if I didn't hurt so much, but it had the desired effect. The glowing bitch in the doorway shut up for a moment, appalled.

Merilanna stared at me with alarm as well. I guess all that etiquette stuff she had spouted earlier was supposed to have had more of an effect on me. Unfortunately, I tend to be a bit indignant about such things.

"Your Lady Ilé can kiss my ass," I suggested. "This is as much her fault as the girl's. She's the one that snipped the Threads of the world and snarled everything in knots. I wouldn't be here if it wasn't for that!"

"Insolent cur! I have another solution to this problem!"

A hint of a dark dagger glinted in her stormy light.

Merilanna shielded me. "Please! Mistress!" She cried, her even tone completely lost, her voice thick with fear.

"What's going on?" another angelic voice – a bit less dramatic but equally insistent – asked from the background.

"It seems our dear *Saduci'i* has taken in a stray cat, my sister," came the hissed reply. "I was about to rectify the matter."

"I conjured her somehow," Merilanna said, desperately shifting to keep herself between me and her dark mistress. "It's not her fault," she cried vehemently. "She didn't want to come here."

The new angel, this one of a slightly less icy hue, appeared at the doorway. Her dark sister yielded her place and drifted into the background.

"Lady Nymaera," Merilanna pleaded, "I'm sorry. I know it is forbidden."

"It is forbidden because it is dangerous, Meri," Lady Nymaera, the new angel, replied as she released her veil of light and materialized before me. Priestly robes, ephemeral like silk, clad her delicate loveliness. Tiny diamonds were woven into her fair, silvery hair. Her eyes shined like stars tinted with amethyst. Her countenance was serene but composed. She waited, eyes on her recaltrant alcolyte.

Long moments of silence stretched; and, in them, Merilanna stilled. With a deep, quiet breath, she composed herself and stood, her stance losing all traces of her earlier passion until she was as a mirror of the calm Nymaera.

"Her name is Lyri," my defender whispered, her tone again even and untouched. It was rather creepy, if you want to know the truth of it.

Lady Nymaera now regarded me kindly – like someone would a lost kitten.

"It's alright, Lyri. No one will harm you."

"Heard that one before," I snorted. "Can't promise the same…"

The priestess glanced to her brooding sister. "I'll deal with this, Ryva," she said firmly.

"Do or I will," snapped the sharp reply.

Then the stormy bitch vanished.

"Thank you, Lady." Merilanna bowed deeply.

Lady Nymaera straightened and regarded both of us, contemplating how to "deal with this." A measured breath and she said, "This place, Lyri…it stands watch over the lands of the dead. It's not safe for mortals to trek here. A step too far and your life would be over."

She found my indifferent shrug a little perplexing, I think. When I spoke again, she looked even more dumbfounded – well, as dumbfounded as an elf can look, I suppose. They've been around a long time so nothing is supposed to surprise them. When it does, they try to fake it. Some prefer incredulity, and some, indifference. Occasionally, it's humility, while others relish outrage. I had already met Lady Dark. She liked outrage. I was curious which façade Lady Light would don.

Oh, well, subtlety is not my thing…

"Your acolyte blew her horn through the Veil. Now, I'm here. The Tapestry is in knots." I looked around at my new cell. This one was made of ice. Delightful. I continued. "Out there, beyond this little, private playground of yours, worlds have collided and what the gods have made has gone to shit. I'll spare you most of the news, but know this: your precious Ilé was the cause of more than her share of this mess. So, before you condemn this girl, you might want to pray a bit. Knees are good for that. You see things differently when you're not looking down your nose."

Lady Nymaera folded her hands passively at her waist and just looked at me. It was better than getting slapped, I guess. Despite my charming demeanor, I'm not a masochist. I'm just a little too pig-headed to stay down when I get kicked. Honestly, when it's due, I prefer to do the kicking. I suppose that's why I kick myself a lot. Different subject – back to the dumbfounded priestess…

"I see," she said finally. "And how do you propose we unsnag you from this twist of fate."

"I don't know. I didn't make up these stupid rituals. Shepherding souls to paradise is your business, not mine. I work the other side of things, you see. I'm more of the 'send them to hell' type.

"As for twirling time around a spindle, I've no answers for that either. Bending the laws of the gods, I admit, is a hobby of mine, but I'm not sure what to do when the laws change altogether."

"You're a very curious creature, Lyri," Nymaera was obliged to comment.

"Guilty as charged," I replied. "Now, how do we fix this?"

Lady Light mused. "Hmm, I guess I need to do that praying you mentioned." To Merilanna, she said, "Why don't you show our guest around while I do."

"My Lady, I don't think Lady Ryva would approve."

"I'll speak with Ryva. There's more going on here than either I or she can 'deal with' alone."

Merilanna bowed again.

Nymaera gave me a courteous nod before getting all glowy again and whisking herself away. Once she was gone, Merilanna sat on the cot beside me and stared at the open doorway. Her expression remained...well, expressionless. I couldn't endure it for long.

"Nice place," I said rhetorically – well, sarcastically – to break through the frigid moment. "How did you get here again?"

The mask of her face broke once more. She looked at me as though startled, but curious. "You want to know how I came to be at Kyrileshar?"

Maybe her ears and brain were frozen. There was enough ice here to do it, obviously. I rolled my eyes and strained for patience. Not my favorite activity. And I hate trying to do things I'm bad at. "That's why I asked."

Memories played across her face. She licked her lips and brought some of them into her mouth. She made words of them there, but they were heavy and low. "There was a raid," she began, giving voice to her past. "It was a very dark night. Fire was everywhere. Everything was burning. I was, maybe, five? Five or six. It was snowing hard and the wind...the wind was howling down from the mountain. I could barely stand. I could barely even see. People were screaming...dying. There was so much blood on the snow.

"I remember my father. I could see his form in the firelight. He had his sword and he was yelling. He was fighting with shadows. They were all around him.

"'Run! Run to the mountain!' he cried. So, I did; I ran. I ran until I couldn't run anymore.

"The wind – in the wind, I heard my mother's voice. She was singing to me, bringing comfort. She told me that everything would be alright."

Merilanna lowered her head under the weight of the visions.

"It wasn't. I awoke in the snow on the mountainside. I should have been dead. But, the Lady had favored me."

She paused in her recitation to smile at me, as if to offer comfort of her own. If her smiles had been silver, I'd have been rich right by now. Despite believing that her cheerfulness is its own, strange evil, I preferred her honest smiles to her creepy mask.

"I wandered," she began again. "Then My Lady's light showed me here. In the Lower Temple, the guardians found me. They carried me up the mountain to my mistresses. Lady Ryva and Lady Nymaera took me in. They told me who I was and who I would one day be."

I leaned forward. "So, you've never left this place?"

Merilanna's eyes were patient. She giggled a little. "No, I have," she said. "I've been away…as part of my training."

My eyebrow quirked but she did not elaborate. Instead, her gaze returned to her memories. Something in her aura matured as she did. There was something there, but she said no more until the reminiscences faded.

"What about you?" she asked. "You're quite the mystery yourself."

I shrugged and shook my head. "Fire, snow, people screaming, people dying…we're not so different."

With every quipped word, the curiosity in her eyes turned to ash. She looked down, regretting the question. "I'm sorry, Lyri."

"Don't be." *Damn, I hate being sentimental. I'd rather break things.* "C'mon," I suggested, hopping up. "I wouldn't want all of this Elven architecture to go unadmired. I think my head has stopped pounding long enough for me to find a new way to make it ache."

Merilanna chuckled, a wicked gleam of humor in her eyes. "You really like stirring the pot don't you?"

Damn, I smiled. Kick.

"Depends what's in it," I answered.

The tour of the tower – for that's what this place turned out to be – was…okay, it was boring. Everything was made of ice and pure and clean and smelled fresh and, ugh…I hated it. Yes, the rooms were soaring and grand. Yes, the snowflakes were sculpted in magnificent ways. Everything was light and glittering. Blah, blah blah. I wanted to smash it all.

Me? A violent person? Whatever gave you that idea?

In my defense, I can't stand pomp and I detest pretense. The whole place pissed me off.

Nonetheless, I survived the tour. Though I wonder if it was longer than it needed to be. My guide apparently knew too many useless facts about Elven architechture. Just as I would think of ten ways to smash the next piece of stonemasonry *exactly like the four pieces before it,* she would give me twelve new and "interesting" facts about it in return. I was fairly certain my growing, growling lack of appreciation was noticed. But she found it incredibly amusing, and she didn't even try to hide her discovery, enjoyed my stormy nature. The best part of the tour, actually, was being inside an ice cube and not being cold. Magic – I hated it, but it had its uses.

One thing that caught me a bit off-guard as the day went by was the sunrise. Why? Because the sun set again after only a few minutes!

Now, to those of you more learned than me, this probably comes as no surprise. Vulgar as I am, standing on a balcony of ice watching Xorconum's Throne barely skim the southern horizon was quite the wonder. I've flown through the stars on the back of a dragon, but, somehow, watching this spectacle amused me, much to my guide's delight.

By the afternoon – alright, I had no idea what time it really was – all that praying was apparently over. Lady Light and Lady Dark called Merilanna and me back into their august presences.

At the center of the tower, at the top, of course, was a circular hall. Great lens of ice formed its walls and ceiling. It really was like being inside an ice cube, albeit one shaped in the form of a fantastic jewel.

Twin thrones facing each other sat on opposite sides of the chamber. They seemed to float in the air, surrounded by light. The two priestesses perched in them, both straight-backed and very proper.

Ryva and Nymaera were quite alike but very different as well. Both were beautiful. Both were adorned with raiment befitting queens. The whole ice and snow theme was maintained splendidly.

Lady Light wore a dress of gossamer silk, a white that shimmered with the iridescence of a butterfly's wings. It seemed to float across her skin, as though she wore a cloud that masqueraded as fabric. Her hair flowed silver down her shoulders and her eyes were a blue-violet shade I've never seen again in another.

Lady Dark, in contrast, wore sleek, black leather, form-fitted to her long legs and wrapped with intricate weaving into a corset around her. Her shoulders were bare, save where the sharp edge of her raven-black hair brushed them. A slender sword, an artful and graceful weapon, rested propped against the side of her throne. On her hip, an eerie dagger capped with a strange pommel shaped like a flower bud rode. Her skin was flawless, without scar or blemish - yet the chill of her storm grey eyes convinced me that this woman did not need scars to prove her battle prowess. Her blades were not decorative.

It was their auras, though, that distinguished them most of all. Ryva's was like vaporous quicksilver scintillating around her frenetically and crackling with lightning. Nymaera's glowed like soft moonlight through morning mist, a pale spectrum of colors that winked lazily.

"Come forward," Lady Light commanded.

Merilanna stepped forth between the two thrones on silent feet and into the center of the chamber, eyes submissive, held low, her face impassive and blank. I walked a step behind her without all the deference, studying the two judges seated on high.

"First," Lady Light began, "Our Lady has affirmed all that which has been said. The Threads of the Tapestry have indeed been twisted by the fate of our world. The aftershocks of events beyond this holy mountain will continue to reweave all that we know for some time to come. Things once small now reverberate in unimaginable ways. So, while it is true that what you did, Meri, was not foreseeable or deliberate, its affects have carried far." To me, she added, "And, yes, it must be undone."

Lady Dark leaned forward and spoke. Her voice was more imperious and steely. "It will be undone," she said, "but that undoing cannot be achieved from here. To untangle this knot, you must go to where the snarl lies. You must free it there."

Merilanna lifted her eyes to her teachers. "Tell me where I must go."

The two priestesses exchanged counsel with a glance.

"You dared to reach into the past," Lady Dark elucidated coldly. "It is there that the knot is snagged. Your pet" – that would be me in case you're wondering – "is the barb on which time is caught. She is an incarnation of chaos and a defiler of the divine order."

I smirked at that; almost laughed. It was funny coming from a priestess of Ilé, given that her goddess invented my job. I guessed Lady Dark liked to flavor things with her own bile.

Lady Light intervened as her sister bristled. "To undo what has been done will not be a simple task. The Threads are twisted both in Twilight and in the world of the living. To unsnag them, you will have to do so in both places."

"How?" Merilanna asked. Her voice was unnaturally calm.

"The creature with you," Lady Dark answered, "has two souls. One is the girl you stand beside. The other is an incarnation of pure rage. These two must be reunited, but doing so may prove the worse for the world. It will surely be so for you, Merilanna. It was your audacity that caused this and it may cost you everything to undo it." Lady Dark gripped the flower pommel of the dagger at her waist.

"Our Lady is with me. Her will be done." Merilanna bowed.

"You're not telling us something," I challenged, stepping forward. "What is it?"

Again, the priestesses consulted with their eyes.

"Something will be lost if the Threads are set free – not even Our Lady knows what. But, there can be only one world in the end."

"You have a guess."

"Yes, Lyri, we do," Lady Light confirmed. "Time will be respun."

"Time is a tricky thing," Lady Dark interjected ominously. "It orders the world. Set chaos loose upon it and the consequences are never knowable. But, in the end, the Tapestry will reweave. *That* end, though, will not be the same."

"That's very unhelpful, thanks," I quipped.

Before the confrontation could escalate again, Lady Light spoke. "You must travel to the place where the knot was formed and unsnarl it there." Her voice lowered as her tone deepened. "The world is not the same now. Here, upon our mountain, the effects have not yet reached us. Below, there are runs in the Tapestry and they are growing. You must be careful, but you must also be quick."

I stepped forward again. Dire warnings always inspired my rashness.

"What happened to the Waygate?" I demanded. "I take it that we won't be shortening our steps by riding ley lines to solve this."

"Power must flow," Lady Light began to explain.

"And it doesn't flow well through a knot," I deduced.

Lady Light smiled grimly. "No, it doesn't. Nor is it clear what will happen when the knot is set loose. Moreover, our portal here leads from the world to the Halls of the Dead – nowhere else."

A tear caught the light on Merilanna's cheek, silent but not unnoticed.

"What you have done must be undone." Lady Dark hissed at the young priestess as she leaned back into her haughty chair and laced her fingers. "When your steps can take you no further, Little Failure, you will return here and face judgment for your mistakes."

"Return to the Middle Temple," Lady Light directed calmly. "Go. Ready yourselves to travel."

"Yes, My Lady." Merilanna bowed to her mistresses with her palms crossed before her chest and backed out of the chamber.

I eyed the two priestesses but said nothing, then turned and walked away.

Outside the audience hall, I found Merilanna leaning with her back against a wall of ice, panting for breath.

"I'm so sorry," she said.

I scowled. "The gods screw up the world all the time and blame us for it. Some things never change. Let's get moving. I'm tired of this icebox."

Chapter 4: The Lower Temple

The goddess' statue was big.

How big?

Let me describe it this way. Half of the Lower Temple had been erected upon her shoulders. The other half spread at her feet, a thousand paces below. It took half a candlemark to walk from the top to the bottom. That's pretty big.

Well, when you take an entire cliffside and carve an image out of it, that's what you get: a really big statue of a goddess who thinks an awful lot of herself seeming to step right out of the rock to the oohs and aahs of her fanatics.

Grand fun...

What had been an overlook of stone jutting forth from the mountain now wore her wondrous vision of loveliness and majesty. Her arms stretched out before her to the ends of the earth to offer her eternal blessings. There, at the terminus of the promontory, an obelisk of amethystine crystal towered, clutched in her meticulously sculpted hands.

Stairs hewn from the blue granite of the mountain wound about her neck and shoulders forming the trim of her mantle and the neckline of her dress. A processional causeway began where the stairs landed. On one end, nestled between the curves of her breasts, was an altar. On the other, the glittering obelisk rose.

A delicate crown, sparkling with ice in the starlight, rested upon her head. Her hair was regally looped and bound. Her eyes gazed to the horizon. Her face was serene. Apparently, she liked her job.

How was it built, you may ask?

A lot of picks and hammers and no small amount of blood and tears would be my guess. Ilé is the goddess of death, after all, so more than a few of her beloved probably toiled to their ends and sacrificed their all for her to have her face on this mountain. I'm sure she thanked every one of them with a nice hug and a pat on the back on their way to paradise.

Merilanna regaled me with the story of this place as we trudged down the path from the Middle Temple. Admittedly, I didn't pay much attention to her. Freezing no longer preoccupied me as we descended, though it was still damnably cold and windy. I had thrown on a few more layers of fur before we began the trek and Wind-Song was back at my side again. No, what distracted me was the hope that I wouldn't need to draw her. I had reclaimed my own gear, but the thick furs that kept me warm weighed on my agility. Fighting in this bulky stuff would have been ridiculous. I looked like a fuzzy, little bear not a hell-spawned hell-cat.

"That priestess is going to kill you the day you come back, you know?" I said. "If you come back, that is."

Merilanna shrugged. "Same as every other day."

My feet stopped abruptly, and I stared her. Hearing such a bald statement, ripe with boredom at the prospect of death out of someone else…well, it was just wrong. That's *my* line!

She looked out at the edge of the horizon, scanning it before turning back to me.

"We should keep moving, time…" She shook her head as though to shake her thoughts free.

"You said there were guardians," I interrupted the priestess' chatter as my thoughts finally reached my lips. We were near to the ruins of the Lower Temple's outer walls now. From the looks of the courtyards and ancillary buildings within, they hadn't done a very good job of guarding the place. It was a wreck. Rocks and rubble were everywhere. Time had sieged this place, bombarded it, and had won the day…the week…the century. Compared to the sites above, the complex was, well, primitive. Raw stones stacked on raw stones composed every structure. I think the ice and snow was all that held a lot of it together. Still, there wasn't a single stretch of wall completely intact. There were no signs of life.

My guide glanced back at me but did not slow her pace. "Yes," she replied, "they are called the Avharkiden, the Ghost Men of the Mountains. They live within caves beneath the ruins and protect these holy places."

"I'm sure they're very friendly," I quipped.

"Don't worry," Merilanna chuckled. "They won't harm us. My Lady protects us."

On that cue, the priestess stopped and drew forth from beneath her cloak a splendid white horn adorned with silver and blew a long, resounding note that echoed back from the stones below. As well, from beyond the clouds that concealed the world, strange rumbles of rolling thunder rose in answer and filled the air. I had heard sounds like those before not so very long ago on a different mountain. Then and there, they presaged people being buried alive under tons of ice and snow. It wasn't such a pleasant memory.

So, too, I had heard that horn before on the night that this peculiar odyssey began. Then as now, the note rang out with the voice of my kin, the Asgevar.

"Why does it sound different to different people?"

Merilanna held the horn forth and admired its craftsmanship. "This is the Horn of Destiny," she said reverently. "Every soul that departs this world into the lands of the dead must heed its call. For each, its voice is different for every soul has its own destiny. What you hear is not the sounding but the echo from within yourself. You entered this world as a note but you will leave it as a song composed by the life you have led. Nevertheless, the first and the last note are always the same; as you began, so shall you end. 'I am that I am' is every soul's song." She smiled graciously.

I guess my expression wasn't awestruck enough.

Merilanna laughed. "Come," she prompted as she stashed the horn away. "It's a long way to the bottom."

"I guess we don't want to arrive unannounced."

"No, that wouldn't be a good idea. The guardians need to know who comes."

"So they don't eat us," I commented aside as we continued on.

A rather coy smile – not a dismissive chuckle or hand to wave away an absurd remark – answered my little joke. That wasn't reassuring.

"You said they were half-spirits," I pressed. "What did you mean? Do they live here or do they haunt here?"

Merilanna mused for a few steps then responded, "Both. Not everything in the Bright World is bound to one side of the Veil or the other. The Avharkiden are one of those things. They live here, but they also walk in the spirit world."

Sounded familiar. Riding the Cusp definitely had its advantages.

"Do you know what the Veil is, Lyri?" she asked.

As something of an expert on the subject, I considered a snide quip, but chose a more reserved reply. She didn't know me, after all, so I settled on simply, "Yes," instead.

"What about Twilight?"

"Yes. I'm clever. Remember?"

She smiled appreciatively. "Very clever…and most remarkable. To be a warrior at your age – and a demon hunter! That's truly extraordinary! I can only imagine how exciting your adventures have been. You're really amazing."

I flinched. "You don't have many friends, do you?"

The young priestess' smile shied abashedly. "Not really," she admitted. "My mistresses are always busy with very important things. They don't talk very much – other than to instruct, of course. For which," she hastened to add, "I am most grateful. I've learned so much from them. They've lived so long and know – well, everything. I've been blessed, truly." She meant what she said, but there was still something hollow in it.

Some things puzzled me. "So, why exactly are you still here?" I glanced back up the mountain to the Middle Temple and to the sparkling beacon that marked the summit. "It's just you in that whole place. Where are the rest? Why aren't there more priestesses for Ryva to glare down at?"

"There were," Merilanna replied frankly as we crossed into the boundary of the Lower Temple complex. Piles of stone flanked the path leading into the first courtyard. The back of Ilé's stone head was still a few terraces down. "They've gone out into the world. My sisters do Our Lady's will in many places and in many lands."

"Shepherding the dead, yes, yes. I know all about that. But why are *you* still here?"

Merilanna stopped in the middle of the courtyard and surveyed the area, gathering her thoughts. "I've been beyond the holy mountain a few times," she insisted, "but my duties of late have been as a caretaker. I was needed here. Someone needs to call the lost dead to their rest."

She gestured to the expansive ruins. "Kyriléshar stands guard before the doors to Urrel's Hall. I carry his horn and guide the dead through. Few of the priestesses of Ile' have the right gifts to draw the dead, much less sing their souls. Fewer still can bear the touch of Urrel's Horn." She tipped the horn towards me.

"It magnifies the power of my song and extends my reach to the lost."

"That's what you were doing when you brought me here?"

"In part. It's a daily ritual."

"In part," I repeated, "but this time you did something else – something you were not supposed to do: You called to your parents."

Merilanna nodded. "In part," she hedged again. "Every year, on the day that they died, I call to them. Their spirits never reached Urrel's Hall. So, I pray that they will hear and will find peace at last."

"But you did something different this time. What was it?"

Regret bowed the priestess' head. "I went too far." She breathed the emotion into the wind as she readied her full confession. "There is a ritual. I found it in the temple archives, in an ancient codex that dates from the Second Age. It allows one to speak to the dead even through time – a communion of sorts. I used it…and all of this happened."

"You tossed a pebble into an ocean and capsized a fleet." The absurdity of the image left me shaking my head. "Don't worry, priestess, all the world's a shipwreck these days."

"All power has a cost." She frowned.

"I still don't understand how you were caught up in this though," Merilanna admitted. "These rite were for the dead, not for the living."

I just looked at her, letting her struggle with the conundrum. At last, a little epiphany washed over her expression.

"You – you're dead," she chirped her perplexing conclusion, like a child gleefully solving a riddle.

"Occasionally." I smirked. "But it never lasts."

"Hmmm…" came her odd reply as her eyes shifted away from me.

A grave thought resurfaced in my reverie. *Maybe, this time it would be.*

Merilanna started to say something excitedly, but I held up my hand. "If you're going to say I'm a wonder…or anything else like that – don't! One more compliment from you and I'll throw you off this mountain."

Resignedly, my guide laughed. "Alright, I won't tell you what you already know."

Her grin was infectious and her eyes sparkled happily, so I let her slide – not down the mountain! What kind of monster do you think I am?

Anyway, momentarily, she set her eyes back towards our next footsteps. "Let's go," she said. "The guardians won't stay in their caves forever, and we need to get to the lower gate before they rise."

I concurred and we got moving. At the landing where Ilé's arms outreached, though, I stopped. More stairs lead off to the sides and wound down the goddess' sleeves and through the folds of her dress to the ruins below, but they would have to wait. My footsteps were drawn a different way.

"The Tear-Stone," Merilanna said behind me as I slid towards the otherworldly obelisk.

Once again, I felt like the proverbial moth.

"I've seen things like this before," I commented just loud enough to be heard above the whipping wind. I could feel the energy emanating from it. The fur on my outfit began to prickle as I closed.

"Don't touch it," the priestess warned. "It is Death's door."

Heroes of the Third Age: Merilanna

I smirked back. "And I came through it."

"Then don't touch it twice." Her eyes sparkled with mischief as she interrupted herself, watching me closely before continuing.

"The guardians found you laying at its base and brought you to me."

"I guess I was too foul to eat."

"They said, you were a gift from the goddess."

At that, I turned and scowled sourly. "A curse, actually." I faced the crystal again. "Why is it called the Tear-Stone?"

Merilanna came to my side.

"Gifts and curses can be one and the same, depending only on one's point of view."

She gestured to the stone. "It's not named for the reason you might suppose," she explained. "Yes, in times past, the grieving gathered here – that is true. But, before then, there were others that stood here, and they did not come to weep for their departed kin. The Tear-Stone was here before mortal death ever came to be – before even the Elves wondered at its mystery."

I cut my eyes askance and regarded her as she reminisced. "It's a Waygate," I said plainly.

"Yes," Merilanna agreed, "but also something more."

"A Palesciaton," I added, my tone just as even.

The priestess gave a little half-snort, half-chuckle, closed her eyes, and shook her head with wonder. She folded her lower lip beneath her upper teeth to refrain from saying what she was thinking, not daring another compliment.

I spared her. "Yes, I know a lot of things," I said matter-of-factly, rolling my eyes back to the purplish crystal. "It's a doorway to Urrel's Hall, but it also opens to the heavens themselves – to the Palescia."

Merilanna nodded to the truth of it. "My mistresses say that it has stood here since before the Tablet of Tears was written."

"The story of how the world began."

"Yes. As it goes, when Chenayan Toni, the World-Mother, beheld her daughter, Pri, whose name is Narianna also – the daughter of tears – she wept with joy and sorrow: joy for the world that would be born in Pri's image; sorrow for the pain that would come as the river of time began to flow. The tears that were shed at that moment fell from the heavens and seeded the world, filling it with waters. This stone is one of those tears. Within it, great power flows."

"But not the way it's supposed to," I surmised. "Mordûn made a mess of that."

"Mordûn?"

"It's a long story, but the fire in the sky in the south you saw – that was Mordûn's doing. He was some sort of demon, but not one risen from the shadows of the Dark World. He came from out there." I pointed to the star strewn firmament. "My friends and I fought him on a mountaintop like this not so very long ago." I cast another glance to the priestess. "Your goddess made that mess. Now, I have to clean it up. So, don't judge yourself too hard for what you did. The gods are opportunists. I've no doubt their hands are in all of this. It's what they do."

I wanted to touch the obelisk, but I heeded Merilanna's warning. Shaking my head, I left it be and returned to the stair.

Like I said, it took nearly a half candlemark to make the descent to the lower part of the Lower Temple. Once on level ground again, our pace quickened. Dallying at the obelisk had cost us time.

That was an irony given that lost time was exactly what had cast me into this situation in the first place. The "me" that was now was not the "me" that was before. The disappearance of the village and the appearance of the unspoiled wilds on the far shore had hinted at my fate. I had crossed over the river into a tangled skein – from one epoch to another.

If Lady Dark was right, somehow, I – this portion of me – had been cleft from my dark side and tossed back to a time before my cursed blood ever even flowed. I wondered grimly what had become of my shadow. Without the light side of my soul to temper it, what horrors had it done? Had I become the demon that Fhaed was now obliged to hunt? He had faced me like that before and it had nearly cost him his life. Those memories haunted my steps once more

Merilanna was jabbering again.

"When we get outside, there's an old road that winds down to the valleys. You'll need to stay by my side. I'll have to guide you. You won't be able to see."

"Because of the clouds?" I asked.

The priestess' met my incredulous gaze with a look of firm certainty. "These aren't normal clouds."

I groaned. "Cloud magic? Seriously?"

She laughed.

"The Veil is very thin here; but, as we move down the mountain, it thickens. Where the clouds lay, it is easy to lose oneself. Everything is white. For the unwary, death is close at hand. I will lead you through, but you will have to trust me."

That's a hard one.

"Alright," I agreed.

A series of plazas remained for us to cross before we reached the last gate – well, the last gaping hole in the rock walls, that is. We had only entered the first when something moved in the shadows and caught my eye. It was time to meet the guardians, I supposed.

"We have company," I whispered, drawing Merilanna's attention to the lurking creature.

Instinctively, my focus scanned the rubble to our flanks expecting an ambush. The tactic was basic, after all. One predator makes itself known, fixating its prey, while its pack mates sweep in to spring their trap. To my chagrin, I neither saw, heard, nor smelled anything.

Prior to my current condition, my senses would have ferreted out every flea sneezing within a thousand paces. As it was, only the damned rock and snow registered in my perceptions. It was when the latter charged at us that I recognized how close we were to the Avharkiden dinner table.

"Run!" I shouted.

My feet were in motion before Merilanna's startled eyes spied the first hulking brute. She didn't follow – seemingly frozen in her tracks.

Alarmed, I spun. She was fumbling with her damned horn! Destiny was about to pay her a fateful call.

The Avharkiden were ferocious looking monsters. Covered head to toe with long, white fur, it was easy to see why they were called ghosts. Against the wintry backdrop, they were practically invisible. Inaudible was a different story. While stalking us, we never heard them; but, when they leapt from their hiding places, there was no escaping their bone-chilling howls. They came from everywhere.

Long of arms and short of legs, the beasts moved with simian bounds, jumping through the ruins with terrifying speed and agility. They almost seemed to materialize from one spot to the next without ever crossing the space between. I knew a lot about that little trick.

Sharp nails equipped their huge hands and dexterous feet. Fangs like ivory daggers sprouted from both their broad upper and lower jaws. What modicum of flesh was visible was eerily blue. Only their eyes flashed with deeper color. They seethed with red, befitting the beasts' lust for our blood.

Wind-Song flashed with starlight as I spiraled, my boots writing the story of my imminent death in the thin layer of snow that covered the plaza's paver stones. It was too late to run.

Through the caterwauls, I heard a sickening thud as time seemed to slow. Through the corner of my eye, I glimpsed my guide as she sprawled. Her horn flew from her hands upon impact just shy of her lips. A jagged stone the size of my head bounced a short distance away and scattered crimson as it rolled across the white drifts to a stop.

There was no time to assess her wounds.

From all sides, screaming white terrors closed in. All hope of calming my thundering heart abandoned me. It's hard to focus when everything is a blur.

Nevertheless, I managed to set my feet. Even without my demonic investitures, I still had my training – not that a firm, martial stance would do much good against creatures five times my weight and twice my height.

Somehow, I sighted the next missile that flew our way and avoided it in the only way that I could: I dove face first to the icy ground.

Spitting snow, I couldn't even scream when claws snatched me up. It was in that moment that I was grateful for the thick layers I wore. The beast's nails did not reach my skin. My steel, though frantic, did find its.

I'd like to say that the stroke was masterful. Honestly, though, it was purely reflexive. But it flashed true. Wind-Song's edge split through monster's cheek and slashed open its broad, flat nose. For a ghost, its blood was red enough.

The Avharkiden's howl of rage became a yowl of outrage. The pain I dealt drove the mad beast-man into a frenzy.

I might mention at this point that I cannot fly. If I could, I would have done so.

The monster flung me skyward as my sword's arc finished its work on its face. Like a pitiful, stuffed toy, I pinwheeled through the freezing wind towards a pile of rubble. Had the snow not mercifully drifted there before my arrival, I am certain that the crunching sound that accompanied my landing would have been from my bones. Instead, rather, the frosty mass cushioned the blow and swallowed me whole.

Dazed, I heard Merilanna scream out an odd, brutal melody. Terrified, I swallowed my heart before it suffocated me and battled my way out of my white grave. Ingloriously, I spilled out of the snowdrift, expecting a grisly sight.

To my amazement, the priestess was not dismembered. She had not regained her feet yet, but her arms and legs were still attached to her body.

Around her, a circle of Ghost-Men had been flattened by some magical force. They were alive, but seemed separated from their faculties. All were clutching at the wind aimlessly from their backsides, their legs spasming and their bodies convulsing. It looked as though the lot of them had been blasted by a lightning strike. My nose, though, caught no such telltale scent in the frigid wind. Whatever she had done, apparently, it transcended my mundane apprehension.

Outside the circle of the fallen, more of the creatures staggered. Some were holding their heads as if to keep them secured to their shoulders. All bloodthirsty intentions had been crushed instantaneously. Those that could do so were already retreating, returning to their shadowy lairs.

Merilanna's fear-filled eyes scanned the scene frantically. Relief flushed through her as she spotted me stumbling back to her.

My earlier admonition was repeated as I arrived. "Run," she said breathlessly.

I concurred and nodded eagerly. The Avharkiden were down, but they weren't going to stay that way.

Steadying each other, we hustled from the plaza.

My ribs ached and my companion wore a nasty smite on her right shoulder. Blood stained her sleeve.

Merilanna snatched up her horn along our path.

It wasn't a very graceful retreat, but we had survived the dinner bell.

Chapter 5: Beyond the Clouds

"Let me look at that," I said.

Merilanna winced as I peeled the sleeve of her tunic-dress away from her injured shoulder.

The wound was nasty. The rock had left a jagged gash of torn skin and bruised muscle, but no bones appeared broken.

"You're going to need a sling for your arm."

I tugged off my furry gloves to do the job.

"I'll be fine," the priestess argued weakly. Her eyes were still glazed from the shock. Her breaths were rapid with pain. "Pain is an old acquaintance. I have faith in My Lady."

I glowered. "It won't heal properly if you don't..."

Merilanna raised her good hand and stilled me. She lowered it slowly and began to whisper an incantation.

My frown darkened. Have I mentioned I hate magic? Anxiously, I cast a glance back towards the ruins of the Lower Temple that was now – hopefully – beyond a stone's throw behind us up the mountainside. Nothing had emerged...yet.

It began to snow, provoking my ire more.

I started to interrupt her. I needed to wrap that wound, and we needed to keep moving. But, before my protests aired, my words got caught in my teeth. Divine power filled the priestess' aura. The snow around her shimmered and settled, gathering most unnaturally upon my companion's injury. As it did, her suffering melted away.

"Thank you, My Lady," she exhaled in relief.

I leaned towards her and examined the red-stained snow. Gently, I wiped the smear away. Beneath, her skin shone, unblemished and unharmed.

Merilanna was looking at me. Her smile had returned.

"You see," she said warmly.

I sat back on my heels. "Yea, I see," I said dourly. It takes a lot to impress me, of course. "If she's going to protect you, she should yell 'Duck!' next time."

Another squashed snort of laughter as she apparently considered my suggestion.

Absently, I scooped a palm full of snow and scrubbed my hands. With that, we got going again.

As the clouds and my apprehension began to thicken, I asked the priestess, "What did you do to them?" Afterall, it was a useful trick.

"My lady has given me certain gifts. Every soul has a song. I simply disrupted theirs," she answered with typical, sacerdotal abstrusity. "They'll be alright."

"Can you do that to anyone?"

Merilanna chuckled lightheartedly. "If My Lady wishes it and my will is strong enough. I *am* only a servant."

"You hear the soul-songs of others, don't you?"

"Of course."

"Even mine?"

Ilé's priestess paused and pondered the question. "Yours," she ventured, "is quite different from any others I have ever heard."

"How?"

"It's hard to shape words to fit what I hear in you." We continued our descent. "You're…complicated, but I know you're very bright and very dark. But more bright than dark. A good person," she offered sweetly after a moment.

I snorted. *Good at causing trouble.*

"I know you have been through a lot – far more than anyone should," she added. "But, I know you're a fighter. The chords in you are very deep and very powerful. I know you are loyal and very stubborn. I like that about you."

The clouds had obscured the world completely now.   From the emptiness, my guide said, "Take my hand." I had little choice, so I did. Merilanna held my mitten firmly. We walked on.

"Is that how you do it – with soul-songs, I mean. Is that how you guide souls to their heavens?"

"It is. Within every soul, there are refrains that sing of the divine. Every god or goddess has his or her own song. It is the role of the Death-Maidens to lead the devout to the heavens."

I was curious. "Where would you take my soul, then?"

Long was the silence that followed. "Hell," was what I expected as an answer. "I don't know," came the reply instead. The bewilderment that tinged the priestess' voice almost amused me.

"Don't worry about it," I chuckled darkly. "The gods don't want me anyway, I promise you that."

"That's not so," Merilanna objected with a surprising degree of passion. "It's just, well, your song is more complicated than any that I have encountered before. I hear in you a holy chorus. It's like all of creation is wound up in you."

All of destruction, you mean.

A thought occurred to me. Yes, that sometimes happens. No, my brain does not hurt when it does. "Can you hear a soul's dark secrets?" I was – or used to be – especially good at that little trick.

"Yes," the void responded, squeezing my hand gently.

"Can you hear mine?"

Again, the hesitation. "In a way," Merilanna hedged. "Your soul-song is a conundrum."

"Most people would call it a mess." I could almost hear her grin.

"Not a mess," she laughed. "A symphony so grand that it overwhelms."

I harrumphed dubiously. "Just wait until you meet my dark half." I changed the subject. "How do you suppose my two soul-songs were torn apart?"

More pondering; more silence. Maybe I was hurting her brain.

"I'm sorry. I'm not really convinced that your soul has been torn in two. It's more like…well, like that part is asleep."

"Or not yet awake," I supposed.

"Yes," Merilanna agreed readily. "Exactly like that. The strings are there, but they are waiting to be strummed."

My cursed blood has yet to be born.

"Time," I muttered. "I was cast out of Time. Now, I'm before what I will be."

"Before your dark song began to play, perhaps," the priestess concurred.

"So, how do I start it again?"

"I think the answer to that lies where the chords fell still. That's where the tangled knot in the Tapestry is."

"Right. So, how are we going to get there? Walk?"

Merilanna squeezed my hand again for reassurance. "If we have to, yes. For now, we'll head to Asgevarheim and see what help the Jhar can offer. His warriors will know the fastest way south through the Fellenrev."

"And if he won't help?"

"He will. I can be *very* persuasive," the priestess promised. "Men like Jharin Bearslayer understand the importance of an afterlife. Without one, their legend will die. He'll help us. He knows who I serve."

Hours tired our tongues as we continued our descent from the holy mountain. The monotony of the trek was highly disconcerting. The priestess had warned that everything would be white. She was wrong. The night seemed perpetual in these lands. It did not relent. Thus, like my disposition, everything was black within the clouds. Our banter earlier had forestalled some of it, but not all. Being blind to the outside world left my vision no choice but to turn inward towards my imagination. There were always demons for me to battle there. I spent most of the climb brooding and seeing hungry wraiths.

The clouds were indeed magical. They were also maddening. Mercifully, before I was consumed by my own horrors, we breached the lowest layers and reemerged onto the mountainside. It was as if we stepped from Oblivion back into existence. Below, a narrow valley extended northwesterly before us to the sea.

"Something's wrong," Merilanna announced at the instant that the world appeared. "We should see the fires and smoke of the settlement from here. The coast is just there" – she pointed – "a day's travel."

Scanning the panorama, I affirmed the darkness. No telltale glimmers of light adorned the horizon. The world was a field of black. Only the frozen ocean in the distance glowed. There, the sky painted it faintly with curtains of color in hues of green and purple.

Tired though we were, worry spurred our heels, and we hastened our pace down the icy, rocky path towards the wood-line. Ahead, the pines looked like sharp teeth, eager to devour us. Snow weighed heavily upon their boughs. The drifts grew deep about them. Once we were away from the windswept slopes, it became clear that speed would not be possible. Freezing – for me, at least – seemed never more certain.

Merilanna had said a day's travel. "More like a lifetime," I grumbled under my breath. At least, it would be a short one. Reaching our destination would not be part of it in the end, however. As it was, I was already knee deep in snow and plowing deeper. Soon, I would be buried in it.

I shook my head. Riding Twilight, none of this white hell would have hindered me. I would have skimmed the snow like a breeze.

Merilanna looked back and watched me struggle. She turned towards me and offered her hand.

"I can carry you. It will be slower, but we'll still get there."

Unlike my own hedge trail of broken snow, her feet weren't sinking in the blasted stuff. Ile' was the goddess of winter, too. Damned freaky priestess witchy powers.

"Not in this life or any other." I growled.

"Alright," she mused, her face turning towards the sky then turning to look back towards the trench behind me. "If you insist."

I hate this weakness. After an hour more, I begrudgingly took her up on her offer. She graciousness saved her; I told you so, and I graciously didn't kill her.

Still, we had no choice but to push on into the steep valley.

To add to our misery, it began to snow harder not long after reaching the trees. A northerly wind returned our eyes to near blindness, whiting out the world once again. Soon, we were forced to find shelter and burrowed beneath the branches of a large evergreen. There, at least, we found a bed of drier needles and a break from the blizzard.

Nevertheless, my limbs were frozen. I couldn't feel my feet, and my brain wasn't much better. It's hard to think with ice in your skull. I could barely move. All I knew was that when I stopped shivering, I was done for.

A glimmer of amber light spared me. At some point, I had passed out. It was the light and the warmth that revived me.

The priestess had sparked a humble fire amidst the pine needles. It wasn't much, but it brought life back into my limbs and defrosted my mind.

"Are we there yet?" I joked weakly. I grimaced; my throat hurt.

A warm hand brushed my hair from my face. "The storm will pass. Then we will get moving again."

I realized that I was cradled in Merilanna's lap. She sat with her back to the tree trunk, holding me like a babe.

I frowned deeply and looked away. "Right," I groused. "Death favors me and now I have a priestess as a nursemaid."

"I'd rather be a friend," she replied lightly

"Friends are dangerous things. Hard to find, harder to keep." I quipped.

"That…is very true." She stared into some memory and left me in silence.

"How long have I been asleep?"

"A day, perhaps. I'm sorry."

I growled. Moving hurt, but I forced myself to sit up slowly. "Sorry? For what?"

Her eyes were downcast, avoiding mine. "For all of it. For bringing you here. For the pain I've caused."

"Stop," I snapped, though with less exasperation than normal. Apparently, freezing to death is exhausting work. "We've been through this already."

Merilanna's hung head nodded. "I wasn't thinking."

"You were feeling," I countered.

"Sister Steel warns me against that."

"Some people are better at being heartless than others…wait! Sister Steel? That's what you call her?"

Merilanna grinned mischievous. "Sister Silk and Sister Steel – though I would never let them hear me say it."

"Steel fits." I grinned back. Then stopped to survey our little cubby. It reminded me of another from a lifetime ago. I had been cold and scared then, too, hiding from the raiders that had destroyed my innocence and my world. Now, the cold was no different; and, admittedly, I was scared but not for the same reasons. Death and I had worked out our differences, you might say. No, my worry was for someone else. The fool had better be taking care of himself. If not, I'd kill him!

The priestess and I said little for a long while. I abandoned her lap, of course, and huddled near the fire. She had no need of its warmth. I envied that.

"Ilé keeps you warm?" I asked.

Merilanna's smile flickered in the firelight. "Not exactly."

My brow rose at that. She glanced at my puzzlement, then returned her gaze to the fire before saying, "From my mother – a gift of my blood."

"Your mother?"

A little nod edged with sadness.

"She was born of the winter wind – not of the earth but of the sky. It was for the love of my father, a mortal man, that she chose to walk upon the ground."

Merilanna looked over at me, another enigma. I'm not sure what she expected to see: horror, disdain, incredulity, or something else.

"My mother was a Sylph," she said plainly. "These mountains were her home." A dreamy expression crept across her face. The story of her parents' love glowed from her eyes as she recounted it. "As a boy, my father was very adventurous. He would climb these mountains, beyond the clouds, determined to reach the sky. It was there that he first heard her singing in the wind. He said it was the most beautiful thing he had ever heard.

"Through the years, he came back over and over. He would play his pipes and she would come to him, singing. He would watch her dance, whirling as a breeze in the snow, and they would whisper their secrets to each other." Her eyes held mine for a moment. In them, I saw such joy. "They were so different, but love brought them together. He asked her to be his wife. She wanted nothing more. So, she begged the heavens to let her be with him, and the gods granted her wish. They gave her a mortal life, and she went with him – back through the clouds, down to the world below. I was born of their love." I watched as Merilanna's happiness faded away as the story grew dark in her memories. "It could not save them."

Silence – save only for the crackling of the fire – weighed between us for a while. I could see the rest of her tale play across her face, painted in the shadowy light of the fire.

"The sisters raised you after that," I concluded.

Merilanna drew a full breath, filling herself with fresh composure. "Yes. The Avharkiden found me on the mountain and brought me to Kyriléshar. I was a wretched creature then. Ryva called me an abomination, too." Her smile was warm. The girl had a gentle heart.

"Those temples have been there for a long time," I commented, "and the Tear-Stone...even longer."

The priestess acknowledged the truth of it with a simple nod.

"People say," I continued, "that the Shining Folk left the world behind, that they couldn't stomach war; so, when it came, they abandoned their lands and fled beyond the mountains. Some of that, I know is true. But not all of it. Not all of the Elves left; I've met some. They weren't cowards. Your mistresses stayed in this world to guard the Tear-Stone?"

"Yes. And to serve Our Lady." Merilanna studied me, considering whether to ask the question that filled her mouth. Finally, she asked, "Who do you serve, Lyri?"

Saw that one coming...couldn't dodge it.

How to answer? It wasn't that I hadn't thought about it. It's just –
How do you explain breaking and unbreaking reality to fix something
the gods screwed up?

The priestess waited patiently but expectantly.

"No one," I snorted. "I think that's how it was meant to be. Whatever
I'm supposed to do ends up being the opposite of what I end up doing
anyway. I guess, Lady Dark was right about me. I am chaos." I amused
myself with my own musings for a moment. "Sometimes, it takes chaos
to show the gods what they've already broken. That way the bones of
the world can break again and then heal the way they're supposed to. I
break things. That's what I do."

"I understand," she nodded. "That makes sense."

She could had no idea what I was blabbing about. I didn't begrudge
her. She listened and tried. I shut up after that.

My throat hurt and I wasn't in the mood to waste more time explain
the inexplicable. I rubbed it indignantly. I was catching a cold: another
mortal misery I had thought behind me.

Demons don't catch colds! I snarled to myself.

"I'll gather some more firewood," Merilanna offered shortly. "It'll
need to dry out for a while, so I'd best get more now. There's no
knowing how long the storm will last."

I nodded and watched as she pushed aside the heavy boughs to reenter
the howling wind. It wasn't easy. Two feet of new snow had already
mounded against the limbs. She basically had to climb out of our hole.

Beyond the meager, orange glow of our fire, the world was deathly
dark and unbearably cold. There was nothing I could do about it. I
didn't want to admit it; but, in reality, I was a lot smaller than I pretended
to be. Alone, anxious, shivering, and miserable, I reacted in my usual
way: I got pissed off.

By the time the branches shuddered and peeled aside with my
companion's return, I was a spiteful, furry, little badger all wrapped up
in myself, my knees pulled to my chest and my glare smoldering from
within my hood.

"I think it will let up soon," Merilanna assuaged as she settled back in
beside the fire and added a few more branches from our drier pile.
"When it does, we'll get moving again."

It was small-talk, of course: just sound to fill the void. I think she was
used to talking to herself, actually. Stoking a fire and other mundane
things didn't usually require narration. I could tell she was nervous and
restless. Being helpless does that.

I didn't stoke the fire of our conversation, though, and her gabbing eventually died down. Silence returned. I closed my eyes and accepted it.

'Soon' turned out to be two more days – if you can count that faint glow in the sky that only lasts a few minutes as a day dawning. The time, at least, allowed us to get better prepared to move on.

We practically had to climb the damned tree to get out of our hole; but, once out, we had a new trick at our disposal. During the interim, the priestess and I had woven branches and sack cloth into somewhat serviceable snowshoes. They were clunky and awkward contraptions, but they kept me on top of the five new feet of snow that blanketed the mountain forest, forestalling our icy burials.

I gave one last look up the mountain. There wasn't much to see. We were beyond the clouds and Kyriléshar was lost in them once again.

"Let's go," I said.

Chapter 6: Forgotten Yesterdays

"There was a village here."

I watched as the priestess staggered ahead of me and turned about slack-jawed, her hands fanned wide at her side in utter bewilderment. She looked back to me as if to say, "I'm not mad!"

What I saw was an empty shoreline covered with rocks and snow. Thick ice covered the seawater.

Merilanna continued. "There were fishing boats and a breakwater." She turned and pointed to the steeply rising terrain behind me. "There – there was a chieftain's hall and, over there – there were houses riding the cliff. A road wound this way and that. I remember coming over this ridge and looking down into the lights shining up at me like jewels." She shook her head in disbelief.

There was nothing there.

The fjord, hooking back into the land, would be the perfect site for a village, though. The cliffs would guard it from the wind's worst. Add the breakwater she described and the sea's fury would be restrained. We were still a few hours from the open shore of the ocean, but well within easy reach for Kyrgevar mariners. So, yes, a village would be prosperous here. But, there was nothing. Just the wind and my guide's plaintive voice carried on it.

"How much farther to Asgevarheim?" I asked.

Merilanna shrugged. "Half a day more along the shore – if it's even there…"

I trudged up beside her. Her thoughts darted behind her eyes, searching desperately for some explanation. I already had one. The priestess reached it also. Her gaze settled upon me. "I told you," I said. "I break things."

"This wasn't *your* fault."

The span of implications suddenly overwhelmed her. She exhaled and shuddered. Wordlessly, she looked back towards the cloud-shrouded mountains where her temple-home was hidden.

"They knew," I said flatly.

Merilanna's long stare reeled back and settled upon me. "How?" she challenged.

It was my turn to shrug. "I don't know. They're elves. Who knows what they know? The world speaks to them in ways I don't understand. But" – I nodded assuredly – "they knew."

The priestess shook her head. "They couldn't know."

There wasn't much strength left in that challenge. I wasn't sure she was even arguing with me. Her dispute had seemed to turn inward.

"Why wouldn't they say something?" she asked herself…and maybe me.

I answered anyway. "Wouldn't have mattered. When we came down off the mountain, we left their world behind. Up there is a sanctuary. Down here is reality, and it's broken all to hell."

She stared back towards the mountain temple, furrowing her brow as she chewed on her thoughts. She looked back towards the forsaken shore for a moment before back to the mountain again with suspicious eyes. "What is an avalanche if it is not one snowflake placed perfectly, tettering on transcendence?" The priestess' words were barely a whisper nearly stolen by the breeze. She was reciting words that had been spoken to her by her teachers that were now beginning to make sense. Her frown deepened. "They should have said something." She declare more firmly, and directed the comment to me.

"Did Ilé?" I asked, scoffing. "She never said anything in your prayers, either did she?"

Merilanna looked away, crestfallen, jaw tight.

"No," I stated for her. "She didn't. The gods never explain themselves. So, neither did your mistresses. They just expect us to go fix things." I looked around us. "We're not in the world you remember. Those yesterdays haven't happened yet and there's no guarantee that they ever will."

The priestess nodded, acknowledging what was still difficult to comprehend. "I had not expected the effects to reach this far. Has the whole world been unraveled? Is everything being rewoven?"

I, too, was beginning to realize how screwed up things were. I, too, was grasping the implications. The more I did, the more it frightened me. The more it frightened me, the more angry I got. I ground my teeth to keep my curses inside.

I guess this is what breaking the bones of reality feels like.

Merilanna was pondering. It was easy to tell. She was talking to herself. "Without the Jhar's warriors," she was saying, "finding our way south will be impossible. There are thousands of miles of wilderness. I don't know the way."

I resisted the urge to put my back to the north wind and point straight ahead...barely! Something suddenly occurred to me me though. "I have an idea," I blurted.

Nonplussed, Merilanna regarded me.

"Shetra – she's a companion of mine and a seer – she came to Asgevarheim to ask Bearslayer for his help in the war. He refused, but that's not the point. Shetra used Clangrym, a Circlestone in the Silverwood, to travel here. There must be another Waygate nearby. If there is, maybe we can use it!"

"Yes," Merilanna agreed. Energy returned to her voice. Her eyes shined again. "Yes, there is one. It's on the hill above the Bearslayer's hall."

"Good. That's where we're going."

"But, Lyri, how will we open the gate? I don't know the rituals. Such portals require magic. Don't we need a Waystone?"

I smirked. "I am a Waystone."

Well, I used to be. Or something similar.

The priestess cut me a dubious look.

"You yourself said that my soul-song sounded like all of creation. There's a reason for that."

Merilanna's smile broke and beamed. "Alright. It's worth a try."

The jaunt to where Asgevarheim would – or might – one day stand took, as Merilanna had said, about half a day more. Of course, the perpetual night made that accounting somewhat obscure.

When we arrived, exhausted, the scene was as barren as it had been at the site of the missing village. Here, too, the topography I looked out across seemed perfect for a town. The shore formed a natural harbor.

Pack ice filled it at the moment, but it could be bustling in the spring and summer with ships.

"That's the hill," Merilanna said, pointing to the highest rise overlooking the crescent-shaped, coastland.

I could see the Circlestone even in the dark. Auroras limned it. Its silhouette, like that of a crown atop a baldheaded king, was distinct.

Impulsively, I wanted to run the rest of the way there. The icy daggers that filled my straining lungs, though, made that impossible. I had been chuffing along for hours, spurred by both my stubbornness and my eagerness to escape this frozen hellscape. My legs protested the urge as well. They were numbed to the bone by the cold, so pressing through the Ilésian headwind would take time.

Companionly, Merilanna embraced me about my shoulders. "We're almost there," she exulted.

Scarcely another footstep fell before I grabbed her arm. Experience warned me of something. "Wait! It will be guarded."

The priestess heeded, looking down to me expectantly.

"Places of power always are," I explained.

Merilanna's head bobbed, agreeing. "We'll circle around, then, and see what's there first."

The tree line was well removed from the coastal plain. The severe winds would not allow the forest too close. A rocky tundra spread inland for miles before the forest took hold to any measurable extent. Thus, we were left exposed as we weaved our way through the snow and undulating terrain. It was dark, but the glowing lights that washed over the sky did provide some dim illumination. We couldn't see much, but I was sure that whatever might be out there had sharper eyes than us.

Waygates are ancient structures. They were built by elementals long before the elves came along. Their primordial magic still protects them; and, from what little I had learned, there were always guardians nearby.

It was unnerving, then, that our approach went unchallenged.

Moth to a flame...here I go again.

"There's great spiritual power in these places," Merilanna commented as we marched across the windswept plain towards the circle of stones.

These, I noted, did not bear their brothers upon their shoulders. There were no lintels. Instead, the plain about the foot of the hill was covered by an array of stone boxes. Well, they weren't actually boxes; but, in the dark, that's what they looked like. Most of the cromlechs were about the size of a small hut. Four flat rocks topped by a fifth formed the structures. There were dozens of them – an army camped beneath the crown of their king.

"Guardians," I muttered darkly.

"The tombs of the ancients," the priestess whispered reverently.

Undaunted, I led the way and began weaving through the strange mausoleums. Their rocks were rough, irregular slabs. No stone cutter had hewn them cleanly from the earth. It was as if giant hands had scooped them from the jagged shoreline where the sea had bitten them from the land and had stacked them just so. In the dim light, I could faintly discern flowing symbols chipped into their faces.

"These are elven marks," Merilanna said, puzzled, tracing her fingers through the grooves of one. "They aren't *kaelvrot*. I had always assumed that our people had made them as places to bury our dead, but no."

I frowned back at her.

"Sorry." Merilanna smiled sheepishly and took her hand away from the stone. "I touch things."

"Bad habit," I grumbled.

She grinned. "But I always learn so much!"

Returning my glare to the ascent, I continued to trudge. My guide languished behind, still befuddled by the strange markings.

"They're names!" the priestess suddenly proclaimed, stilling my steps.

"So?" I shrugged. "Gravestones usually have names."

Merilanna blanched...I think. It's hard to tell in green and purple light. She looked around at the assembled rocks, aghast. Quickly, she flitted to the nearest, then the next nearest, then the next. "These are families."

I mulled here words. "The elves left, remember. They didn't stick around to fight." I glanced back up at the Circlestone. "I guess some of them left from here."

"Recently," Merilanna added. "The carvings aren't all that weathered; they're almost new." Another thought hung on her face for a moment. "Where did they go and when??"

I puffed a cold cloud of breath and shook my head. "Away. It doesn't matter."

"Away" was what I had in mind as well. I clambered on with renewed urgency.

At the top, hundreds of feet above the ocean of ice, I stopped and marveled. The ring of stones were towering, far taller than most I had seen in Einhervaldheim. Within their midst was a single obelisk that dwarfed the others. Its tip speared the sky and shimmered incandescently. Only the Valstone in Valistad was its superior. In splendor, though, this rock was incomparable. Flecks of crystal-like scales adorned its surface, holding the aurora's glamour. Rime grew from its edges and shimmered with iridescence.

"Someday, the council of elders will meet here," the priestess behind me said musingly, reflecting upon a future yet to come. "They'll pray for guidance."

We could use some of that, but my knees where too obstinate to bend. I wondered how long it would be until my kindred bowed here.

My thoughts were fleeting on the subject. It didn't matter. What mattered was getting back to where I started and fixing this mess as quickly as possible. The longer this went on, the worse it was going to get. Of that, I was certain.

"Lyri?"

"Merilanna?"

She chuckled at my exasperation as I paused and turned back to her.

She chewed her lip for a moment looking at me, then up at the stones, then at me.

I raised my brows.

She blew out a sigh, her mind settled. "I made you a gift." She pulled a tiny braid of her hair from around her neck and drew it over her head.

Weird.

A snowflake sparkled, irrediscent in the weave of the hair necklace.

"A hair necklace. Really?" Escaped my lips as a deadpan reply.

Merilanna snorted, her eyes crinkling with humor.

She snorts too much. She should just laugh.

"I didn't have a proper lace." She shrugged nonchalantly. "I made do with what I had. It isn't much – just a small bit of finding magic in case we get separated."

"I hate magic."

Her head tilted, considering me. "You shouldn't hate yourself, Lyri. Its not healthy."

I rolled my eyes but held still as she dropped her little fetish over my head and tucked it beneath all the blasted furs.

Magic. Inside, I shuddered.

I drew another deep, cold breath and blew my ruminations into the depths of my mind. Then, without ceremony, I stomped into the center of the circle and regarded the giant, shiny prick in front of me.

Merilanna swallowed her priestly reverence and followed a bit more tentatively. She didn't say anything, but I could feel her eyes on me, watching intensely and waiting.

Earlier, I did mutter something presumptuous about being a Waystone, I think. As I stared up at the rock not knowing what to do, I hoped that my comment was a tiny understatement and that some flourish of brilliance would happen. So far, though, the monument was ignoring me.

Now what, genius?

From what I understood of my genesis, I shared souls with Auril the Weaver, a goddess that everyone thought was dead, and with Dyerbazog the Destroyer, a perfectly magnificent dragon with a sleeping disorder. Ilé had worked all that out, which I still wasn't sure was a good thing or a bad thing. Originally, I think she did it to inflict me on the gods – some sort of vengeance for evils done to her – but I wasn't really sure any longer. I guess the gods screwed each other over as much as they did mortals and deserved whatever enmity she bore.

Anyway, as it turned out, all of her scheming ended up saving the world from a darker fate than me. I'm pretty sure that wasn't part of her plan.

You see, there is this war that keeps happening over and over again. Narianna, where we are, is called The Bright World. I don't always share that opinion, as you may have noticed. Morthalin, the Dark World, keeps trying to gobble her up – it's a demonic thing. Don't try to figure it out.

Well, ever so often, these Waygates I keep chattering about line up with the Dark World and demons come over for dinner uninvited. A sort of world war thing happens when they do. We call it a Shadowfall. And, we are in one now…though, given my current predicament, I'm not sure which one.

This time…or the last time – I'm getting confused with all the chaos going on – some dark lord named Khazul Mordûn showed up from beyond our little neighborhood spat and decided it would be the perfect time to invade, clean up the scraps, take over both worlds, rule for eternity, etcetera, etcetera. But, I guess he underestimated what resurrecting a goddess and waking up a dragon would do to his plans. That's where I came in. Too bad for him.

Everything else that you've been reading is what came after. I was, to use the terms I just mentioned: cleaning up "the scraps" when we met – chasing down demon-infested Dyards.

Now, all of that aside, it turned out that my connection with Auril made me especially good at using the Waygates. After all, the Threads of Creation she wove were twined around them. I suppose, as well, that this special talent left me especially vulnerable to the mess that the wars within wars caused. Lucky me.

So, here we are.

"Can you open the gate?"

I knew she was going to ask that...*sigh*.

My shoulders slumped. Without responding, I took a deep breath, reset myself, and straightened, trying to focus.

There was supposed to be swirling lights and heavenly music playing by now.

Nothing.

"It's broken," I said dourly under my breath.

The priestess heard me.

"Broken?" Alarmed, Merilanna entered the ring and moved quickly to my side. As she did, the air began to shimmer and whisper a ghostly song.

I grimaced and winced but did not face her.

"It's working!" she exclaimed. "What did you do?"

"It's a god thing. You wouldn't understand," I blabbed before turning about.

The priestess was wide-eyed and grinning childlike. "I've never actually been inside a Waygate," she confessed. Her gleeful gaze lit upon me. "How does it work?"

I looked around at the growing helix of light for answers. Something sparkled, but it wasn't the whirling motes of ley lines that caught my attention. It was Merilanna's horn!

"Waystone," I declared, pointing at the dangling device.

Caught off-guard, the priestess did not immediately understand. She looked down at the instrument and lifted it up, puzzled.

"Urrel's Horn?" she asked. "But it's not a stone."

"It doesn't have to be a stone." I shook my head impatiently. "Most are, but some aren't." I spread my arms. "I'm not a magic rock, but Waygates open for me."

Merilanna did not seem convinced.

"How can that be? " She frowned considering the new puzzle. "It is a tool to call the dead to their destiny. It amplifies my song and extends my will farther than I can reach alone. How else would I be able to draw them from across all lands to the roof of the world and lead them to their afterlives?"

"Yes," I argued, "at the Tear-Stone. But, somehow, its magic has to do with the Waygates, too. It snatched me from a Circlestone, remember? It plays notes heard by every ear as familiar. It's like, the ley lines all point to the horn and the spirits flow."

The priestess nodded as she began to understand.

"So, if I blow Urrel's Horn, every Waygate that hears will connect here. Maybe. Do you think you can find the line that leads back to your friends if I do?"

Time to fess up a bit.

Resignedly, I shook my head. "I don't know. Whatever happened to me at the river, I think it's holding back my power in this as well. I can't tell where the lines go. I can't hear them the way I could before."

Confusion creased Merilanna's brow. "So, what are we going to do?"

"All I do know is that we can't stay here. If we ride this light, we could end up anywhere – maybe somewhere worse."

That optimistic smile again lit upon the priestess' lips. "I have faith in My Lady. We have to try."

I don't!

I really hated saying it, but I did. If Ilé wanted me dead, I'd already be dead. "Alright," I conceded. "Do it."

Merilanna nodded, put Urrel's Horn to her lips, and blew.

Light exploded around us.

Chapter 7: Guardians

After trumpeting, the priestess began singing. I don't know why. I guess she was swept up in the moment. For that matter, we both were. Waygates do that. They swarm with light and sling you away to wherever the Threads of Creation that touch them go. If you know what you are doing, you can pick the path. If you don't, well, you end up somewhere.

Generally speaking, Wayfarers – those that know what they are doing – call to their desired destinations. Every stop along the way has a name and every name has its own special power. Waystones carry within them that power. They know the names of those places to which they are attuned. It's sort of like they listen; and, when the name is spoken – or sung or screamed or whatever – they wake up. When they do, the Waygate opens to where that name is telling it to open. So, I guess the easiest way to think about it is that a Waystone is a keyring and a Waygate is a room with a door or doors. A Wayfarer knows which key to use and which door to open.

Sound simple? It isn't.

Most people cannot tell one key from the next. The Elves could, but not people today. How all this works had been forgotten and most of the Waystones lost. The Waygates were still around, but what they were –

people made up stuff to explain them. The only thing that had seemed to endure was that they were magical and, to a lot of folks, either holy or unholy. That made sense. Wizards and priests loved the places. Even if they couldn't use them for what they were intended, they knew that power flowed through them. It was no wonder, then, that churches and temples and shrines and magic towers and all sorts of other high and mighty places were built around or on top of them.

As for me, I'd had the displeasure of being tossed around the Bright World and beyond like a child's ball by these things recently. Yes, the trips were awe inspiring and dazzling, but the process still bewildered me and made me cringe. No, it didn't hurt; it was just...weird.

Apparently, Merilanna liked it.

She blew her horn of death and away we went. I did mention that Waystones don't have to be stones, right? They just have to carry the names of the places the Waygate knows within them. That's important because not every Waygate knows the name of every other Waygate. I guess some of them don't talk to each other. It's like a worldwide web. That probably makes more sense to you than to me. Fancy folks call it the Tapestry.

So, anyway, Merilanna blew her horn and the Waygate exploded with light and sound – and I don't just mean Merilanna's singing. That came later. When Waygates open not only is there always lots of flashing, whirling light, but also a flourish of music. It sounds like music, at least. All of creation is filled with divinely orchestrated compositions. Open a Waygate and all of those channels of sound come streaming in. The first few times it happens, your senses overload. Then, when the trip is over, the euphoria fades and your feet are back on the ground – just ground somewhere different from where you started...usually.

I say "usually" because that's not what happened this time.

Merilanna blew her horn of death and the Waygate opened. Light and sound swallowed us up and the priestess – probably smiling ear to ear – started singing along. Now, I realize that last time she did this she was calling to her dear, departed parents' spirits – she said as much. This time, though still ridiculously beautiful, her song was different. I remembered the first song very well. I had chased it down and it had brought me here – to Kyriléshar, anyway. This song was much more soaring and complex. I don't sing – be grateful for that – so I can't really tell you all the technical things that singers do when they are singing, but I can tell you that her song was pretty damn amazing. It was almost as if she was engaged in a dialog, a musical discourse with reality itself.

So much for me being a Waystone and some sort of Wayfarer virtuoso. The priestess had a gift. I was just an enigma with an ego.

Later on, I wondered in retrospect whether hanging around with Elves most of her life had anything to do with her talent. Maybe, maybe not. I do think that being the daughter of a Sylph did. Air elementals were always singing.

The Waygate opened. Light and sound swallowed us up. Merilanna started singing. And we ended up standing in the circle of stones right back where we began.

I blinked and shook my eyeballs and eardrums back into focus.

Looking to the priestess, I started to ask the obvious question, but held my tongue when I saw her expression. She wasn't smiling. In fact, she was slowly turning to look back over her shoulder with that wide-eyed look of apprehension that says, "Oops."

For the record, "Oops" is never a good thing.

The song had been interrupted.

I sighed and turned also, following her timorous lead. A foul-tasting word formed in my mouth before I ever saw the "Oops."

"Guardians," I groaned, exhaling out my exasperation.

There they were: Elves - an army of shimmering, scowling specters clad in bad attitudes and gleaming, golden armor, pointy spears and swords leveled at our hearts to say hello.

Slowly, reflexively, Merilanna raised her hands, offering a peaceful surrender.

Me? I raised my hands, too. The only difference was that I had a sword in them and a peaceful surrender wasn't what I was offering. The priestess and I have slightly different personalities, you may have noticed.

The most decoratively dressed Alurishi knight spoke.

It's funny how an elf's voice always sounds so melodious. Even when he's ferociously telling you that you're about to die for daring to trespass on his people's sacred lands, it sounds so proper and refined. You almost want to say, "Yes, please!"

Thankfully, Merilanna didn't.

Instead, she started jabbering back in the Aluri tongue, apparently catching "Shiny Pants" off-guard.

The thing about the elven language is this: despite what your ears hear, your brain knows what's being said – if the speaker wants you to, that is. Neither the priestess nor the knight shared with me their banter.

For my part, I wasn't all that impressed. In fact, I sulked. The elven army wasn't paying me much attention. They were focused on the priestess. Stupid bastards! I was the one with the sword! Okay, so I'm a snarling runt. That doesn't give anyone the right to ignore me! Happens all the time, though. Being underestimated is the mistake that my former enemies have often made – once!

I got bored with the grownups talking. Pleading for my life wasn't something I was good at anyway. I never practice.

"Did someone mention dying?" I taunted, shifting my stance and leveling my blade towards the gleaming guardians. "Who's first?"

Merilanna gasped. That stopped the chatter at least.

The elf commander's eyes narrowed within his fine helmet. He shifted his own stance.

Finally, a little respect!

"Please," Merilanna interjected her words, her hands, and her body between us. "We mean no harm."

I peered from behind the priestess, matching my snarl with that of the looming elven avatar. "I'm still deciding."

The elf's spine straightened. It was easier for him to look down his perfect nose that way.

"These lands will not be infested by your kind," he hissed – it was very pretty sounding, I thought. "Enough has been sacrificed. We will yield no more! Return to your horrors, humans. Never again dare this path. For if you do, you will surely die!"

I yawned. I couldn't help it.

"We won't return," Merilanna promised. "We're just trying to find our way south. The Threads of Creation are snarled around this girl's fate. If we don't get back to where the tangle began, death may be all that awaits any of us."

The knight's stern glare settled upon the priestess. It started to ease as he looked at her. Compassion, it seemed, was more readily attainable when someone beautiful is asking. Puppies get petted; slugs get stomped.

"Whatever evils your Shadowlord has brought," the knight said firmly, "we are beyond their reach. If your necromancers have poisoned these lands, then the death they have sown will be yours to reap." His countenance hardened again as his eyes fell upon me. "We will not save this demon from her fate."

I smirked.

His attention snapped back to the priestess. "But I will gladly see her gone from here."

With that, the knight stepped back. His army did as well. Once all were beyond the ring of stones, he raised his gauntlet-clad hand and intoned some piece of a song.

Merilanna watched and listened intently.

The light began to swirl again and the elf's voice twirled into it. Just before the energy swallowed us whole once more, I caught the knight's eye and, still smirking, waved goodbye.

It hurt my feelings that he didn't wave back.

Not really.

This time, the light and accompaniment shot us away. Even before my eyes and ears caught up, my skin registered the change in scenery. I was so happy! It was warm!

Happiness never lasts long, of course.

Yes, it was warm. Warm turned out to be those few seconds before hot sets in. So, to be completely accurate, I was happy just long enough to realize that Elves can't be trusted any more than anybody else. They have a mean streak, too. They also have nearly immortal lifetimes to refine vindictiveness into an artform. Elves like artsy stuff.

Now, before you judge shiny pants too harshly, let me back up for a moment and toss in some perspective.

Before we opened the Waygate, unannounced and uninvited, there had been some pretty bad stuff that had happened. Bards have tried to put it into more flowery language, but the basics are this. The Elves had lived in peace for centuries all over Narianna. It was pretty much their world. Then, a big Shadowfall happened. Armies of beast-men – ancestors of we humans – marched up from the south filled with demons in their souls. What followed was an apocalypse and a genocide. The Elves were the recipients of both. Some say they left, withdrawing into magical sanctuaries, so that, mercifully, the war would not go on. Others claim that they were decimated and were forced to retreat or be completely exterminated. Personally, I think it was a little of both. Regardless, you can begin to understand why we humans are not very well loved by our Elven neighbors. In this case, Merilanna and I came knocking at their door while the wounds were still very fresh. So, don't judge Shiny Pants too harshly. He did let us live…sort of.

Ok, enough of that.

The dazzling white light that swallowed us up melted into a hellish red glow. The pretty music descended into a rumbling, grumbling growl. The heat hit us and so did an overpowering, sulfurous stench.

Merilanna wasn't singing anymore. She was retching.

Admittedly, I was too. The moment we arrived where the noble knight had sent us my nose and throat exploded. My eyes seared and everything in my head became goo. The scorching air braised my skin. Oddly enough, being clad like a furry bear spared me the full brunt of it. Not much was exposed to cook.

The priestess fared far worse. I guess the Elven knight's compassion wasn't that great. I heard Merilanna raise a choking cry, "Lady help us!"

Blearily through my evaporating eyes, I saw a windswept cloud of red cinders sweep over her like a swarm of flies. Everything they touched flared with fire, peppering her silky dress with black burns, singeing her white hair, and stinging her perfect skin with blisters.

Frantically, I surveyed our new hell. We were on the slopes of a damned volcano!

All around us, liquid fire surged. Waves of rotten gas rode the orange rivers. Plumes of ash rained down. Much of it glowed, still burning, ablaze with the earth's fury. Even the jagged, obsidian island where we stood smoldered from below.

Whirling about, I spied a twisted pillar of rock. It, too, pulsed with its own inner, fiery rage. Encircling us were its attendants. We were in the midst of another Circlestone.

"Ardra," I wheezed. "The bastard sent us to Ardra!"

For those of you that can't tell, Ardra isn't a very nice place. I've visited on a few occasions and can confidently report to you that it was hellish every time. I don't recommend it.

But it wasn't always like this.

Once upon a time, as the story goes, Ardra – called Elyarsa back then – was a beautiful land surrounded by soaring, snowcapped mountains, spanned by emerald green, forested valleys, and filled with a sparkling blue lake. At its center, there rose the tallest and grandest of the mountains, Altairas. It stood as an island ringed by the pure waters flowing down from the countless, majestic waterfalls. Here, the Elves – Iridescians, they were called – lived in abject luxury and loved their little piece of paradise, their city floating on islands of flying rock like a necklace of glittering crystals about the mountain. While the rest of the world was going to hell, they were all snug and comfy. That is, until the Destroyer showed up and wrecked their world.

You see, while the Elves were ignoring their responsibilities, all sorts of bad things were happening outside. Secure in their own arrogance, they didn't notice the demons beyond that were tormenting the dreams of a particularly powerful dragon named Galandrake. Poor Galandrake tried to get the Iridescians' attention to help him, but they couldn't hear his screams. Apparently, their music and laughter was too loud.

So, when Galandrake finally cracked up and went crazy, he was more than a little irritated with the Elves.

How irritated?

Well, let's just say that he flew up to the heavens, told the gods to kiss his ass, then turned tail and dropped like a meteor on Elyarsa Altairas. Everything went bad at that point, and he burned the Iridescians' dreams to ashes. From then on, he was called Dyerbazog the Destroyer.

We're related.

Ardra is what was left and it's still burning.

There is more to the story, of course: a dead goddess' resurrection, saving the dragon from his madness, and so on. But I told that tale earlier, so you will need to go back and pick it up from the beginning yourself. I'm a little busy with this one.

Back to it.

Merilanna was on fire. That left her pretty much incoherent, which is understandable.

My own garb was smoking. I only had a few seconds before the furnace set little smoky bear alight as well. Thus, the practical choice was clear: get the hell out of here!

Options were not great. We were surrounded by lava on an island of volcanic rock being snowed on by burning ash and being fanned by flaming gases. My joy was almost indescribable.

I did the only thing I could think of: I snatched Merilanna's horn and blew it so hard my eyes crossed.

As you might guess, a random toot on a magical horn isn't much of a rescue plan. Desperation, though, has a way of muddying higher thoughts.

The Waygate didn't open. No light. No nice music.

So, I blew it again…and again…and again.

Those seconds I mentioned were almost up. I was about to be a fireball. I've been one before; it's exciting, but not fun.

With what little vision I still managed I could see that Ilé's priestess was doing her best to fight fire with ice. Put the two together and you get a lot of steam, so it was hard to tell if she was winning. She was no longer on fire. That's good. But she was in the middle of an erupting geyser of her own making. That's bad.

I would have marveled more if something hadn't answered the horn's call and distracted me. Luckily, I didn't wind the thing right. If I had, a horde of lost souls might of showed up for directions to their afterlife and been pretty peeved with me. Instead, something with a slightly better attitude appeared: a grinning demon.

How, you may ask, is the arrival of a grinning demon a better option than being cooked by a volcano?

Please remember that part of my problem here stemmed from not being able to access my dark powers. All along, I had assumed that sorcery of some sort had stripped me of my shadowy half and that the knot in the Threads had tossed me back in time to before my curse was conceived. While all of that made some twisted sort of sense, it turns out that the theory was only partially correct. Indeed, my black flame had been extinguished when I crossed the river. What I didn't realize was that it was only the fuel for that fire that had been removed, not my inner spark. All of that elysian purity had just robbed me of my stock of coal. You can think of it as an unwelcome bath. All my dirty parts had been washed clean. Unfortunately, those dirty parts are what I use to annoy the gods.

Then, a demon shows up – probably for a quick snack – and all my predatory senses reignite.

Thank you, Mr. Demon. It's so nice when your meals are delivered.

Demons come in lots of flavors. I tell you this because I doubt that many of you have munched on a demon before. Some of you...and I know who you are...have. But most of you haven't. So, let me explain a little bit about demons.

First, as you may have deduced, there are lots of different kinds – ergo, lots of flavors. Lots of kinds; lots of flavors. Make sense?

Let's start with the Shadowfalls.

Like I've mentioned before, there's the Bright World, Narianna, and the Dark World, Morthalin. Between them, there are countless portals. Most of the time, these gateways are locked up tight – and for good reason; but, from time to time, like clockwork, the Bright World and the Dark World get cozy as they dance through the cosmos and the locks start to break apart. That's bad news. When it happens, dark things from Morthalin cross over to pay their respects. These are the Shadowfalls.

I suppose, if you lived in Morthalin, you might call them Lightfalls or something...nevermind.

Anyway, they start small – barely even noticed. Then, year over year, they get larger and larger and more and more common, until, finally, you have the grand affair: a Greater Shadowfall. After that, things wind down. Whoever is lucky enough to be left when the smoke clears has the pleasure of picking up the pieces and carrying on. It takes centuries for it all to play out.

Okay, demons...

Demons live in Morthalin, but they love to vacation in Narianna. When the Shadowfalls are small, only little demons can make the trip. When they get bigger, bigger demons can come over. Once the Greater Shadowfall hits, every demon in hell lines up for a chance. Thankfully, the high season is short, and the biggest gates close before they can all show up.

You also have gatekeepers – guardians – here in Narianna whose job it is to keep the riffraff out. Unfortunately, not all posts are manned and some that are – like the Unholy See of Armadar – are staffed with pro-demon supporters – like the Morarmadin. This makes things complicated for everyone who happens to be anti-demon, which is just about everybody else.

The most common sorts of demons are what we call Shadows. These little guys are found everywhere – just like normal shadows. And, like normal shadows, they don't have physical bodies. Instead, what they love to do is hide out inside a host where they can stir up trouble. Contracting a Shadow is sort of like having a diabolic flu. Their hosts go from being nice and friendly one minute to cruel and hateful the next.

Shadows, you see, feed upon strong emotions. The darker, the better. What is worse, they are contagious, spreading and multiplying from one host to the next like...well, like the flu. Whole regions can be infected in no time flat.

Getting rid of them is tough, too. Sometimes magic works. Priests do what they can to help, but they're often overwhelmed by the sheer number of cases. When armies are infected, things get really bad fast. Bloodlust is hard to stop. Don't believe me? Ask the elves. They can tell you plenty about genocide.

After the Shadows, there are the Shadow Demons. Shadow Demons have physical bodies when they want to. You might think of them as grown up Shadows. After a Shadow has gorged itself like a caterpillar on hate and suffering, it breaks from its chrysalis host and becomes a Shadow Demon.

Shadow Demons can take on the physical aspects of their hosts or just slip around as a Shadow doing particularly evil stuff. Over time, they get more and more powerful and scheming. They can be a real problem.

Next are the Shades. Shades are pretty messed up. They are the offspring of Shadow Demons and mortals. It's rare, thankfully – I think it's gross – but it does happen. In Morthalin, it apparently happens a lot. Whole armies of Shades have marched from the Dark World in the past.

These twisted creatures, while only half-demon, are, with very few exceptions, wholly evil. Able to move through the world undetected by normal means, the wickedness they can do is impressive. There's no telling how many hold positions of power and influence. Never trust a politician. One well-known is the aptly named Shade Prince of Armadar, Tyvervexius, High Priest of the Morarmadin. His schemes for world domination are legendary.

There are other types, of course, but those are the most identifiable of the Lesser Demons.

Then, there are the Greater Demons.

These creatures come in all shapes and sizes but are, as I said before, unable to enter Narianna except during the Greater Shadowfalls. When they do show up, though, you can't miss them. They have all the scary things you probably think of when you imagine a demon: horns, hooves, wings, tails, fangs, fire, claws and scales. All that stuff epitomizes the Morkyri – that's the name scholars use for them.

I've met a few. Some were just hulking brutes. Others were titanic monsters that could level an army singlehandedly. Needless to say, they're always a problem. I really have to have an appetite where Greater Demons are concerned.

So, to summarize, Shadows can range from snack-sized to meals, Morkyri can be a full-on buffet…well, to me anyway.

The particular demon that came to dinner today was of the shadowy variety. It had expected a quick bite, so I gave it one.

Merilanna was its intended target. Shadows love strong emotions. Pain, fear, desperation, anger: all those were wrapped in her into a tasty morsel for the fiend. Steamed priestess was on its menu.

Actually, it was the steam around the priestess that saved her. Without it, I probably would not have spotted the Shadow in time. But, the steam gave just enough contrast. I saw it as it swept in behind her.

Typically, when I am on the hunt, the Shadows that infest men's souls call to me. I can see the darkness inside. I can feel the corruption, the sin.

The thing is, the Shadows can also sense me. My presence inflames them like the bellows of a forge. My own darkness fans theirs and they go crazy, unable to hold back their darker urges. For their hosts, this means bad things are about to happen. It's hard to devour a Shadow without killing the host, especially if the infection has corrupted the host's soul beyond salvation.

This hunt, though, was different. My inner darkness had been pretty well extinguished, so the fiend didn't even notice me.

Merilanna startled – which was impressive given all that was distracting her at the moment – when I sprang her way. She had no idea why I came racing and shrieking like a hellion towards her with my sword in hand. I'm pretty sure the sight was as bewildering as it was terrifying, especially when my furry, little outfit burst into flames about half-way there.

Poor Merilanna. I would have to apologize later.

The Shadow saw me too late. It was just about to wrap its claws around the priestess' soul and duck inside her body when I struck. Of course, this was not a physical blow. Remember, Shadows don't have bodies. It was more like a bass swallowing a minnow. I pounced and gulped the demon down, drawing its darkness into the hollow, black hole in my soul.

I don't think Shadows have eyes really; but, if this one did, they flew wide as saucers just before its dark essence was slurped into my emptiness.

It was quite refreshing.

I didn't waste any time burning the energy I gained.

Tossing off the flaming cloak happened in a flash. The next flash happened as the Waygate surrendered to my will.

One of the problems with Ardra is that the Tapestry of Creation was incinerated when Galandrake fell. The Waygates of Elyarsa were destroyed and the ley lines connected to it were shredded. Repairs were underway, but these were far from complete. So, as the Circlestone's magic yielded to me, I realized that our troubles were, likewise, far from over.

I shouted into the cacophony that shrieked at us as the portal opened. Where I wanted to go didn't really matter. Away was the best I could manage as a destination, and nearby was the furthest reach of my acquired power supply. Too much chaos filled the Waygate to do more.

Crackling lightning and mind-numbing noise delivered us from fire to water an instant later. Unfortunately, it was hot water.

Apparently, the nearest Waygate was submerged beneath a simmering, mineral spring. My screaming instantly became a swarm of bubbles rising in front of my face. Frantically, I followed them and ascended towards the sunlight filtering through the bad tasting brew.

I was only vaguely aware of Merilanna as the two of us squirmed our way onto the pool's muddy shore. I heard her coughing – a sign of life – as the water drained from my ears and from her lungs. The stench of sulfur still filled the air.

Exhausted, spitting brine and gasping for a breath that didn't burn my throat, I wormed over onto my back and stared at the tranquil blue sky and the white clouds drifting lazily through it. Xorconum's warming rays bathed my skin.

Funny, I didn't feel that relaxed.

Glancing aside, I spied the priestess on her belly and elbows not far away. She looked absolutely wretched. I guess I looked no better.

"Are you alright?" she croaked.

"Fantastic," I answered sourly, spitting the aftertaste off of my tongue.

Chapter 8: Shackles

The pool from which we crawled was very pretty. A rainbow of colorful minerals had collected around its edges. Dripping the mineralized brine, I stood up to appraise our surroundings before my energized senses returned to normal. The charge my snack had provided was fading fast.

We were on a wide, marshy plain covered with thick clumps of tall, sickly gray grass. These formed a maze of shoals and marked the higher ground. Between them, prismatic pools of burbling water steamed, carrying all sorts of pungent odors into the lightly blowing wind.

To the south, the Fangs of Ardra rose. Fire filled the jagged serrations and black clouds of ash rose from their summits. A broken landscape fanned out from the slopes of the volcanic range and reached our way. Thousands of geysers hissed amidst the stepping hills.

North, waving grasslands spread as far as I could see. East, distant, ice-capped, purple peaks marched connecting north and south, framing the verges of the prairie. West, the fingers of the southern desert clawed into the plains. Farther, rising clouds hinted of more mountains.

I knew they were there. I had ridden a Thromnyr pony in their shadows a long time ago.

"Where are we?" Merilanna asked.

"The Midlands," I replied, "somewhere south of the Weary Way."

"The Weary Way?"

"It's an old road that armies have taken from the north for centuries. It leads to the Gauntlet – fortresses that hold back the darkness of the south."

"You've been here before."

I nodded. "On the road, yes. But when that was, who knows."

Merilanna seemed to understand my quandary. Were we standing in "now" or were we standing in "then"? This whole being kicked back in time thing gave me a headache.

The priestess looked around us, taking in the dreary scene and scents. Neither appealed to her, apparently. I couldn't really argue with her grim countenance; it mirrored my own.

Merilanna's survey mired as she beheld the fires of Ardra. "So much pain," she whispered. "So much sorrow."

The priestess couldn't bear to look at it. She lowered her eyes and turned her face away, deeply affected. I watched as quakes of anguish trembled her being. I could almost hear her heart breaking as waves of horror shook her beauty and withered it. Grief covered her.

"I know," I consoled solemnly.

It was the truth. I did. The aftershocks of the apocalypse that claimed Elyarsa Altairas lived on inside my soul. Dyerbazog's blood flowed in my veins, carried to me by my progenitor, the Shadowlord, Darkyr. Dark sorcery had put it there to fire his rage as he marched north and led his army against those fair lands which would one day become Einhervaldheim, my home. It was his curse that I bore, contrived – in part – by Lady Death herself. Part of me remembered it all.

"I can hear them screaming," Merilanna said hushedly. Tears slipped from her grimacing eyes and slid through the valleys of her face. "A song of a thousand years would not see them all to their rest."

"Yea," I replied softly back, nodding slowly. I forced a deep breath into my lungs and looked away from the nightmares that filled my mind. "We have to get moving," I said with the exhale. "We're a long way from where we need to be."

The priestess affixed her gaze on me. Strange, I thought – she was the adult, yet innocence peered from within her soul, begging me, a child, to lead her away from this suffering.

"C'mon," I said again and offered my hand. She took it and we began the next steps along our path together.

We didn't talk much as the day passed. That was probably for the best. My mind was in dark places. Merilanna, too, seemed caught up in her thoughts. We walked and let the earth soak up our melancholy one footstep at a time.

Around the noontide, our trek – primarily north and west – delivered us to the verges of a dead forest. The gray skeletons of twisted trees littered the land. Whatever splendor might once have been here was turning to dust. Only the gray ruins of the mighty trees remained. New plants: spiny, prickly, and stinging, clung wherever they could find a foothold in the rocks. The terrain was eroded into a maze of snaking canyons filled with the carcasses of yesteryears. Wind and water had clawed the bare earth, carving these scars as the desert was crawling north. Black sand snaked through them, spread by the hot southern winds.

I didn't recall a place like this in my previous travels. The grit was familiar, of course, but not the hollow wood. Arrokyr, called the Wallows, lay farther to the south and west by my reckoning; but, again, that was a memory of something that might not yet be. The world was vast, and we were small. Stubborn reckoning was all I had to guide us, and it was out of date.

In the shadow of a rocky outcrop overlooking the wide valley ahead, Merilanna and I took shelter from the searing glare of Xorconum's Throne. It was only slightly cooler, but we welcomed any relief.

Salt crystals – an unpleasant gift from the waters of the mineral springs – clung to our charred and tattered clothes. More hid in our hair. We had only been walking for a few hours, but our skin was turning to cracked leather as well. Everything itched. Everything scratched, burned.

"Some ice would be nice," I said half-jokingly to the priestess.

Merilanna managed a small, apologetic smile. I could tell that her condition was no better than mine. Thankfully, the injuries we had sustained earlier had been healed. My shadowy snack took care of mine. Ilé's grace had tended to my companion's. What we were dealing with at the moment were the woes of traveling through this bleak, scorching wasteland.

"When the power She blesses with runs dry, My Lady blesses me with her forbearance that I may learn to endure and grow stronger."

I snorted. "So, no ice."

Merilanna's smile shrugged, answering wordlessly.

"Then we need to find some water – and not the stinky kind."

The priestess scanned the parched terrain. I let her look, knowing there was nothing to see. While she did, I tugged my boots off and rubbed at my poor feet. The briny bath we had suffered had soaked my leathers through. Drying out had split my skin thereafter. My toes were a bloody mess. Wincing became my new pastime.

"Oh, Lyri," Merilanna gasped, "let me look at those."

I wasn't in the mood to protest – a rarity for me, so I leaned back and let the priestess examine my wretched feet.

"You should have said something earlier," she scolded. "We could have stopped."

"We can't stop," I replied. "If we stop, we're dead."

Merilanna frowned as she dabbed at my wounds with a tatter from her skirt. "How could you walk on these?" She shook her head despondently.

I tried to ignore the pain, looking to the horizon.

That's when I saw the glint. Glints usually mean trouble. I squinted through the midday glare and tried to see where danger lurked.

Merilanna noticed my intense stare and followed the line of it down into the valley. Standing, she craned her neck for a better view.

"There's something moving down there," she said.

Of course, there's something moving down there! Why do you think I'm staring?

Instantly, there was something moving up here, too.

I grabbed my boots and began to stuff my bloody, blistered feet back in them.

Merilanna turned at my sudden shuffling and protested. "No, Lyri. Wait. What are you doing?"

"Going hunting," I snapped.

"You're going to hurt yourself more."

I glared at her for a second before continuing with my self-torture. "We have to move," I growled. "That's going to hurt regardless." I pointed to the valley with a jut of my chin as I pushed my right foot into its hole. "The best way for me to heal is to kill something."

The priestess of death apparently had no stomach for my plan. She probably blanched. I was impossible to tell. Her fair skin was cooked red. The sun had burned every inch of it.

"I'm coming with you," she announced.

Left boot on.

"Follow," I commanded, "but not too close."

"What if you need help?"

I smirked humorlessly. "I won't."

With two boots on and wearing a foul mood, I scurried from the shadows of our sheltering rocks and descended into the winding arroyos. The dry, rocky terrain crunched under foot as I padded along. Soon, the parched air stole my breath. The taste of iron tinged my tongue as dust and blood from my cracked lips touched it. I had no spit to spit it out.

As the valley rose up around me, the labyrinth deepened, but I was not unskilled in lands like these. As I descended, I fixed several high landmarks as points of reference and oriented myself to them. Picking the right path, I glanced back and spotted the priestess moving gingerly downslope along my trail. Good, I wouldn't have to go far to fetch her.

The valley floor was well-traveled. A dry riverbed leveled the going and hastened it. Numerous tracks were visible, if you knew where to look. The wind and the sand were always moving, so any exposed signs did not last long. However, some areas were low or sheltered, and I found them there – just as an old ranger had taught me to do what seemed like a lifetime ago. I chuckled, musing on the notion that Relteran Martelas would not even be born for centuries yet.

I missed him.

After about a candlemark, I was getting close to where I had seen the telltale glint of sunlight. Xorconum's Throne had edged from its highest point and was on its way to the horizon; but, unlike in the frozen north, its journey would last for many hours more. Days were very long here.

Did I mention that it was hot? I think I mentioned it, but my brain was boiling, so forgive me if I did.

Nevermind.

Skirting along the more shadowed edge of the canyon, I rounded a bend and drew up behind the cover of some boulders. My ears had alerted me that something was ahead. Low, bestial grunts and the jangling of some sort of wagon reached me.

Cautiously, I crept forward, staying low. Peering over a shallow rise, I scanned the area ahead from my belly.

There were three wagons, actually. Each was basically a crude, wooden box with four wheels pulled by ox-sized, four-legged tri-horns – a breed of stocky, frilled, reptile creatures with, of course, three horns on their heads: two on their foreheads, one on their snout.

I guess they have been used in this manner forever. I had seen their like before in Stonefist and Morgaradar as well as on the caravan routes, once upon a time.

Marching alongside the wagons were a troupe of heavily armed, brutish creatures. At first, I thought they were Morok, the Black Orcs that would one day be the scourge of these lands, but I realized quickly – their tails gave it away – that they were saurian: dragon-men of some sort, but sans the wings and shiny scales sported by the infamous Drakkar. These were squat, dark, earth-hued types that I had never encountered.

Whip-masters rode the carts and snapped the teams along. The thirty or so remaining afoot marched dauntlessly forward.

Behind me, I heard the priestess crawling up. I glanced back with a warning look. She heeded and scurried quietly to my side.

"What are they?" she whispered.

I shook my head as my answer. It didn't matter. I could sense the darkness that infested their souls. It was like a foul scent that wafted through the arid air.

"Stay here," I said, pushing away from the rocks.

"What are you doing?" Merilanna asked urgently, alarm and protest mixing in her tone.

"Getting captured," I replied.

"What!"

I grinned mischievously – the absolute opposite of her horrified expression.

"Just stay hidden," I implored. "This won't take long."

Before the priestess could voice her objections further, I dashed off to find a way around and ahead of the marching monsters.

Exhausted and exhilarated altogether, I clambered across the broken terrain and found a spot for my ambush. Thirty-three to one hardly seemed like fair odds, but I wasn't feeling merciful…just hungry – and I don't mean my growling belly.

Just before the lead brute rounded the bend in the valley, I shot out from the shadows and promptly sprawled out along the path the caravan was taking. I had barely assumed my position before the monster appeared. I was certain he saw me, but neither his pace nor those of his fellows following slowed. I guess roadkill wasn't an overwhelming sight around here.

The ground was scorching hot. The heat rose, blurring the world around me. Peeking through my lashes, I watched as the wavy, scaly procession approached. The wagons' wheels rolled along, crushing to dust any hapless pebbles that lay upon their line. Clickety-clack, they came.

It was hard to steady my breath. I could feel my curse stirring with every step my prey took, awakening the shadow of my black soul. The closer the dragon-men came, the more insistent was my hunger. The more it grew, the more I seemed to vibrate from within. The blue haze of Twilight flickered before my eyes. Everything was sharpening. Everything was on fire. The crunching of gravel became claps of thunder. The jangling, clattering, clanging made the earth quake. The stench of the tri-horns, the shifting of scales, the deep respirations of the column: everything flooded the valley and struck me like a deluge. I shuddered as the dark power inside me hissed then growled then roared. I felt my eyes roll back in my skull to stare into my inner darkness. I knew I couldn't restrain it.

I don't remember when the first dragon-man reached me. By then, no rational thoughts remained. My first cogent recollection thereafter was of the priestess' face and her plaintive voice saying, "It's alright…it's alright…you're alright. I'm not going to hurt you…"

Beyond her trembling words and shaken expression, the world had been swallowed by shadows and chaos. Blue lightning crackled wildly through the darkness of my soul. I could feel every jolt searing every nerve in my body. My mind had exploded outward even as all of creation was crushing down upon me, desperate to contain the eruption, desperate to force it to stay within me lest I devour the world.

I screamed and reality shook.

Faintly, I perceived the priestess frantically running to me over the moving earth.

"Lyri!" she shrieked, throwing herself towards me, grasping at my shoulders, frantic to shake me free from my nightmares before they dragged me from the world altogether. She pleaded for me to return, to take hold of the storm I had brought.

I think I almost killed her before I seized control of the demons my rampage had unleashed.

Her eyes held mine. She was breathing so hard. Her heart was racing so fast, pounding inside her breast. I could see the shadows in her own soul; but, fatefully, I saw the light as well. That's what saved her.

"Come back to me," Merilanna begged.

The Bright World and Twilight slowly began untwisting.

It had been so long since my soul had been drained. I had overdosed on darkness. But, control was returning.

"I'm…alright," I parroted the priestess' words hollowly.

I only flinched a little when she embraced me. She was sobbing and shaking. She was a priestess of Ilé, and she had just met Death. Maybe I wasn't what she had expected.

Over Merilanna's shoulder – she was kneeling as she held me – I saw the carnage I had wrought. It was, as always, horrifying.

There were no dragon-men left. In truth, it was impossible to say which pieces belong to which corpse. Literally, I had torn them apart. The canyon was painted by my handiwork. Blood and gore showed my artistry. It was splattered everywhere, hissing on the hot rocks.

Merilanna leaned back, holding my shoulders to examine me. I could see blood covered her as well. Thankfully, it was not her own. It had come off of me.

Numbly, I looked down my body and held forth my arms. My small hands were soaked. My clothes were drenched.

"Are you hurt?" the priestess was praying to know.

I wasn't – at least not physically. Metaphysically, my soul and the shadows I had ingested were still raging. Dark, primal fire yet blazed behind my eyes. I shook my head slowly and pulled away from her – not hard, but definitively.

Seeking calm, I closed my eyes and steadied my inner flame. Thundering heart. Deep breath. I gained enough control to know that I wasn't in control. Nevertheless, "I'm alright," I reassured. I wasn't sure if I was speaking to her or to myself.

I stepped away from the priestess and walked into the epicenter of my explosion, taking it all in. I glanced back to her. She was still kneeling next to the shadowy nook where I had apparently ended my frenzy. She was watching me, worry still weighing her featuues.

I looked away and more formerly addressed the scope of the scene. Only the wagons and the tri-horns were intact. The lumbering beasts were grunting nervously, but they were too stupid to run away.

Absently, I wiped the blood from my hands onto the skirt of my black and blue tunic and walked to the rear of the first wagon.

Merilanna rose and moved to join me.

I held up my hand to forbid her coming closer. My preternatural senses had already registered what was inside. She had seen enough horrors for one day.

Obediently, she held and watched as I threw the bolt and bar. The heavy door creaked open. I looked. I saw. I closed it and locked it back, but the sight was within me now.

After a dreadful, still silence, the priestess asked, "What is it?"

Seething, I gritted my teeth and strode from the rear of the wagon. Our eyes did not meet. I didn't want to sear her soul. I focused on the road ahead. "Shackles," I snarled and walked past her.

Chapter 9: The Weary Way

She didn't follow immediately. I didn't slow my steps. Eventually she found me and measured her steps to mine. We didn't talk for a long time. It was for the best. Nothing but foul words filled my mouth anyway. I think the priestess knew it and wisely held her own tongue lest she provoke mine. Night had fallen before my northward march faltered. Atop a rocky rise, I stared into the starry sky, huffing with rage; and, at last, I screamed, my clenched fists shaking at my side.

"Damn you all!"

Trembling with fury, I whipped back towards me solemn companion, tears streaming down my filthy face. They could do nothing to wash away the stains on my soul.

She stood there, Ilé's priestess, compassion wetting her own eyes, and watched me seethe. She was helpless. What could she do?

Wracked with anger, I turned away, bowed my head, and choked down the bile that burned into my throat. Breathing hard, I lifted my acidic glare back to the heavens. The stars looked down, but they did not fall. The gods offered no contrition, no apology. Nothing.

"They were only children," I hissed.

So was I. It didn't matter...

Gracelessly, I collaped onto my ass and sat there on the rock, grinding my teeth and fighting for a cleansing breath, lost in the curses that filled my mind.

"They brought them from the north," I said numbly into the hot, dry wind that blew across my shoulders and caught in the matted tangles of my hair.

I heard the priestess shift and attend my words. She gave me space, sitting downslope from me in silence, waiting for my fire to burn lower.

"War is like this," I added stoically. "It's always the worst for the innocent."

"I'm sorry, Lyri," Merilanna replied softly, earnestly.

I glanced over my shoulder and shook my head. "It's not your fault." I looked back to the sky. "It's theirs."

I folded my knees to my chest and buried my forehead against them. There it remained for a long while. When I lifted my eyes again, the light of a small campfire played shadows across my face. I looked to where it glowed and saw the priestess sitting there, deep in her own meditations.

She offered a gentle smile up to me as I moved to join her, flopping down opposite the flames.

"It will attract trouble," I said, tossing a clump of branches onto the pyre as if to dare it to come.

Merilanna nodded but left her gaze upon the fire.

"I don't know why the gods do what they do," she confessed. "I don't know why they allow any of it. The ideals of justice, the nature of laws. One is too fluid and one too strict. Yet evil is evil but we do not see them act to stop it. I sometimes think that the gods are too much like people. Or, perhaps, it is more terrifying to ponder that people are more like the gods than we choose to believe.

"Why do they reach out their hands to save one, but turn their backs to another's desperate cry?" She smoothed the fabric of her tattered dress over her leg absently. "Why do they proclaim themselves Bright but allow the Dark to florish. It's unfair. We ourselves are creatures of shadow – a mold of dark and light shaped by the choices we make on who we shall be. Even in the dark – we may choose to scream. Or not. Every choice has its price. Even the footsteps of heroes are filled with blood."

She found a tattered edge of her dress and traced its rough edge.

"I am all too aware that the Gods of Light have their shadows. Is not Urrel one such as these? And did he not commit such crimes, too? Yet, still he rules over Death. And the people of many lands worship him as 'good'."

She looked across the fire towards me.

"In a way, this gives me hope. If there is such darkness in the Light, then there must also be such light in the Dark." Her small grin was a wry twist. "It is a truth overlooked, I think, because of its nature. For such a thing *must* be a shadow. The golden court of the Aesyr with all its priests blinded by the shine of it, may never see such a shadow as anything but evil. But not everything in the light is good. Not everything in the dark is evil. And a shadow, in deepest of darks, may seem bright indeed.

"It must be so…this is the Balance. But it does bear us back to the same 'why'. If the gods are held to the same measure, why do they not act to stop the invasive evils within their power and sight? It is by our choices and actions that we shape our world: darkness or light."

I blew a long breath into the wind. "Because they can't stop it."

She looked at me now, waiting for me to elucidate.

I shook my head and shrugged. "It's the Balance. Some good. Some bad." I looked out into the darkness of the night. "I just always seem to be in the bad part."

I guess that made sense to her. Her smile flickered as she mulled my words. "Forever a struggle, so swing the scales to and fro."

That, I left unanswered and, thus, self-evident.

"Even the gods can't change that," the priestess rued.

"Or won't."

"Perhaps."

I was seriously screwing with her religion – not on purpose or to be mean; but – well, I don't know why. I just say what I think before I think what I should say, I suppose. Though, she is a priestess of Ile', so who knows what she really understands.

"Look," I tried to explain, "all of this is a game. Life. Death. It only means what we allow it to mean. It's everything and nothing. We decide if it hurts or not. We decide if it matters…if we care. Caring is a choice; but, if you don't care, nothing matters. Someone told me that once."

"Someone that cared about you," the priestess discerned.

I shrugged.

Her smile had returned as her heart lightened. "I can see why your friend loves you," she said.

"He doesn't love me," I snorted, arguing with feigned indifference. "We just put up with one another. Most of the time, I want to kill him."

"Ah, now I *do* see."

I scowled.

She smiled coyishly.

It was time to escape this girl-talk, so I hopped up. "I'm hungry – for real food." I scanned the darkness. "We might as well not waste the fire. I'll bring back something to put on it. If the light doesn't summon demons, maybe the smell of my cooking will."

Merilanna grinned. "Be careful."

She wasn't quite sure why I rolled my eyes at that as I vanished into the night.

Surprisingly, neither the campfire nor the roasting rabbit brought monsters to our table and we ate in peace. The morsel wasn't much, but it did quiet the growling beasts in our bellies a bit.

When the meal was over, Merilanna settled into her cozy bed of sand and stone.

"You sleep," I instructed the priestess. "I'll keep watch over the dark and make sure it behaves itself."

Merilanna started to protest. But, instead, she surrendered with a weary nod. She was too exhausted to spar over the point, I guess.

"Wake me in a few hours," she urged.

"Sure."

Of course, I didn't.

Tired but restless, I returned to my place on the top of the rocky rise. There, I sat and surveyed the road ahead. It wasn't really a road, of course – not a fancy one with paver stones and level trekking. No, it wasn't like that. What would one day be called the Weary Way and would lead countless young men to their deaths in wars against the monsters of these southern lands was now only a wide, battered trail – one blazed by an insidious army that prowled unchecked into an ill-prepared world. Though months, perhaps years, had passed since the main body had stomped north, the scars worn into the lands of the living and the dead were still clearly evident. What lingered also was a vile, spectral stench that saturated everything. Even the forest had been consumed by its evil; its arboreal spirit drained away.

In the days that followed as Merilanna and I crept along, we discovered abandoned camp after camp, marking the infection's advance. It was chilling.

Tonight, though, I let my memories lead me north along the Way. I remembered a thousand-thousand deaths. I remembered friends – family – that had been murdered by these endless horrors. I remembered the *Skyran*'s wickedness and my quest for vengeance against Armadar's harbinger. I remembered sweet Miss Whinny, my gentle pony, and our long, arduous travels together. I remembered everything, every awful step that had brought me into and out of these godforsaken lands. I had a hell of a lot to remember.

The moon rose in the wee hours and bathed the wasteland before me in her pale glow. I didn't need Toni's silvery light, but neither did I begrudge her for it. As it were, I could track every cricket within a hundred paces through the pitch anyway. My shadow gave no heed to the black around me, and every spirit that wafted through Twilight was mine to see. There weren't many. Everything living or dead had been devoured.

Nonetheless, several times during the night, scavengers did appear. A gangly pack of wolves circled our camp, but they didn't dare to come near. I guess the smell of the dragon-men's blood on me was enough to hold them off. Lucky for them; wolves and I don't get along. That's another story.

Just before dawn, I woke Merilanna. I don't think she was surprised that I had not roused her for a turn at the watch.

"How far?" she ventured to ask as she joined me on my lookout.

"For the living, a couple of months – maybe more. It's at least half that far to Blackrock Crag."

"Is that near your homeland?"

"No, but it was my home once…or it will be someday. Just depends how you look at it."

Saying nothing more, I plodded down the rise and into the footsteps of evil. Strange it was that I was following the very path that would someday lead to my own creation. But my life is nothing if not an enigma. Irony and I are well-acquainted.

There's not much to tell during this part of my tale, so I won't bore you with it. All-in-all, the going was uneventful. The land flattened and spread wide. The dead forest fell away to waving grasslands – though,

I will say that there were a lot more copses of scrub and trees than would remain in later times.

Yes, occasionally, something hungry would come by for a bite, but I bite harder and faster.

So, basically, we walked...and walked...and walked.   Merilanna talked...and talked...and talked – when she wasn't singing.

Somehow, I managed not to kill her.

"Who do you talk to on the mountain?" I asked. "Or did you save all your thoughts on the hope I'd someday arrive?"

She giggled. "I talk to the wind.   It doesn't mind.   But only with respect.   While it is usually kind, the wind is *always* listening."

I stared at her for several long moments.

"Yours is a special kind of insanity, isn't it?"

She tilted her head and thought for a moment then shrugged delicately. "Probably."

Honestly – and it's not easy for me to admit it; and, if asked, I'd vehemently deny it – I sometimes enjoyed her banter...sometimes.   If you've ever been on a long road-trip, the distraction of having someone singing or jabbering in the background passes the time. It gives the mind something with which to occupy itself: a sort of madness, I guess, but one that's more or less tolerable.

As it were, my recollection and my estimate proved accurate. A month went by and the landscape began to change.   Contours appeared on the eastern horizon that quickly grew into snowcapped mountains.   Hills began to roll around us.   Escarpments and outcrops of rock broke through the green skin of the world and rose from the plains.   Small streams bled through them and pooled in isolated lakes that appeared in the low places. These latter, too, would not remain when I walked this way in the future.

Again, there were more trees lingering in these lands than I had known. Still, the grandeur of the forest that once covered the Midlands had long since faded. I could only imagine how it might have looked in centuries past.

Despite my wistful daydreaming, though, the rank smell of contamination that I had been following for weeks still clung to the world.   The supernatural scent spiked late on the forty-second evening of our march.   By the forty-third, the ethereal reeking reached my companion's nose.

"What is that smell?" she asked.

"Death," I answered the Death-Maiden plainly.

As night approached, smoke tinged the sky and marked the source. It rode the northerly winds and brought our eyes to a spot on the horizon. There, beads of orange light flickered hungrily.

We did not camp that night. By its midst, we were looking up at the crude, stacked stone walls of a fortress. Bonfires lit the rocks from within and sent shadows crawling across them. A wide gate closed off what lay inside, but the grunts and growls of dark tongues climbed out and reached us. They promised what I had foretold: death. Rotting corpses and heaps of bones covered the steep hillside from where the wall grew. Skulls were stacked along it like buttresses. Dark, ragged flags rustled in the wind atop.

I glanced at the priestess. The ghastly sight had contorted her face.

"So many lost souls," she whispered her horror. Her expression strained with her desire to do her goddess' work.

"Don't sing for them," I said firmly. "There's black magic here. I can feel it."

She nodded. "I sense that. What are we going to do?"

We had options? I suppose we did.

Skirting this stinking hell-hole was the most prudent. If you knock on Death's door, she's likely to open it, they say. Giving this place a wide berth, then, was the sensible thing to do. But, as you may have noticed, I'm rarely prudent or sensible.

Options? Eh, who cares...

"I'm going to see what's in there," I declared, "and you're going to head west and circle north. I'll catch up with you there."

"No."

Short word...very long on meaning.

"Yes," I answered back.

"Lyri, no. These souls aren't alone. This is a pit, deep and wide, but overflowing. There's too many for you alone, I suspect. Definitely, it's too deep a dark for me to pull you out of before you drown in it. It's too dangerous."

I cocked my head to the side and stared up at her incredulously. "For them, maybe. I'm going in."

The priestess hissed her rebuttal into the gusty breeze after me as I slipped the Veil. She sounded a bit frustrated and a lot afraid – for me. I probably should have listened to her; but, of course, I didn't. A month of walking and her talking had eroded my patience. Though the charnel stench was overwhelming, the cache of shadows within this rocky box was dizzying my good sense – not that I ever claimed to have much of it. There was evil here. My darkness hungered for it.

Walls – of the mundane sort – are no hinderance to me when I'm riding the Cusp. Horizontal and vertical are the same, more or less. So, it was with ease that I overtopped the rocks and came to survey the bowels of this accursed dark-hold.

For those of you that remember my early travels and may be wondering, yes, you and I have been here before. I have burning memories – or memories of burning, to be more accurate – of this damned place. But, that's no matter. It's in the past, er, in the future. Oh, whatever! The Turanian garrison, Skullborough, would eventually sit on this rise.

Inside, a rather impressive number of ugly creatures milled about. Most were humanish – two arms, two legs, one head, lots of hair. Others were more beast-ish – a cobbling together of manlike forms with those of all sorts of other things. Some were gangly; some were squat; some were scaly; some were shaggy. All were grotesque. It was as if Armadar had dropped every monster it could find into a pot and stirred them up until it had a brew of horrors. In a word, it was pandemonium.

Yes, I know lots of big words. I'm a kid, not stupid. Besides, I'm writing this quite a bit after the fact, in case you're wondering. Be thankful, too. Sentences like: "See Lyri run. See Lyri jump. See Lyri kill everything." are boring, don't you think?

Okay, back to the pandemonium.

There were lots and lots of demons. Shadows infested the army within like fleas. It was practically ablaze with them. The same black arts that had crafted their flesh riddled their souls. That any semblance of order existed at all in their ranks testified to a single, frightening fact: something bigger and darker commanded their submission.

As I scanned the rock and timber hovels that littered the space within the walls, where that bigger, darker something dwelled was not hard to surmise. Near the center of the fortress was an ominous keep. It, like the stocky structures that ringed it, was crudely constructed: stacked up rocks, no masonry, no mortar, no artful design. It was, however, a lot bigger. Giants had laid those stones and smashed them into place. Whereas the camp was low, the donjon towered fifty feet and spread over a hundred. Its jagged roofline was crowned by flaming cauldrons and ragged banners that waved in the smoky wind. A single ramp, a causeway lined by pillars made of rocks and skulls, led to its great, yawning maw. More fire burned hungrily within its hellish throat.

It was homey. I sort of liked the place – in a morbid, I'm-going-to-destroy-it-all sort of way.

Emanating from inside, beyond the oh so welcoming glow, a deeper darkness called to me. Therein was the lair of the biggest beast.

Below my perch, a trio of ogreish fellows were fornicating with a fat sow. The female – I think it was female – was leaning with her back to the wall and holding two of her playmates enthralled, one in each hand, let's say, while the third slathered on his knees beneath the overhang of her rolling folds.

I'll spare you more details to keep the page in front of you from catching your last meal. You're welcome for that.

From my pocket, a pair of shiny friends rolled into my hand. The little, silver orbs orbited in my palm smoothly at the slightest caress, ready to spin death. I would not deny them that pleasure long.

With a flick of my wrist, I sent one to work, holding its twin tightly as an ethereal thread, thin as spider's silk, unwound between them. At my will's command, the voyager flew and looped, weaving unnoticed among the abhorrent revelers below. Another snap of my wrist and, like a fisherman setting his hook, death was deftly spun.

The fourth of the group, his face stuck someplace dark, disgusting, and stinky, was unaware that the party was over. I think he mistook the female's convulsions for something else.

Grinning devilishly, the troll peaked up and over his whore's pallid flesh but could not find her eyes…or her head. Blood flowed down the slope between her sagging breasts and mixed with the grime and sweat that covered her. Jerking backwards in terror, he sprawled on his ass and elbows. Throwing his head from side to side, he realized that his alone was still attached to its shoulders. Both of his buddies had lost theirs as well, their corpses having collapsed left and right of him into the black mud. He had been wholly oblivious to their anticlimactic end.

Something between his legs caught his frantic, fearful gaze. In his desperate, hasty retreat, he had kicked it as he fell backwards. At last, two lovers' gazes met. Her eyes were wide and transfixed; his were wide and shaking.

I snorted, snapping the slug's terror up to me. I was a mere silhouette against the night sky atop the wall.

"Ah, love," I pined.

His frothy mouth opened to scream. I threw my balls down his throat and sliced the sound from within him before he could.

The Aylehsi orbs whirled back to my hand and plinked together, tolling a final note before I stashed them away.

Springing from the wall, eddies spun along the Cusp in my wake. A quartet of shadows rose from the carnal remains of the doxy and her boys. I sailed through and snatched their black flames, devouring their sins before ever my boots touched the befouled earth. It was wretched energy, but it fueled my hate.

I put it to good use.

There were, perhaps, a thousand demons in this pit. Even for me – Merilanna was right – that's a bit too many. So, I chose a more judicious route and slipped deeper into Twilight to evade their notice. My focus was upon their master in the keep anyway, not the mongrels at his doorstep.

Blue and grey, the lands of the dead washed by me in a blur. The fortress and all the monsters within it were but watery apparitions that only hinted at their horrors. The nexus of it all, though, remained starkly defined and detailed. The donjon awaited me in both worlds. Its form and power transcended. Magic rippled the Veil.

Before I reached the keep, however, I came upon a courtyard that magnified my anger. Within it, a fleet of dark, boxy wagons waited for their gruesome cargo. Nearby, teams of dull-witted tri-horns were tethered.

Snarling, I moved on.

I stopped before the first rocky pillars at the beginning of the causeway leading to the mouth of the keep and eyed the horrific structure. The blue fire within the rocky lamps burned with violence matching my own. It hungered for me to step upon the path.

A trap.

"Clever," I whispered under my breath. I was not being complimentary. The sorcerer within the fortress guarded himself well. He was smart to do so.

I could not advance without feeling the fury of the flames. Neither my flesh nor my shadow, I sensed, was immune to them. Peril blazed on all sides. Even the cauldrons atop the keep burned with the insidious spell. Wraiths watched from within those fires, ready to deliver their master's wrath.

What I needed was a priestess to hold them at bay, but I had left mine outside.

"Well, Petunia, now what?" I chided myself.

How do you draw a serpent out of its hole? It's not easy. Nothing ever is. Opportunities, though, appear in strange ways. Sometimes, you seed them without even knowing it.

Abruptly, a clamor arose within the ranks of the Grymfolk behind me. It seemed that my handiwork had been discovered. Through the Veil, I watched as a gaggle of brutes lumbered hurriedly towards the keep. A familiar quartet of heads dangled by their hair from the lead lummox's fists. I stepped aside to let the excited procession through.

At the start of the pillared causeway, the troupe stopped as well. They knew the price of approaching closer. There, their leader hefted the four heads and held them up towards the looming keep. He bellowed ferociously, his voice echoing from deep within its stones.

I smirked as the hell-fires burning in the pillars slowly dimmed, granting passage to the unwitting herald of my arrival.

Undetected, I fell in behind the burly band and strode forward to meet their master.

I hadn't intended it, but I hoped he liked the gifts my escorts brought. If not, Wind-Song and I would be glad to offer my heartfelt apologies and my deepest condolences.

Chapter 10: A Dark Parley

You may have heard it said that nothing is as it seems. When you're dealing with magic, that is a gross understatement. Reality molds to the will of the wizard; therefore, it is very subjective. In fact, sometimes reality is not real at all.

For instance, the moment that my entourage crossed the causeway, the seeming of the keep transformed radically. It wavered and dissolved away. Where a gaping gate into hell had been, a resplendent architrave materialized. Twin doors towered at its heart to a shared apex. Complex, golden glyphs festooned every inch of them. They glimmered and gleamed, appearing to snake across the surface, dancing to the flanking firelight cast by two blazing cauldrons.

A pair of colossal dragon-men stood guard with arms crossed and eyes afire to their sides. Their black scales caught the fiery glow. It tinged them the color of dark garnet. Neither monster carried weapons. They didn't need to. Their claws and fangs more than sufficed. Each stood at least twice my height. In all, it was impossible to escape their ominous, hateful glares.

Before the doors, the beast-men dropped to their knees and bowed, faces down and arms outstretched like good little slaves. Their leader released his offering, letting the heads of the slain lull before the doors.

At the rear of the gang, I crouched. Small as I was, the hunching backs of the ogres shielded me from view easily.

Several long seconds passed before anything but the golden glyphs moved. Then, unnervingly quiet, the doors split and a purer, reddish glow spilled forth. A slight silhouette took form between them. To my amazement, not a demon, but a fey boy emerged. His slender figure was clothed by a long robe the color of bleached bone. Delicate embroidery swept across its mantle and coiled down its stole. Tiny crystals accented the serpentine curves. The boy's hair and skin were pale. The former was like corn silk; the latter, like translucent alabaster. His eyes, though, were flushed with blood such that no iris or white could be discerned. Too, his lips were unnaturally red. I gauged him a few years older than me – though, as an elf, he could have been my senior by centuries.

Coldly, the acolyte surveyed the supplicants, his unnerving gaze settling upon the gory gifts. A frown marred his perfect features.

"Why have you disturbed the master's rest?" the boy demanded impatiently. His voice was beautiful but it shivered my spine. I could feel it worming through the air and through the ether of Twilight, entering my mind with meaning though his words were in the tongue of the Alurishi.

Hesitantly, the brute at the fore growled some sort of reply.

The boy's disgust was evident.

"You dare to bring such vile matters before the Great Amon? His Eminence does not trifle with such petty things as this. Seek out their murderers yourselves and add their skulls to the piles. There's nothing more to be done."

The alpha grunt grunted something more. It gave pause to the boy. His head cocked ever so slightly and his eyes narrowed.

"What magic?" he asked.

A second ogre, older and clad in a cloak of shaman's fetishes, was waved forward by the leader. Groveling, the witchdoctor drew a bundle of tinder from a leathery pouch and puffed the embers to life. A wispy cloud of smoke gathered in the air before his tattooed and gnarled face. Still jabbering, he evoked some cantrip and set the pother in motion.

A scene that I knew well enough was animated in the fumes.

Clever.

The boy watched with growing interest as my wraith dispatched the whore and her repulsive coterie until, abruptly, he snapped his gaze away from the scene as if a voice unheard spoke into him.

"Our guest is here," he announced flatly, his bloody eyes affixing upon me.

Confused, the beast-men looked to each other for his meaning, but they found only shared bewilderment betwixt them. It was their leader – I guess that's why he was their leader – that first recognized the prompt.

Like a ferocious bear, he rose and turned towards where the boy looked. He snarled as he spied me.

Feeling cavalier, I tilted my head to the side, smirked, and snorted. "*Humph*, so it's going to be like that, eh?"

Weapons moved, and I disappeared – at least as far as the beast-men were concerned.

Slipping along the Cusp, I flew towards the boy and the open doors. Wind-Song sang as I did. Her pure, ringing notes, though, shrieked unexpectedly as my advance was cut prodigiously short. The Veil crumpled and my flight was instantly ended. It was as if the thin ether thickened to liquid amber. Before I could veer, I was caught in a sticky trap. The blue haze of Twilight shook violently around me, rippling like water as I struggled. I was close enough to bite him; but, strain though I might, I could not sink my teeth or my blade. My defiance had reached an impasse.

Of course, that pissed me off. But, hanging in space and time helplessly before the boy's empty gaze, I composed my outrage and did not reward him with my scream. Acidic words, though, flushed my tongue. Before, I could even spit them, though, he spoke.

What he said stunned me more effectively than any slap could have.

"You're beautiful," he muttered with abject admiration.

I snarled.

His thin eyebrow rose slightly.

"Traitor!" I managed to growl in rebuke. "I know what evil rolls from within this place. I know what you are!"

Now, the boy smiled as I seethed.

"The Grand Magus will see you now," he announced and nodded to the alpha ogre. "Bring her."

Huge, calloused hands seized my arms as others snatched my sword away before hauling me forward on the heels of the acolyte. I watched as the red glow from within the keep swallowed him. I followed. I had no choice. Twilight gave me speed and momentum but not brute strength. Hands and magic held me tight.

Entering the fortress was like falling into a pool of blood. Everything around me was warm and wet, viscous and vile. It felt more like squirming than walking. My senses were saturated by the abhorrent sensations. All I could see was red. It filled my nose and ears. It invade my mouth and throat, suffocating me. Every inch of my skin recoiled as though it was covered with slimy leeches. They were feeding upon me, sapping my will and my life. Through this unholy baptism, I was brought and purified and made worthy to kneel before the master of this place.

My body and my soul were in shock when, at last, I was cast at the fiend's feet. My captors, then, eagerly faded back into the bloody light, retreating from his ominous presence.

Quaking, shivering, I forced my face to rise, still unwilling to submit.

"Hello, Lyri."

I knew that venomous voice.

"Vespirak," I vomited his vile name.

"It's been a long time, my pretty," he chuckled.

The irony of the statement was not lost on me.

"How?"

"One does what one must to survive. You know that. Along the path of my long life, I made arrangements for its end. Like a climber, I anchored myself to the mountain's slope lest I fall too far."

The contempt in my glare was searing. Yet, though my hatred of the creature blazed, I could not help but be dazzled by his splendor. His appearance in this incarnation was startlingly different from that which I had encountered before. Too, this place was far from a dusty old crypt.

Looking about the chamber, I suppose its gaudy grandeur should not have been surprising. It matched its master's audacity.

A circle of columns, each ostentatiously carved of ebon marble veined with red, supported the resplendent dome that capped the room. At its zenith, an eclipsed, bloody sun burned. A constellation of golden, arcane symbols orbited it, snaking across a midnight sky. Along the horizon, a hellish glow, like the last glimmers of dusk, limned the firmament. In the center of this eerie cosmos, bathed in the bloody aura, the Grand Magus, the Vampire-King himself, sat his black throne and stared down at me.

Clad in a flowing, black tunic, open-chested and sleeveless, he was far from the desiccated corpse wrapped in a charnel cloak that I remembered.

First off, he was much younger – though still a grown man easily thrice my years – if years meant anything anymore. His skin was oiled and bronzed and utterly flawless. His body was muscular and toned to the point of being vainglorious. It actually shimmered. Clean-shaven and bald, the lich wore a gold headdress with a cobra rising from it. Across his broad chest, a wide mantle of banded gold, ebony, lapis, and garnet beads fanned. Other kingly jewelry adorned him. Delicate gold chains spanned from his nostril rings to his pierced ears. Spikes of gold knitted the tips of his brows. Magnificent jewels rode his every finger. His nails were polished black and trimmed sharp. Gold anklets wrapped his strong calves. His feet where sandaled; and, like his fingers, his toes were painted and perfect. Gleaming bracers in the forms of serpents cuffed his wrists. Similar bands of gold accentuated his powerful biceps. Kohl mascara masked his eyes and coiled towards his temples. It contrasted sharply with the whites of his eyes but matched completely the deep blackness of his irises.

All in all, Vespirak was stunning: a god – a true testament to the power of his arrogance and ego.

He disgusted me.

As dominating as the Arcanalestri's figure was, I was aware, too, that he was not alone. In the shadowy recesses beyond the columns, dragon-men like those that I had slaughtered stood, maintaining a silent guard. Huddled between them on their knees were the lich's servants: elven children. At least a dozen slave girls waited anxiously, their lives dependent upon satisfying the monster's least desire. No doubt the slightest glance or gesture would send them scurrying.

Nearer, flanking his black, bejeweled, serpentine throne, were his most ferocious pets. Two golden, gilded *arvargr* lounged upon the dais. In the southern lands, these creatures were known as deadly, consummate predators. Here, both wore golden collars.

Like scaly panthers, they watched everything that moved, ready to pounce, ready to do their master's bidding with diamond-hard claws and razor-sharp fangs. Casually, they reposed at his side and eyed me with hungry, beady-black stares.

"You don't seem yourself, my pretty. What's wrong? Did you miss me?"

"I miss not killing you when I had the chance," I hissed.

The lich chuckled. "You haven't changed a bit. I see your fire still burns just as hot now as it did –" his eyes rolled through his dark thoughts as he mused over the paradox "– then." Manicured nails rapped upon the arm of his sovereign chair. "I'm delighted that we have been reunited. You fascinate me."

"Come a little closer and I'll fascinate you to death!"

His evil grin spread. "They'll be time for that, don't worry." The Grand Magus paused, considering another notion. "Yes, time – it's something we both have at our disposal, don't we, my sweet. For me, I drink it in. I savor its purity." His evil gaze swept meaningfully across the children huddled in the shadows. "For you, it is a perpetual purgatory. Still, we are not so different, you and me. Just two sides to the same coin. You devour the dark. I devour the light. In the end, the transaction is what sustains us both."

"We can play 'whose the better killer' anytime you like," I baited.

"Well, that's the thing, isn't it? Maybe we *can* play 'anytime'." Vespirak reclined into his throne and laced his fingers upon his chest. "My lifeline caught me here when I fell. Now, here you are: an angel from my future – fallen into my past." He leaned forward again hungrily. "I do want to play with you Lyri, but *then* rather than now, if such things are possible."

My brow furrowed. "What game are you playing, lich?"

"The long one," he answered. "My end, then, has become my beginning anew. Can you not imagine the opportunities before us? The unraveling of the Tapestry has filled my mind with wondrous thoughts and awakened endless dreams. I mean to seize them all and march into a glorious future."

"You're still just as mad now as you were then."

"On the contrary, when I awoke in my former self – bringing with me the fullness of my wisdom – I realized that madness is only what the simple call that which they cannot conceive. You're not simple, my sweet. You can understand well what I can do."

"All you do is evil," I growled. "You're a monster!" My tone piqued the ears of his two pets.

"A monster?" he laughed. "I survive! It's what we all do. How many souls have you harvested, child? A hundred? A thousand? Do not lecture me. We are all –" his sinister gaze regarded the *arvargr* "– monsters."

I was tired of this useless debate. "What do you want, lich?"

Vespirak's wolfish stare focused hard on me. "I want it all, of course; and, with you here, I see that it is all within my reach far sooner than I had believed."

Uncountable shadows swarmed within the vampire's black eyes. His sins called to me, invoking the darkness in my blood. My eyes narrowed to hateful slits. "Come and get it then."

Vespirak reclined back into his regal chair. His grin did not falter. "Do you know why I love children, Lyri?" he asked innocently.

Grotesque, perverse thoughts invaded my mind and sent tremors of disgust through my body. Before I could heave them from my mouth, the fiend answered himself.

"Because they are so malleable," he said salaciously, admiring his bejeweled hands. "They can become anything…anyone…if properly shaped."

Vespirak glanced to his scaly guards. His unspoken command roused the dragon-men. Following, a flurry of plaintive whimpers and frantic shuffling swept through his captive audience. Then, a pitiful scream broke through, snatching my horror to a hapless elf-girl being dragged forth by a pair of the saurian brutes. Her golden hair fell wildly about her beautiful face. Once it had been lovingly braided. Now it was a disheveled mess. She kicked and fought to no avail. I glimpsed her sky-blue eyes, filled with terror, imploring me, begging me to save her. The necromancer's bloody magic, though, had all but extinguished the strength from my veins. Despite my acidic bravado, I couldn't even force myself to stand.

In front of me, the elf-girl was mercilessly slung.

Sprawled at the vampire's feet, she shot a panicked look my way. The *arvargr* rumbled deeply. Their muscles tensed, eager for her to run.

She couldn't. She was paralyzed and trembled with fear. "Please," she wept.

Vespirak rose and stepped down to her. He kneeled, gently lifting her delicate chin in his long fingers.

"You see, my sweet," he said over the girl's frightened form to me, "anything is within my power."

The Arcanalestri's countenance focused, devouring the elf-girl's terror as he clutched her face and forced her eyes to meet his own. I could feel his spell stabbing into her spirit.

"Leave her alone!" I screamed, slamming my fists into the smooth, black tiles beneath me.

The lich grinned, stood, and let the elf-girl collapse. He returned to his throne, turned dramatically, and sat, satisfied.

I watched helplessly as the fey-child convulsed on the floor, seizing and crying out to the gods to save her.

Of course, they didn't.

I ground my teeth until they nearly cracked. I seethed, panting with rage. More hate filled my throat. The veins in my neck strained; but, before I could launch my bitter roar, the elf-girl unleashed a bloodcurdling shriek of her own that shattered and stunned my wrath.

Horrified, I looked on as she lurched upright. Her frail, lithe figure shook as the necromancer's will took root and grew, impregnating her with his wickedness.

On his throne, he simply smiled wryly.

The *arvargr* stirred and stood with growing excitement. The scales across their necks and shoulders fanned and bristled, quivering as they growled.

Within a lifespan of seconds, the poor child before me transformed. Her fair flesh split and molted. Dark scales erupted from beneath. Her mass expanded abhorrently, tearing apart the thin gown she wore. Her red blood sprayed forth, soaking its tatters and splattering my face.

Her trebling shriek quickly dropped in octaves until it became a hollow, haunting groan. The metamorphosis doubled her over in pain. When, at last, it was over – though the memory would never leave me. The girl was gone and another of the dragonkin stood, hulking, heaving, and horrible.

"So malleable are the fey," the lich gloated. His black eyes were locked on me. "So, too, are the gods, my sweet. You are evidence to that." To the creature he had just created, he said, "Show my guest to her room. We will have much more to discuss later; but, for now, see that she has a warm bath and is made comfortable."

The dragon-"man" turned to me. Only a hint of blue still lingered in her reptilian eyes. Her fanged maw hung open, dripping her own blood. Her claws clenched and reached for me.

Reflexively, I recoiled. It was to no avail. The newly minted monster lifted me with ease and bore me away.

Over its shoulder, I shouted a vow at the Grand Magus. "I'm going to kill you!"

He dismissed the comment with an arrogant backhanded wave.

"Perhaps, later," he said.

Chapter 11: Blood Ties

Now, you might suppose that I was shone to some posh, silky bedchamber after being hauled from the vampire's throne room.

I wasn't.

My new accommodations consisted of an iron cage within the center of a large, dark room somewhere deep below his keep. The chattering of rats and the echoing of dripping water along with the horrid stench of decay provided the place with a delightful and cheery ambience which, I'm sure, anyone with an appreciation of top-quality dungeons would acclaim. My host's generosity was utterly effusive. He truly spoiled me.

As for my nice bath, that came in the form of a bucket of rancid water that was doused over my head by my new caretaker – a well-trained ogre – after I had been stripped down to my bare ass and beaten for a few hours for his sadistic amusement.

Fortunately – or unfortunately, depending upon your perspective – I didn't die from all of the attention that was lavished upon me. A trickle of shadowy energy still flowed through my veins. The dark puissance, though, was only enough to keep me in the game. Vespirak's spells had sucked away the rest of my power.

You're beginning to understand why I detest magic.

I'm a creature created from defiance. What the gods will, I rebuke. It's the dragon blood in me, I suppose. Dyerbazog's fire, vested in Darkyr, my progenitor, burns inside me. With it, I set alight the Threads of Creation and thumb my nose at the decrees of the heavens. It's grand fun.

However, sorcerers do much the same thing. They exploit the loopholes in the Tapestry and exert their own wills over reality. They call it Third Magic – First Magic being what is inherent in creation, and Second Magic being the stuff that priests do in compliance with what their gods command. The problem with Third Magic for me is that I can't always defy what is already in defiance of the gods' laws. It comes down a battle of wills; and, though mine is impressive, it's not always the stronger or the most strategic.

Imagine it this way. I'm a brawler, a street scamp and a wildcat. A sorcerer is a practiced martial artist. Whereas, I throw my fury at things. A skilled wizard can deliver a precise strike to a precise spot and topple a titan. More often than not, I'm the one receiving that finger flick and getting sent flying. I'm a flea, and it sucks to be me.

With Vespirak, I had the added pleasure of being one of his least favorite playthings. Our rather rocky relationship all started centuries from now when I had the audacity to show up in his crypt where he and a group of his lich chums were plotting to take over the world – a rather cliché preoccupation that villains always seem to have. Well, being a part of the world they were planning on taking over and not being so inclined personally, I did what I typically do and told them where they could stick their schemes. So, when you look at it from the Grand Magus' perspective, he is completely justified in hating me.

After a few days of his hospitality, I was developing a keen appreciation for just how put out he was. After a week, I was pretty sure that our relationship was irrevocably broken.

What about Merilanna?

I've been avoiding the subject, admittedly, since "I told you so" is one of my least favorite things to hear.

Don't worry. She does turn back up again. I'll get back to her in a bit. You'll remember that I had sent her far and wide of this place with plans to join back up north of here once I had dispatched the garrison's leaders. That obviously did not work out as I had planned.

Alright...alright, I admit it. I don't plan! You're reading the wrong book if you like strategists. I'm a brat with an attitude. Deal with it!

Returning to my love affair with the lich: We worked very hard to develop our relationship over the coming days. He was a remarkably imaginative sadist and I was an imaginatively remarkable masochist. A perfect couple! The more he tortured me, the more I mocked his efforts. We truly inspired each other. Any time I was feeling a bit dead, he would toss in some wicked soul for me to refresh myself with and away we would go again.

Why?

Well, first off, he enjoyed it. I guess having someone to say no to you when no one else dared to fulfilled some special need in him. But that wasn't the main reason.

Vespirak wanted something that he thought that I had: a way back to the future.

Back to the future. Hmm...I will have to remember that phrase. There might be a story to tell there.

Anyway, all of this joyful euphoria centered around persuading me to tell him how I got here and, by the power of deduction, how I would get back to...you know.

Unfortunately for both of us, I had no idea how time got snagged or how I was going to get it unsnagged. Personally, I still blamed Ilé for this mess. But that didn't change anything. He wanted what I couldn't give. Sadly, our relationship was doomed. On top of that, he was seeing someone else.

Unfaithful bastard!

My heart was broken.

Okay, not really.

On one rather unremarkable morning, I was told to pack my things. We were leaving. You do realize that I didn't have anything to pack, right? That made leaving on time easy.

My caretaker loaded me up in my chariot – read prisoner wagon – and away we rolled. We soon joined a caravan accompanied by a few hundred of Vespirak's lumbering minions and headed north. To my delight, my host was leading the procession surrounded by a grand retinue of his favorite creatures. It was there, as we clattered along, that his infidelity was finally exposed.

Riding at his side, replete in a lovely white outfit befitting an ice queen, was his new paramour: Merilanna!

I told you I would get back to her.

Now, before you get all riled up and jump to my defense, cursing her as a traitorous harlot or something, you should know that her relationship with Vespirak came about under circumstances that were not really meant to betray me. In fact, it was quite the opposite. She was trying to save me.

I guess that when I didn't make it to our intended rendezvous, she had the suspicion that something bad had happened. I had only gone into a fortress filled with monsters and demons, so I can't imagine where she got that notion, but she did. When I didn't return, to her credit, she didn't linger on the "I told you so" part and set to finding me.

Merilanna's approach was quite different from mine. I stomp in. She sashays. It's a subtle difference, I suppose.

Through the bars of my wagon, I watched her work her charms. She smiled and the vampire smiled back. She demurred and the vampire smiled back. She teased and the vampire smiled back. You get the picture.

Vampires usually thrive upon their seductive wiles. They blend into the flock they intend to hunt. It keeps the flock from hunting them. Vespirak was one of the wiliest wolves there was. He was a master at the game. Against Merilanna, though, he was rank amateur.

I had thought the priestess somewhat innocent, sheltered on a frozen mountaintop and away from worldly vices. Seeing how she played Vespirak, I was forced to reevaluate my first, second, third, and fourth impressions of her. There might have been a few more, but who is counting.

Needless to say, while I was entertaining our host's darker desires, apparently, she had ingratiated herself with him and won a place at his side. Not bad. But, after all, she was a priestess of the most crafty, conniving goddess in the Palescia. So, I guess I should not have been that surprised.

Three days out from the garrison, Merilanna and I "officially" met. Vespirak pointed me out to her from across the camp with a fleeting gesture. She and I made eye contact briefly before she giggled and whispered something into the vampire's ear that made him grin very wide. I don't think it was something favorable towards me, but she was playing a game to garner his affection not mine.

I did notice, though, that she had picked up a new weapon. Wind-Song rode her shapely hip. I was glad to see that my old friend was safe.

The priestess and I did not interact for days after that. She was very clever and very careful. Among other things, Vespirak's mind could invade those of others. It seemed that Merilanna's, though, was well-trained. Apparently, he read only what she wanted him to read of her thoughts. With me, it was a different, but with the same results. Too much dragon fire burned in my brain for him to know what I was thinking. Of course, I was always eager to tell him some of my more fiery thoughts.

A forest appeared as the army marched north. We were entering the southern reaches of what would one day be called the Greymere. On the banks of the Wylren River where a little village named Nenn would stand centuries from now, the camps of the lich's allies came into view. We had joined Darkyr's forces.

Looking at this rabble, it pained me to admit that these brutes were my ancestors. Not all of them, of course. Just the ones without the tails and horns. I should also mention that not all of them, regardless of their species, were alive. That didn't seem to matter much, though. It was a necromancer's army after all. Rot was just another in a vast collection of foul smells that followed this horde. Nobody seemed to care how much meat you had on your bones so long as you could still wield a weapon.

Upon a rocky hilltop beside the river overlooking the cantonment was a grim keep very much like Vespirak's in appearance. Unlike the Grand Magus', though, this one seemed to be of the mundanely evil variety. No purple fires burned about it.

It was to there that the Arcanalestri and his select entourage rode.

I was a little miffed that I wasn't invited.

Instead, as the vampire's army mingled and its leadership hobnobbed, I was left to count the bars of my wagon again: one, two, three…Damn! Still the same number.

Night arrived right on time and the place really came alive – except for the dead things, of course. They just faked it. Apparently, a lot of the army preferred the darkness, especially the ones with the tails and horns that I mentioned. This is also to say that, no matter the hour, the party never ended. It just changed shifts.

As for Vespirak, I guess he was too busy to tuck me in tonight. Oh, well. I'd survived without cuddles before.

In fact, other than a few curious glances or sniffs, I was all but forgotten. The sight of just another prisoner wagon drew no special notice. Shipping captives was a commonplace enough occupation in this war just as in others. I wondered how many elves had died in this accursed box.

Shiny Pants definitely had every reason to hate us.

Through most of the night, bizarre caterwauls and the constant beating of drums entertained my ears. I kept my eyes closed through most of it, not to sleep – I rarely did that – but to spare myself the bulk of the depravity that the demons here were enjoying. They were a rowdy, horny bunch.

It was sometime during the wee hours that I was finally invited to the party. The dark fire in my soul was barely an ember, but its glow still caught the eye of one of the least brutish brutes. I guess the littlest troll wasn't having as much luck with the fun and games as his bigger, burlier buds were. So, he came over to pay me a visit.

I, not being a trollop for a troll, played hard to get and scooted to the center of the wagon to avoid his advances. Not one to be denied a girl that couldn't say no, he clambered to the rear door of the wagon and, after checking to be sure no one important was watching, took a swipe at the boxy lock that secured it with his crude hand ax. Clearly, he wasn't the best soldier in the army either. A half-dozen blows later and the mechanism finally broke.

By then, I had huddled into the farthest corner of my cage and did my best to cower. It wasn't my best performance, I'll admit. I'm not very good at cowering.

Nevertheless, the worm opened the door and came stalking in all cocksure and badass. He was jabbering the whole time and licking his thin lips as he crept near. His chipped ax swung side to side like a conductor's wand, accented whatever it was that he was saying so fiercely. I could see that he was shaking with excitement. Exuding dominance, I suppose, was a heady sensation for him.

Nearly naked save for a layer of filth and a few rags I had scrounged, I did my part and whimpered, drawing up into a little helpless ball.

He liked that.

With a growl, he slammed his ax into the wooden floor of the wagon inches from me and crouched, looming.

I think he was telling me how much fun we were about to have. Such a charmer, this one!

Through the matted bars of my black hair, I watched as he readied to grab me. I could almost see the flicker of my dark flame reflected in his hungry eyes. There wasn't much of it left, but I hoped it would be enough. I didn't want to disappoint him.

The troll's hands moved closer, his long fingers and dirty nails wagging eagerly. His breath chuffed and made a wet, wheezing sound. He was very excited.

I was, too.

Overwhelmed with lust, at the last moment, I sprang at him and threw myself into his embrace.

He wasn't expecting that and recoiled reflexively.

I hit him with everything I had left. Had he been bigger, who knows? As it were, he caught me but still toppled backwards, sprawling with a wildcat on top of him.

Frantically kicking and flailing, he tried to get me off.

Not like that, you dirty-minded reader. He was trying to escape!

At one point, he succeed in reversing our positions, pinning me beneath him. He grinned wickedly, assuming that victory was his. That's when I headbutted him in his crooked teeth, corrected his assessment, and changed his expression.

Stunned and staggered, the troll staggered back to get his face out of range. Blood sprayed from his mouth as he spat curses at me. Hate filled his eyes and he lunged for his ax but froze the instant he realized it wasn't there.

His horror snapped to me.

"The party is over!" I hissed as I put his nasty weapon to use and split his wide eyes farther apart, wedging the blade squarely into his skull between them.

A quick jerk and the ax was free of his head and his service. A rush of shadows spilled from his soul as his blood geysered. I savored both.

Wheeling about, I snarled and scanned the darkness, letting my inflamed, predatory senses transcend the Veil. I knew the troll's sins would not sustain me for long, but I didn't need long.

With a burst of fury and desperation, I flew from the wagon and onto the Cusp. I know I should have fled into the night; but, remember, I'm not strategic. While the shadow still burned inside me, towards the keep I ran, a revenant on a warpath.

Along the way, I nibbled, cutting a vile throat or two or ten, fortifying my rage. By the time I reached the rocky hill, I was nearly delirious in my rampage. Screams from the camp were beginning to catch up with me. I wasn't being subtle or, as Fhaed would say, careful.

Into the fortress' maw, I dashed just ahead of my heralds' cries. In the shadows of the bailey's towers, I buried myself deep, cloaking myself in thick layers of Twilight in the courtyard. There, I waited for my prey to emerge.

I didn't have to wait very long.

Within moments of the alarm, Vespirak and his compeer, a monster of a man in black, leather armor, stepped out from the donjon. I could feel dragon fire blazing in his blood. It sent shockwaves through my soul.

Shadows boiled wildly inside of him. I closed my eyes and fought to steady my breathing, focusing hard to keep my dark fire from swooning. As for my nemeses, both held their composures firmly as they received the reports from the camp.

Hearing the accounts, I think the vampire smirked.

I like when my handiwork is acknowledged.

His towering companion, though, seemed far less appreciative and barked something at the soldiers that sent them scrambling. His words reverberated to me through Twilight. They sounded almost like my Asgev tongue, but not quite. But that didn't matter; their meaning was clear enough: "Find her and bring her to me!"

I was flattered. My hosts did care.

Seizing upon the distraction, I shot into the keep and stole my way into its great hall. Unlike Vespirak's, this place was far from posh and palatial. There wasn't even a throne. In fact, it actually looked like a respectable war room.

At the far end, beyond a long, glowing firepit, a large table dominated the chamber. Stone figurines were arrayed upon it like some giant game board. Rivers, mountains, forests, and coastlines were represented. Placed throughout these, some pieces marked strongholds while others identified gatherings of troops. It looked like the boys had been busy. Conquest was complicated work, I guess. There was definitely more to it than march here, burn that, kill them, and march on. Those were just the basics. Vespirak and his large friend played the game more expertly.

I was tempted to move some of the pieces around just for the fun of it, but I decided not to. They would only move them back, and I probably wouldn't be around to enjoy their grumbling anyway.

The booming sound of the great doors to the keep slamming shut resounded to my ears. The vampire and the warlord were returning.

I glanced at the figurines.

"Alright, Lyri, what's your next move?" I challenged myself.

Dark fire blazed inside me. I needed to use it or lose it. For the moment, though, I chose a different option. I dove deeper into Twilight…and, just to be sure that I never, ever would be detected, I hid under the table. That always works, right?

"She won't get far," Vespirak assured the commander. His voice filled the space between the giant's echoing footfalls.

"What is she?"

Humph, that I understood. As I burned through the shadows that I had harvested, the languages their mortal coils had spoken sifted into my mind slowly. Replaying their sins was like a crash course in their guttural tongues. In Twilight, meanings transcend sounds anyway. It had taken a while for them to root in my head, but I was starting to learn fast. That my own native tongue had grown from this gruff dialect was disheartening but it still helped.

"A demon, of sorts," Vespirak replied. Together, they stepped back to the arrayed table, giving me an excellent view of their kneecaps.

"Why is she here? Why did you bring her?"

"She is a gift for our master."

The big man's voice frowned. "A gift?"

"Yes, a gift. That little monster was spawned in these lands. She could prove quite useful in their conquest."

Nice lie.

"There conquest is well in hand, Magus. Do you doubt that?"

The vampire shuffled. "No, of course, not."

"Good." The warlord moved something on his table then added, "She is your gift, so she is your problem. Do not let her become one for me. Understood?"

Did he just threaten the almighty Vespirak? I think I liked this warlord.

"Be assured, Lord Darkyr, she will not."

Lord Darkyr? Lyri, you're an idiot! Giant warlord filled with dragon fire – who did you think he was, the court jester!

After my initial panic attack, I lost my mind completely and grinned. I almost broke from my cover and screamed, "Surprise, grandpa, it's me!" But I didn't. That wasn't the first impression I was going for. Actually, no impression at all was my preference.

"I have something she wants," the vampire was saying as I tuned my senses back into their conversation.

The table creaked as the big man leaned across it towards the necromancer. "Explain."

Vespirak's polished toes wiggled as he, too, leaned forward conspiratorially.

I wanted to cut them off; but, again, I refrained.

"The priestess," the Grand Magus replied smugly. "Her soul and the girl's soul are bound."

Bound? I don't like bound!

"Bound?" echoed the warlord.

"A spell, divinely crafted. It weaves between them and binds their destinies. I sensed it the moment the priestess appeared. She is, I think, oblivious to it."

"Bound by who?"

The warlord was still stuck on the word. So was I. He sounded worried and little miffed. So was I. I guess there wasn't a figurine on his table for an unexpected new player.

Paranoia is a common disorder among megalomaniacs. For me, it's just a hobby. Okay, it's an addiction, but I'm not trying to conquer the world, just piss off the gods.

Speaking of which...

"Ilé, I should think."

"Ilé?"

He doesn't know who she is.

To quote a certain Nagari friend of mine who you haven't met in this book, "Interesting."

The vampire didn't actually have to breathe, but he drew in and exhaled a deep one before continuing. "Ah, Ilé – she's new."

"New? Are you saying there is a new goddess in the world?"

I could hear Vespirak's sharp fingernails tapping rhythmically on the tabletop.

"Given when we are," he answered cryptically, "yes, that's exactly what I'm saying."

Darkyr leaned back and relieved his burden from the table. "What does this goddess want?"

"That, I think, is still undecided – well, beyond vengeance, I suppose." Vespirak, too, moved off from the table and paced slowly, selecting his commentary carefully. "She was recently ravaged by the god of death and lifted into the divine court – something you might say, she resents."

Darkyr snorted. "And what does this priestess of hers have to do with your little gift?"

"Another mystery," the Arcanalestri replied.

"I don't like mysteries," Darkyr countered sharply. There was no missing the threat in his voice. A heavy game piece slammed hard against the tabletop. "Solve it and find this demon-girl of yours. I don't have time for your games or those of the gods."

The vampire stopped pacing.

"Of course, Lord Darkyr," Vespirak assuaged. "Time is very valuable. I understand that very well."

A bow and the lich departed. He was going for Merilanna, I surmised, so, I slipped away and followed. When I hazarded a glance back, the Shadowlord was staring across his table my way. It was also the way the vampire had gone, though. I hoped he wasn't looking at me. Truthfully, I didn't wait to find out.

Chapter 12: Web of Ice

Vespirak made his way back to his quarters directly. Deep in the Cusp, I stalked after him.

Not unexpectedly, his accommodations were fancy – at least as compared to the spartan furnishings throughout the rest of Darkyr's keep. I could smell the incense and perfumes long before he reached his door. A single dragon-man, his scales like polished ebony, stood guard outside it. I wondered what poor elf-child had been sacrificed to make the monster.

It was truly sad that such beautiful beings as the Alurishi were so vulnerable to sorcery. It was as if they had no immunity to its plague at all. The gods had done a terrible job of preparing them for the Shadowfall. Were the Aesyr inept, naïve, or just that stupid? I didn't know, but I still pitied the poor wretches that suffered for it.

I guess it's the difference between spirits and souls. The former are very susceptible to what happens to their world. Cut Narianna and they bleed. The later are more enduring and able to withstand such traumas. Cut Narianna and they cut back!

Alright, enough philosophy. Apparently, I've been talking to Rasha Khan too much.

Rasha Khan? Oh, he's another acquaintance of mine you won't meet in this book. Interesting fellow: a Rhakashi, a leonine warrior and philosopher. We've chatted a few times. He's wise and furry, but not exactly cuddly. Fierce and loyal, he's one of those guardians of the world that cuts back both with his claws and his sharp mind. I like him.

Back to necromancer who I don't like…

Vespirak strutted into his chambers like the audacious, golden peacock that he was and was greeted immediately by his lovely paramour, Merilanna.

"There you are, my pretty," he said warmly.

'My pretty.' Hey, that's my pet name! Should I be jealous?

Merilanna glided into the vampire's embrace and bestowed a kiss on his lips. "Is all well?" she asked innocently. "I heard cries in the dark. I was worried for you."

The golden-skinned lich smiled and held her at arms' length admiringly. "A minor squabble between some of the rabble – nothing to concern yourself with. I have dealt with the matter."

Adoration flowed across the priestess' lovely face.

Silently, I slipped to a shadowy alcove and watched the two of them play games with each other. Both were skillful dancers – metaphorically speaking. If I didn't know her better…at least, if I hadn't weighed her soul in judgement back on the bloodied road, I'd have truly thought she betrayed me. Everything she did rang true. It was unnatural and I hated it.

Vespirak glissaded past Merilanna and moved to the only window. It was an arrow loop, actually, but it provided a view of the courtyard below. I supposed that the rectangular room had been a storage area or small barrack recently. Whatever it had been, now it served as the lich's lair and was furnished with a comfortable four-poster bed, a small, well-crafted dining table for two, and a splendid armoire. All wore the hallmarks of elvish artistry. I didn't remember his entourage lugging these things here on horseback, so I presumed they were already present – spoils of war.

"May I ask, my prince, how long before we continue north? Lord Darkyr's hospitality is, well, charming, but my heart desires to return to my homeland."

Vespirak smiled back to the priestess evilly. "You miss your lands of snow and ice."

Merilanna blushed and demurred, but her countenance turned dark before she replied firmly saying, "I do. It has been many years since the *shi* court imprisoned me and exiled me to these hinterlands. The war you bring brought my liberation. To the elves, punishment is overdue. Now that they are broken, I would return to my goddess' shrine and see it cleansed. Let what blood flow that must. My Lady will judge the fallen."

"You truly hate them, don't you?" The vampire smirked and stalked back to the fuming priestess. "You, of sylph blood, a fey child of the winds, hate them that much? I wonder."

Merilanna stiffened and lifted her face to the golden god beaming down at her. "Doubt it not," she snarled indignantly. But there was a dangerous sensuality to her growl as well – enticing and seductive. She was baiting him.

Vespirak took it. "Was it not Urrel, the god of these heathens about you now, that claimed your lady's innocence?" He stroked her hair, aroused by her icy fire. "And yet, you ally with them, not her kin and yours, the elves?"

"Don'Ellithyran's court did nothing to aid My Lady," Merilanna spat. "They were cowards and fled before your master's banner ever flew over these lands. The death god of the Urgrym did as they do. Nothing more.

He claimed the spoils of war like the animal he is. I do not blame the beast for its nature, but I do condemn the *shi* for their willful arrogance and faithless abandonment of the holy mountains. They left her innocence unguarded! They betrayed her when they fled. So, yes, I damn the elves to every hell you bring them." Her back stiffened as she lifted her face closer to his, daringly. "But do not believe that I hold anything by scorn for these filthy monsters beneath your sandals either. They are dogs and swine; but, at least, they do not give pretense for what they are."

"You are born of their blood, too," Vespirak observed, baiting her as well. "Your father was no better than his god. In truth, they are the same. He ravaged your mother's innocence. How else would you have been conceived, my pretty?"

"I killed him already," Merilanna hissed. "His blood is frozen in the ice of the holy mountains."

"And your mother?"

The priestess' fury ebbed and drained as sorrow filled her voice. "My birth was her death," she said softly.

Vespirak shook his head, confounded, and laughed. "And still you pray to the goddess of death."

The tears that tinged Merilanna's eyes trembled as anger reignited in them. "My Lady has given me the strength to endure this world's wickedness," she said and reared again defiantly. "She is not the bringer of death, she is the guide of the fallen. She is my protector and my pathfinder, true and unwavering. I follow her and she never fails me."

The vampire regarded her with admiration. "Such fire and such beauty," he said, his hand moving to caress her cheek with the back of his fingers, the motion leading her tears down her face.

Merilanna's eyes locked on his. Her bosom heaved as her heart pounded. "I will see the holy mountains again," she declared. "I will return to my home and raise a temple to her."

"I believe you will," Vespirak replied. His broad hand slipped behind her hair; his fingers cupped her head. Then he kissed her with a primal fierceness. Her locks rippled in waves across her shoulders and down her back as his mouth devoured hers then moved passionately to her neck.

In the ethereal shadows, I gagged and tried to look away as he lifted her bodily into his arms and crushed her petite form against him. Still, I could hear his fangs pierce her skin and was drawn back to the macabre, lustful scene. A gush of passion escaped Merilanna's lips as she arched backwards, her wide, inverted gaze looking straight to where I was.

Heroes of the Third Age: Merilanna

Surely, she could not see me in Twilight, but her pink lips quivered nonetheless, mouthing my name as lascivious ecstasy overwhelmed her. Her eyes rolled into her head as the vampire fed. Her lithe body shook with unearthly pleasure, ensorcelled by his venom. The wet patter of her blood resounded from the stones of the floor, dribbling through her silvery white hair.

Magic was flowing fast. They both were weaving its web. Horrifically, I could feel what she was feeling. I recoiled at the shock.

Suddenly, Vespirak's fangs snapped free from her veins. He reared like a cobra, still holding her dangling in his arms triumphantly. As he exhaled his lust, his cold, black eyes dropped towards my shadows and pierced them. Merilanna's stare, swooning and exsanguinated, lolled towards me.

"Run," her shivering lips said without sound.

"There you are," the vampire purred. "I knew I would taste you in her blood."

The priestess collapsed as Vespirak sprang into the Veil to claim me. Stunned, I tried to escape, but my dark fire guttered and the fiend was upon me. All thought of the troll's ax evaporated from my mind. It clanked back into the solid world as I was lifted, one steely hand wrapped around my small neck.

Reflexively, I struggled, kicking wildling as I clawed at the monster's wrist. Without my speed, my strength was useless. He had me. I couldn't even spit curses, clutched in his grasp.

"You are a remarkable irritant, my pretty," he laughed.

A chill raced through my body, freezing my motion.

The silvery sheen of a sharp blade erupted through his throat before he could finish his chuckle. I stared in awe as Wind-Song fought to free me from my torturer.

But the vampire was not nearly slain.

Whirling about, Vespirak threw me hard across the room, tearing my sword from Merilanna's hands as he spun. The armoire caught me. Its beautifully carved doors shattered inward. My body broke against them, but they yielded just enough to spare me a crushing blow.

Nearly blind with pain, I saw the monster seize the priestess, trading my throat for hers. With his other, he reached back and pulled Wind-Song from his own. Her blade was not wide enough to sever his thick neck by a mere thrust. The attack had succeeded only in stopping his annoying jabber.

Blood sprayed from Vespirak's lips as he vomited a curse at the woman in white caught in his claws. His venom painted her red with his rage.

Wind-Song clattered against the stone tiles, discarded.

Merilanna's fate was no better than mine. The lich lifted her with ease and threw her away. Her body snapped the nearest bed post before slamming into pillows and headboard. Limply, she crumpled. I could hear her wheeze wetly.

Summoned by the clamor, the dragon-man sentry burst into the room with serrated sword in hand. The creature scanned the commotion, looking for danger. Neither Merilanna nor I posed any. We were stunned and nearly insensate. The vampire's rage, though, was not yet sated.

It's hard to read a dragon's face, but I guess the one it wore was bewilderment.

Vespirak spun to the draconian guard, the blood of his countless victims spilling down his broad chest. More boiled from his throat through his fangs and through the gash in his neck. Unintelligibly, he splattered some order into the air.

Unsure, the dragon-man withdrew a step.

It's compliance was too slow, apparently. The Grand Magus backhanded the air between them. A shockwave cracked the distance, whirling dust and candle smoke violently. Its blow caught the sentry and blasted it back through the door from which it came. A dreadful sound, like stomping on snails, thundered from the hallway outside ending the guard's duty.

Vespirak turned menacingly back towards the pitiful sound of the priestess' agony and eyed her helpless condition.

I shifted in the folds of the armoire. My own blood stained the rich apparel revealed therein. Splintered wood crackled as I struggled weakly to free myself. My dark fire sputtered and fought to reignite.

Bitterly, the vampire stalked to extract me. Little could be made of his gurgled words beyond that they were curses.

"Leave my sister alone!" Merilanna cried. Her voice was strained and shrilled by pain.

Vespirak ignored her. His perfect nails, now dripping red, latched hold of my rags and snatched me from the company of his silken wardrobe. Hanging like a tattered doll held by my throat once more, he leaned in close to glare at me.

Dazed but defiant, I snarled back.

I could only discern one word as he berated my insolence: "Mistake."

Heroes of the Third Age: Merilanna

As his grip tightened and my vision darkened, I nodded my feeble agreement and wheezed, "Yes, it was. Yours!" Then, viciously, I grabbed hold of the golden chains draping between his nostrils and his ears and snatched them from his ugly face.

The vampire threw back his head and howled, fountaining more blood into the air.

With what little reservoir of black fire I retained, I speared the gash in his exposed neck with my fists and thrust his golden trinkets down his throat.

Vespirak choked.

Behind him, Merilanna invoked her goddess' wrath as well. An icy spell slid from her bloodied tongue. The lich's undead grasp, already unnaturally cold, burned into my skin with frost. The red haze filling the air around us crackled and popped as every droplet exploded. Crystals of ice erupted from the showering blood. Too, that which flowed in the vampire's veins grew hoary. Spikes of frozen enmity pierced his skin, shredding his glorious, golden form from within. Stutteringly, as the goddess' damned him, his horrific visage chattered down to regard me with his hate. I watched with glee as the ice wove its web across his eyes, covering them with tiny, jagged prisms.

My black fire resurged as the lich's spell broke. Ferociously, I kicked out from his grasp. His fingers shattered as I flew free.

Thus began the fall of Vespirak. I tumbled to a crouch, ready to spring away, and watched in delirious, wide-eyed fascination as the fiend's figure cracked. The sound of it was thrilling. His expression was fixed with disbelief.

I grinned so wide.

"Your time is up," I taunted.

An instant more and the Grand Magus shattered like glass.

On the bed, the priestess, her hand still outstretch to deliver her goddess' judgment, collapsed.

I rose as she fell and waded with my arms wide to embrace the pyre of ethereal black flame that engulfed our foe's shards. A hurricane wind of evil blasted my soul, lifting me into its tempest. A thousand lifetimes worth of debauchery and sin swept and swirled inside me. I was awash in darkness so deep that I left my mind and body behind and simply spiraled into the monster's wicked world. All that he had done, every sinister act, consumed me. I drowned in the deluge, lost in the dark.

I would have remained lost had not a song reached my heart. It was a lullaby that brought me back.

My eyes fluttered and found the light. The priestess was cradling me once again in her lap, her hand stroking my hair as she hummed, sound whispering along my soul with silken fingers.

"There you are," she said down to me, smiling gently.

I exhaled and blew a window through the swirling blackness to clear my view of her. Thoughts and memories, like the riffling of a deck of cards, were falling back into place.

Still confused, my senses awash in screams and nightmares, I glanced about our surrounds. That only added to my befuddlement.

We were in the forest.

Something moved and, catlike, my eyes shot that way.

A black-scaled dragon-man sat nearby and added wood to our campfire.

I jerked upright, my hand flying to my side where Wind-Song should be. She wasn't!

"It's alright," Merilanna assured, though she was wise not to try to grapple me. "He helped us escape."

I shook my head to clear the tangle of bloody images that warred within.

"What?"

I recognized him. It was the dragon-man that Vespirak had struck down with his backhanded spell.

"She saved me," the creature added, his voice cavernous and profound. "You both did. Her Lady's song freed my spirit and her touch restored my flesh. Your fury led me to freedom."

Still reeling, I struggled hastily to my feet and scanned the wilderness. "Where are we?"

"The Greymere," Merilanna answered calmly, "somewhere northeast of the Wylren."

"How – how did we escape?"

"We followed you," the dragon-man replied.

Merilanna nodded but looked down as the weight of those memories revisited her. "You cleared our path, Lyri."

I couldn't remember that, but I knew how I did it. Shadows yet hissed inside my soul and whispered of their doom. They remembered very well.

"Darkyr?" I wondered aloud.

"He follows," the dragon-man said simply.

Idly, I brushed down the sides of the long, woolen tunic I now wore, gathering my composure. I think it must have been a cloak once, but it had been split and refashioned to cover my small figure and was now more a tabard-like dress. A simple, plaited cord bound it about my waist making me appear like an odd little monk. Cloth wound with leather strips clad my calves and shod my feet. All-in-all, my apparel was crude and quickly worked but practical.

"Where's my sword?"

Merilanna pulled a bound bundle of sackcloth – a makeshift backpack of sorts – from beside her and drew Wind-Song from its midst. From a small satchel, she retrieved a wrapped kerchief and handed my Whisperer to me as well. "I kept them safe," she assured.

The rapid rhythm of my heart slowed and settled as I set the shiny orbs to dancing in my palm. I exhaled and finally refolded my legs to sit by the fire, suddenly exhausted again.

A small braid of hair looped over my head, the tiny snowflake shimmering with the firelight.

"Again?" I ask, weary, but without a fight.

"Of course!" She moved and took a seat beside me. "If not, I might get lost." Her eyes crinkled with impish humor. I ignored her.

"Do you have a name?" I asked the dragon-man.

"I did," came a low, rumbling reply, "but it was stolen from me by the magus."

"So, I gave him another," Merilanna added.

"I am Eindrac," he said proudly.

"Eindrac." I nodded, savoring the taste of it. "It's a good name." I looked to the priestess and gave her a wily smile.

For you barbarians that can't speak the noble Asgev tongue, "Eindrac" means good or blessed dragon. That's why the name fit.

"So, what's the plan?" I asked after the pleasantries passed. "Besides running I mean."

Merilanna pulled her knees to her chest and stared into the yellow flames, thinking. "We still have to get you back to the Circlestone. After that, I don't know. I hope all this will be resolved when we do."

"How do we get there?"

Neither of my companions were forthcoming with a ready answer. That was, unfortunately, to be expected – at least as far as the priestess was concerned. These weren't her lands. As for Eindrac, I wasn't sure.

"Do you know these lands?" I prompted the dragon-man.

"I did once," he said, his voice subdued.

"But those memories were stolen from you as well," I concluded for him.

This was very aggravating. We were in dangerous lands in the middle of a war and had no guide to see us through them. Einhervaldheim would be my home in a thousand years. Right now, I was as lost as the priestess and the dragon.

Of course, there would be landmarks: rivers, mountains, and even some of the ancient stone megaliths to point the way, but this Silverwood was still a vast and alien land to me.

To be honest, I wasn't that great at navigating it the first time I tried. Had it not been for Kel, the ranger, and – as much as I hate to admit it – Aras Azzar, the Black Orc, I probably would have died there then. My new traveling companions weren't going to be of much help finding the right path.

I brooded for a while then said, "We need to find the Grymryl Road. It will take us to Olde Asgevan – or whatever stands there now. The Clangrym Stones may show us the way from there."

"What are these places?" Merilanna asked. "I mean, I've heard of Olde Asgevan. The *Einholdte* – the gathering of clan chieftains – meets there. Correct? But what is the Grymryl Road?"

I shrugged. "Bits of an old road. There are pieces of it all over the Silverwood." I glanced at Eindrac. "The *Shi* built it. Do you remember that?"

The dragon-man shook his head slowly.

"Right," I grunted. "Well, it should be in this forest; and, I think, it's probably a lot easier to find and follow nowadays."

"We'll head east and see if we can find it," Merilanna offered. "North and east should take us where we need to go, eventually."

"Roads will be watched," Eindrac warned.

Merilanna and I exchanged troubled looks.

"Yes, they will," I concurred.

"We've managed to evade Darkyr's army so far," the priestess reassured. "We'll just have to be careful."

A question popped into my mind. "How long?"

"What?"

"How long have we managed to elude them so far?"

"Almost a week."

"You've been lugging me along for a week?"

"Following you for most of it, actually. We only caught up in the past day."

"The path was not hard to follow," Eindrac added.

"Then why haven't they caught us," I challenged.

"You killed everything that came," the dragon-man answered evenly.

I shook my head in frustration, rattling what little brains I had stuffed in my skull. I couldn't remember much, just fleeting images of monsters and the evils they had done. Perhaps, that was merciful.

"She sang for you every day," Eindrac said simply. "At last, you came and laid your head upon her lap. I was glad for that for I saw my own death in your eyes when first you stepped from the shadows."

I regarded the dragon-man. "Don't take it personally. I do that to everybody. Still, I'm sorry," I said honestly.

"Do not be. You are fierce. You have the blood of dragons in you."

I sighed and said, "The blood of one, anyway." I shook my head, dismissing the rest of what I was going to say. Finally, "It's complicated," was what I offered.

The dragon-man seemed to accept that and asked nothing more.

"What about you?" I ventured. "You weren't always a dragon. Vespirak made you, right?"

Eindrac nodded.

"So, your blood is elven."

Another nod.

I extended my query to the priestess and asked, "What was his fascination with dragons? Why change elves into dragon-men?"

"I'm not sure," Merilanna admitted. "Perhaps, it was because commanding dragons displayed his power best."

"Perhaps," I allowed. "But, as arrogant as he was, I'm surprised he didn't brag about his plans more." Something else didn't add up. "The first dragon-men we met were guarding wagons filled with dead elven children. That's hardly a glorious errand."

The priestess' affected countenance showed that she agreed with me. Hauling corpses for hundreds of miles didn't make much sense. Where were they taking them and why?

Now, the necromancer was dead and the answer to those questions was probably lost as well. Of one thing, though, I was certain: Vespirak had a plan. Dragon-men and dead elven children were part of some scheme.

A thought flared. "Eindrac, did you ever escort such a caravan?"

"Yes."

Electric looks shot between Merilanna and me.

"To where?" the priestess sued.

"The Grand Magus' ziggurat in the dark city he called Amonarca. It lies in a black, broken land filled with fire."

"In a rift valley?" I asked.

Another nod.

I gathered Merilanna's attention with my seething glare. "Garadar," I said assuredly.

She did not know the word and beseeched me to explain with her puzzling eyes.

"A city – once beautiful – but charred black and twisted cruel in the age after The Destroyer came. I ruled its underworld for a time." My words were chilled and I confessed them flatly. Inside, though, I burned as old anger swelled and a flood of dark, smoking memories filled me. Some were bittersweet. Sweet because it was there that I had met Fhaed, the man I loved but, cursed forever to be a child, could never love with a woman's heart. Bitter because it was there also that I had killed him in throes of rage befitting the foulest of demons.

I guess we all have monsters in our stories. For me, I was the monster in that chapter of my life. None blacker or more wicked have I ever faced than the one I had been then. Only an undue blessing from one of the gods I despised had saved my friend and, in turn, though I deserved it not, saved me as well.

I never fully reconciled with those days. Thinking on them now gnawed at my soul.

"There," I continued, "a race of sorcerer kings ruled: the Amons." A derisive snort escaped me. "I suppose their rise to power is only just beginning given when we are in the weaving of the world."

"And the children?"

I blew the bitterness from my tongue and made room for my wicked conjecture. "I don't know. But Garadar stands in a place called – or will be called – The Cut. When Dyerbazog destroyed Elyarsa Altairas, the elves beyond came there to pray for the spirits of their lost people. They built shrines all over those damned mountains. Vespirak made dragon-men and he sent dead children back to that place. Why? I don't know. But he was a necromancer and his ambitions were grand. Gaining the power of the dragon and the elves – that's something he would seek."

Merilanna's brow knitted tightly as she struggled with what I inferred. "But why dragon-men? And what purpose could dead children possibly serve?"

I shrugged. "When Dyerbazog burned the world, his fire and fury made dragon-men of the elves. It changed them just like the lich's spell did."

"Yes, they're called the Drakkar," Merilanna agreed. "I remember that from my teachings. Even in the icy north, I've heard of them. They rule over the black lands of Ardra where the mountains forever burn."

"That's right," I said. "As for the children, who knows? Maybe the vampire meant to use them in some dark spell to slither his way into Ardra. Whatever his plan was, it was bad."

"And it's over," the priestess stated firmly. "He'll do harm no more."

I shied from her sure words. Vespirak was dead, but he had been dead before. That's the problem with liches. They don't stay dead. That's why their liches to begin with. The Arcanalestri defy death. Their magic always seems to find ways to escape it.

Merilanna read my thoughts in my countenance. "No matter what happens," she said gently, "we'll beat him and all like him. We're stronger together."

I wanted to believe that, but optimism wasn't my strong suit.

"We'll see," was all I could muster.

Later, still in the midst of night, my mind racing through all that had happened, I returned my gaze to the patient priestess. "Thank you," I said quickly then looked back into the depths of the campfire.

Merilanna smiled her gentle smile. "We are together in this, Lyri," she said softly. She truly meant it.

"Vespirak said our fates are woven together. Our souls are bound." I set my troubled eyes on her again. People I cared about always died. I didn't want that to be her fate. "Do you know what he was talking about?"

Merilanna retreated into her thoughts for a moment then shook her head. "No, but I won't deny it's true either. I can see a silvery thread spun between us. It is My Lady's doing, I think."

I frowned deeply and looked away. "Right," I groused. "You called me sister." I accused. I was in one of my moods – you know, the dark, brooding, emotionally prickly ones. "Not a good choice," I rebuked.

"But a choice I've made and will not change, nonetheless. I do not fully understand it myself, but…you are my sister. It sings true in my soul regardless of a silence in yours."

I looked at her sharply. "You're a good liar, you know." It was an awkward compliment and caught her off-guard. "The lich," I explained "You had him caught in your web. That takes talent."

She looked away, embarrassed. "I did what I had to. Every good lie is seeded with truth."

I wondered how much she had said was one or the other. "Your father? Mother? The story you told him?"

Merilanna lifted her face back to me. The firelight shone on her fair skin. It seemed to glow.

"I told you the truth. I told him what his evil heart would believe. I needed him to trust me and hate bridged the distance to that end."

I smirked – I never smile – and nodded. "Like I said, you're a good liar."

"Thank you," she chuckled mildly.

"Get some sleep," I suggested. "It's a long road ahead."

Merilanna smiled – she never smirks…I think.

Eindrac just sat and watched the fire burn. His thoughts were harder to see behind his dragon's face.

Chapter 13: Where Giants Tread

They say the Oröm built the great stone monuments that lay scattered across Einhervaldheim. Most smart people agree about that. What were they for? That is what they argue about.

When I was growing up – which is a weird thing to say since I'm stuck in my ten year old body even though I am now, for those of you keeping count, nearly fifteen – the skalds taught us that the standing stones were there to protect our lands and that they had powerful spirits that guarded them. As for the Circlestones, everybody knew they were gates to magical lands – some good, some evil. According to the grey-beards, the Grymryl Road had been a gift from the Earth King, Klakispar, to the elf king, Don'Ellithyran. Maybe that was so. It's hard to imagine hundreds of elves moving the gigantic rocks needed to build the thing. The notion just didn't fit with what little I knew of the *Shi*-folk.

As a note and aside, I don't know what the Grymryl's original name was. In Asgev, "grym ryl" means "the giant's path." So, that's what I call it. I'm sure the elves had a prettier name for it.

The Gyrmryl Road was, as we had suspected, easy enough to find. Unlike in my future time, it had not been swallowed by the forest and was in much better repair. The paver stones were nicely fitted and trimmed by a clean-lined curb. The grand trilithons that marked the miles – I guess they were miles or something equivalent – were upright and their lintels were set snugly in place. The words and symbols that were carved upon them were clear and distinct. I couldn't read them; but, despite his transformed state, Eindrac could. So, reaching the road proved a great boon. The only problem was that the names etched upon them meant nothing to us, Eindrac included. The best we could do was pick the proper direction and start walking.

Overall, for a land under siege, the scenery along the causeway was idyllic. The Alurishi had gone so far as to weave the landscape around it. Flowering vines and hedges trimmed the rocks. Grass and ferns bordered it. There were way-stops along its course where we could rest and enjoy a view from a high hill or have a cool drink at a merry stream running nearby. Despite the ravages brought by the invading monsters, the Grymryl and its smaller, intersecting thoroughfares remained a wonder to behold.

This is not to say that the road had not suffered, however. In places, it had been defiled, its beautiful landscaping hacked away and destroyed. Some of the trilithons had been toppled. Some had been scarred, their words chiseled away. Some areas had been trampled under the marching feet of the wicked hordes and turned to mud. So, though it endured, even the Grymryl Road was not spared.

As Eindrac had warned, it was also watched. There were many predators prowling about its path. Deserters from Asteranoth's army found the Grymryl to their liking in their new professions as brigands. It wasn't long before we encountered the first of them; or, shall I say, I encountered them.

The problem with a good ambush is that the ambushers have to be good at ambushing. Now, normally, hiding in the forest along some carefully selected spot in the terrain where you, the ambusher, have all the tactical advantages is the key to success. When some oblivious and careless ambush-ee shows up at the chosen location, executing the ambush is simply a matter of popping up, weapons brandished, and claiming your booty. If done properly, the ambush-ee is caught totally by surprise and is left incapable of resisting you and your carefully laid plans are richly rewarded. No mess. No fuss.

I suppose that was the strategy the first brigands we met had hoped to employ.

At a certain, choice spot along the Grymryl Road as we moved through the foothills of the Greymere, our little trio came upon a narrow meander flanked by outcrops of overgrown rocks. Visibility was limited by the rolling land and the leafy foliage such that, though the road itself was unimpeded, our path forward was obscured by numerous twists and turns. Leaving the road was not an option, of course, as doing so would involve climbing, something we, the typical, carefree travelers, had no interest in doing. Thus, we, the ambush-ees, were in a less than perfect position.

For the brigands, on the other hand, the location was absolutely perfect. The rocks provided cover and elevation – two things any good brigand appreciated – and, while perched atop the outcrops, they were in an excellent place to do their jobs waylaying passersby quite effectively. One group would introduce themselves from above, kindly asking for submission from the ambush-ees, using their arrows and spears to get their points across, while a second group would jog in to reiterate those propositions more directly once the expected compliance had been achieved. Then, it was a simple matter of collecting the rewards of their clever schemes, heading back to their secret camp in some cave somewhere, and celebrating. Not a bad life, I suppose.

But there was a problem, a small oversight on the part of our prospective ambushers: Me.

Long before their spotters spotted us, I spotted them. Now, don't go blaming the brigands. They did their best. They were well-hidden, well-prepared, well-informed, and well-marshaled. Normally, the game would have been theirs. Unfortunately, for them, I was hungry; and, though they were concealed and alert, the shadows in their souls were scented long before we came frolicking along.

By the time, the priestess and the dragon-man appeared at the appointed ambush spot, I had filled the darkness in my belly and was waiting for them.

"Horses?" I suggested, offering the reins to a pair of stout mounts to my companions as they rounded the corner.

Merilanna stopped and stared at me. "You shouldn't run off like that," she chided mildly.

I shrugged and walked over, leading the animals. Both shied from Eindrac, snorting nervously.

"Where did you find them?" Merilanna asked – though I could see my black fire reflected in her eyes and knew that she knew from whence they came.

"Their previous owners won't be needing them," I replied simply.

Eindrac approached his proffered mount slowly, his scaly hands splayed as benignly as possible towards the jittery animal. Words in the *Shi* tongue whispered from him. Still, the horse was not soothed. It nickered and pulled hard upon its lead, stomping its hooves upon the paver stones.

The dragon-man withdrew a pace and lowered his reptilian gaze. "I am far removed from the spirits of this world now," he said sadly. "The scent of death is upon me."

I frowned. "I *am* Death and the blood of The Destroyer himself runs through my veins, but even I can ride a horse."

Eindrac regarded me gloomily.

"She fears how you look," Merilanna suggested.

The dragon-man conceded with a nod.

"That I can change," the priestess said, stepping between the animal and the monster.

Eindrac and I watched with curiosity as Merilanna gently caressed the horse's nose. "Shh, easy girl," she whispered. "No one's going to hurt you."

"Or eat you," I grumbled under my breath impatiently.

Merilanna shushed me with a glance, then returned to her ministration. "See only me," she said to the mare.

A soft lullaby hummed from the priestess' lips.

I felt the ripple of Ilé's magic shiver my spine; but, even as it unnerved me, the horse calmed and lowered its head suppliantly.

"Good girl," the priestess said softly, stroking the animal's mane, her cheek laid gently upon its forehead. To Eindrac, "She will not oppose you now."

"You have charmed her?" the dragon-man asked, his voice pitched with wonder.

Merilanna looked to me and then to him and smiled. "My Lady has removed her fear of death. She has quieted her spirit."

"Good. Let's get moving," I said.

We three mounted and we did. I rode with the priestess.

Travel on horseback, of course, was much swifter than padding along on foot. Riding the Cusp would have been even faster, but I don't think either Merilanna or Eindrac would have approved of the method. Slipping across the Veil was something mortals could do. All it required was that they die and become ghosts. Neither of them would have enjoyed that process, I'd wager. Even if they had, there would have been the prickly matter of reincarnating once the trek was done; and, though the priestess might argue otherwise, I was not convinced that Lady Death would be so charitable and oblige. Therefore, I didn't suggest, "Let me kill you and this will go faster." My magnanimity is so unappreciated.

Three days of uneventful riding brought us to the banks of a swiftly flowing river. A great, stone bridge spanned it. Seven arches made the crossing.

"I know this bridge," I announced excitedly as it came into sight.

Merilanna looked over her shoulder to me as I slipped from the saddle.

"This is the Thaedrimar River," I explained, hustling ahead. Midspan, I stopped and stared west and pointed. "Tyresvrad is there – where the Asdrimar and the Thaedrimar meet."

"Tyresvrad?" Merilanna queried.

"Yes, Tyresvrad…my home village."

The priestess gazed that way the returned her eyes to me. There was sadness in them and pity in her gentle smile.

Instantly, my enthusiasm waned. I was a fool…again. "Where my village will be," I corrected. Anger tinged my tone.

"Where you will be born someday," Merilanna offered, "as a blessing to the world."

I scowled at that. "I don't think you know what that word means."

The clip-clop of the horses' hooves resounded as they began their crossing.

"Oh, I'm sure I do," the priestess countered mildly. "You've been a blessing to me, at least."

"Now, I'm sure you're mad."

Merilanna laughed. It was hard to sustain my glower when she did. Her brightness overwhelmed my darkness.

"And what about you?" I snapped at the dragon-man. "Am I a blessing to you too?"

Unsure of how to answer without stoking my fire, Eindrac looked to the priestess for help.

"The answer is yes," Merilanna instructed.

Trapped, Eindrac's head swiveled between the two of us. Committing to the reply, though, eluded his tongue. "You are –" he hesitated, choosing the next word carefully, "– frightening."

Merilanna bit down on her bottom lip and sniggled.

I frowned some more and crossed my arms, glaring up at the mounted monster. "Some dragon you are," I scoffed.

"I was a musician's apprentice," Eindrac retorted softly, musing on the revelation.

"You remembered that?" Merilanna asked. Notes of excitement filled her voice.

Eindrac's eyes darted left and right as if he were reading some chapter of his life in his mind. "Yes," he gasped. A low trebling sound echoed from deep within him. "I remember. I played a silver flute."

I shook my head and sighed. "The world is at war and the lich is recruiting flute players. No wonder he lost."

"Lost?" Eindrac responded.

"Not yet, but he will."

Merilanna nodded, affirming my report.

"How do you know?" Eindrac implored.

"I just do."

The dragon-man started to press the point, but was rudely interrupted by a deep, thundering bellow and a massive rock. The latter struck Eindrac hard and carried him from his saddle with ease and into the river. The former followed the attack and announced the deadly toll for daring to use the bridge.

My eyes flashed to the hurler. Its ambush was much better. I never saw it coming.

Upstream, a mass of boulders, an Oröm, erupted from the rapids and drew back its arm to catapult another stone our way.

"Ride!" I yelled to Merilanna.

She couldn't. She was fighting just to hang on. Her horse was rearing, startled by the attack. It's rider-less companion pranced wildly, equally upset.

"Get Eindrac and get out of here!" I screamed, slipping simultaneously into the Cusp. Once submerged, I flew across the water towards the elemental and braced for impact.

The Oröm never saw me coming either. I exploded from Twilight at the last second and slammed into the rock-monster's chest. I gritted my teeth, knowing damn well that this was going to hurt.

I was not disappointed.

The elemental could throw a mean stone. Eindrac, if he was still alive, could attest to that. I, by contrast, *was* the stone, and I was hypersonic when I exploded into its chest with a clap of thunder.

Imagine traveling faster than thought and slamming into a rock wall. That's what happened.

The wall shattered and I splattered.

Apparently, Merilanna caught the impact out of the corner of her eye and screamed. I didn't really hear it. I just glimpsed her face in the instant before I turned to mush.

Dying sucks.

I'm good at it, but it still sucks.

In this case, I guess it saved the others from being pulverized.

I'd get better, of course. Excruciating pain is exhilarating. It let's you know you are alive, right?

The moment I felt it, I knew I was on the mend. Again.

Sounds wormed their way into my mind long before my eyelids fluttered. I could hear voices; and, at first, I wasn't sure if they were echoes of memories or actually being spoken. The little snippets of speech were jumbled and slurred to my ears. I couldn't discern the language.

Movement.

I was being moved, being carried along. The cadence of footfalls jostled my shattered body, branding my every awakening nerve with agony. I must have groaned, because my litter bearers abruptly stopped, and the chatter of excited voices coalesced around me.

Someone was poking at me.

The taste of my own blood was in my mouth. A horrid click shot lightning through my closed eyes as my jaw reset into place and more of that exhilarating pain I mentioned blinded my senses. After that flash of misery, clouds of color rained across my vision. Wherever I was, it was dark, but I could discern the flickering yellow of firelight.

Had I blasted through the Oröm's chest into some subterranean realm?

Okay, that's a stupid thought, but you try thinking when your brain has been splattered and let's see how you do.

Shadows became form as first one eye and then the other rolled back into their sockets.

The excitement was growing. The chattering was as well. At least the poking had stopped.

Silhouettes bobbed in the firelight of torches around me. Big, yellow eyes caught their glow and shined it back at me. Gasps and hoots filled the smoky air.

I pulled myself together, the dark curse in my blood working its magic to mend my flesh and bones. I writhed as my broken skeleton was re-knitted with muscles and torn organs slithered back to where they were supposed to be. My restoration was far more torturous than my destruction and far slower as well. That gave me time to truly appreciate my decision to become a human catapult shot.

The spectacle I gave kept my audience at bay, I suppose. Once my head and my neck finally realigned, I appraised my situation.

Kith!

Everywhere I looked, there were kith. Big ones, small ones, fat ones and tall ones. All around me, their mouths open and their expressions agog, they stared down at me in utter amazement. Some carried torches. Some carried spears. Some carried other litters bearing a variety of corpses: animal corpses.

I was amidst a hunting party. Or was it a scavenging party. I didn't guess it mattered much.

A crude mat of braided vines that spanned between two wooden poles bore me. My bearers had dropped me to the ground and scurried away as I stirred and came back to life. I imagine that resurrection was not something with which the goblins were all that familiar. My wheezing, rasping return to respiration had scared the hell out of them. Several had their spears lowered at me like I was some sort of wild boar. Others had their spiked clubs and flint knives in hand. I counted two-hundred of them – but that was before my faculties returned, my math corrected itself, and I realized there were only twenty.

One of the bolder kith jabbed at me with his spear and jabbered something. My Twilight-lit senses gathered the blather and hinted at the meaning. My apprehension was still scrambled, but I think he said, "Evil spirit." I've been called worse.

Dark fire was racing through me now. The pain was nearly gone.

Slowly, I pushed myself up from the litter and into a sitting position. Reflexively, I spat the blood and bile from my mouth, coughing it from my throat, and freeing my tongue to speak.

Curiously, I detected very little evil burning in the souls of these creatures. Some of them were sadistic. Others were meanspirited. Most, though, were what I would describe as simply run-of-the-mill bad. In my experience, seeing into the blackness of souls as regularly as I do, the kith ranked, more or less, as average in the wicked category. I'd met a lot of beings that were far, far worse.

Still, I wasn't in a charitable mood. "Get that out of my face before I stuff it up your ass!" I warned the boldest goblin. My words were meaningless, but my tone was very clear.

A few more spears jabbed the air in front of me, but all of them fell back a step or two.

"Where are my friends?" I demanded.

Neither Merilanna nor Eindrac were in sight. I wondered if the dragon-man had even survived. He had been unseated from his horse by a flying rock. That didn't inspire much hope. As for the priestess, she was capable enough, but I wasn't even sure I had felled the Oröm.

"Quiet, demon!" the somewhat less bold goblin barked.

Some of the kith had appeared with nets clutched in their fists. They wasted no time using them.

My dark fire was burning low, but it was far from out. Before the nets were cast, I slipped to the Cusp and vanished. From the shadows farther down the tunnel, I watched as the kith panicked and started howling in terror, spinning wildly as they searched for me. In seconds, the entire band broke and raced away, frantically speeding past me and deeper into the darkness as if their hair was on fire.

I snorted, watched them go, then turned my toes back upslope. A hint of night air wafted from that way. I followed it to the surface and emerged from the goblins' burrow. The entrance was located beneath the root ball of an enormous, fallen tree.

Night, indeed, covered the land. Around me was the ancient Silverwood, but there was no sign of the Grymryl Road. The creatures' rank scents, though, were everywhere. I nosed for the freshest path and struck that way, following the trail like a hunting hound.

Half in and half out of Twilight, it did not take me long to return to the river and the bridge. It was only a few miles. Unfortunately, there was no sign of Merilanna or Eindrac. I did find the stoney carcass of the Oröm, however.

"Gotchya," I said with grim satisfaction.

To any other eye, the dead elemental would have been just more boulders in the stream. The stain of blood splattered on them might have been of interest, but I doubted that anyone could have conceived the details of our encounter.

Amidst the rubble, I found Wind-Song and my Whisperer. Both had survived the impact far better than I had. Disturbingly enough, the thin hair braid the priestess has adorned me with had never left my shattered neck. I fiddled with the fetish. "You're not much good," I said. "Aren't you supposed to be a lucky charm or something? Guess I'll have to do the finding of the priestess myself."

No sooner had I stopped berating the forget-me-knot than a pall swept through the woods, silencing the stirring of its creatures. My hackles instantly rose.

I ducked behind the Oröm's broken body and peered towards the bridge downstream. The clatter of hooves on the pavers reached me promptly thereafter. A vile wave of magic followed, washing over me as the first of five riders appeared on the southern bank. Though riding fast and hard, I could still tell they were undead. Their foul aura sent ripples through Twilight. The living world shivered with revulsion.

Four crossed quickly. The fifth curbed his nightmarish mount – also dead – and scanned the river. A spectral light limned his figure. More intensely, it glowed in the hollows of his eye sockets. His spectral stare settled on me.

Wrapped in the Veil, I prayed he had not seen me. As his sword slipped its sheath, though, I abandoned that hope.

"Damn," I groaned under my breath.

Crouching, I gritted my teeth and readied, but the wraith-rider did not close. Instead, he fanned his great, black sword my way slowly as if searching for a bearing with a compass. Fatefully, the tip of the blade dipped and pointed straight at me. I could feel its icy touch upon my soul and recognized the insidious metal: Shadowsteel.

My heart froze.

Shadowsteel is a horrible thing. It eats magic, ravaging it no matter its form. I'd suffered its curse before. No power, no matter how strong, could resist it. The black fire inside me guttered as the sword's aura sought to inhale its heat.

I dropped behind the Oröm's corpse and put my back to the thing's head, fighting to save what I could my fire. I closed my eyes tight as my ears strained to hear the death-bell toll.

The clopping of the hell-horse's hooves resounded as the rider rode on. Or so I thought. My sigh of relief was short lived.

Above me!

Standing on the Oröm's face, the wraith appeared and drove its blade down. I shrieked and scrambled away. Only the sword's aura grazed me, but it was enough to strip my flames and eject me from the Veil. In the rolling water, I splashed and spun, going under then breaching, gasping, wracked by terror.

Effortlessly, the dark blades-man glided towards me.

I couldn't run. I was caught in the current and barely able to swim, drowning in unearthly fear as the revenant stalked my soul.

Pure malice emanated from the wraith. Blue-white fire blazed around it, igniting the air and the water. It's sword rose to deliver its merciless stroke. I saw my doom and I was afraid.

The blow fell. It's arc was unerring. But it was not complete.

A powerful force intervened, one that held dominion over death and struck in my favor.

The wraith exploded in a flash of ghostly light. It was if some giant blew out a candle. Wisps of ethereal smoke lingered for a moment then dissipated, absorbed into the blackness of night. The creature's sword splashed into the river near my feet.

"Lyri!" a frantic voice cried from the northern shore.

Stutteringly, I shifted my gaze to my savior.

Merilanna splashed into the rolling water and waded with desperate speed to reach me. She struggled across the slippery stones, falling twice before gathering me.

"Meri," I sputtered. I was so cold. I was shaking so hard.

"It's alright. It's alright."

Behind her, the dragon-man appeared. I hadn't even seen him; but, admittedly, I had been slightly preoccupied pissing myself.

Together, my friends carried me to shore. Merilanna wrapped me in her cloak and did her best to comfort my trembling. Had I not been so afraid, still in the grip of the wraith's aura, I would have cursed myself and berated her succor. But I was far beyond my usual snarky, stubborn defiance. Desperately, I clung to her like a babe.

"We have to move," Eindrac declared.

Merilanna and I both followed his gaze back the flowing water. A whirlpool of spectral light was spinning above where the damned sword had fallen. Even now, its wielder was being restored.

There was no argument. Eindrac helped Merilanna to rise; and, together, we ran for our lives. Well, truthfully, they carried me away.

I don't know how far we ran or for how long. Everything was a blur. The darkness of the forest swallowed us.

Panting hard, Merilanna said, "It won't stop coming. It has the scent of her soul."

"There are four more of them," Eindrac noted.

"If the others join the chase, we'll never get out of here."

"Leave me," I wheezed.

Merilanna's face hardened with determination. "No!" To Eindrac, "We have to find holy ground."

The dragon-man scanned the primordial landscape. His expression was unreadable, but I could see no hope in his eyes.

"Tyresvrad," I whispered.

"Tyresvrad?" Eindrac's dragon eyes shot to me.

"Your village?" Merilanna remembered.

I nodded weakly. "There's a Sentinel Stone. It's on the high hill."

Merilanna and Eindrac's eyes met and concurred. "Sacred ground," they said in unison.

"We'll be trapped there," Eindrac cautioned.

"I know," Merilanna exhaled, "but we'll dead if we stay here. I could only dispel the wraith, not destroy it. It's too powerful. We'll figure out our next move once we reach the Sentinel."

Resolved, we set off again, following the Thaedrimar west and north.

Dawn broke as we reached a reached a clearing adjacent to a bend in the river. Another, smaller branch cut from the northeast and merged at this point. It was the Asdrimar. I was home.

Rising above the convergence was the high hill. I had sat upon its slopes innumerable times in my early childhood. I had sledded down on snow and rolled down through wildflowers. I knew this place well.

At the crown of the hill, a monolith stood watch: a Sentinel Stone. The runes and pictograms chiseled into its surface were a wonder to behold in the morning light. I had never guessed there were so many. The Veil was thin around the towering rock.

To its base, I was carried swiftly.

No sooner had I been delivered than Merilanna's hands were to the sigils and symbols. Eindrac stood nearby, his gaze watching the woods, expecting dark company at any moment.

"What are you doing?" I asked.

"Looking for a door," the priestess replied cryptically.

"A door? What door? It's a watcher, not a Waygate."

Merilanna wasted no time on the argument. Her hands were flying across the stone's surface. "They're all Waygates," was all she said.

I saw Eindrac's spine stiffen and shot my attention to the cause. Five dark riders had appeared along the river's course below.

"They're here," he announced.

Merilanna hesitated, drew a deep breath, then redoubled her examination of the carvings.

"Got it!" she cried.

I glanced to the stone. A series of glyphs were aglow.

"What did you do?" I implored.

"Awakened the path."

"To where?"

Merilanna bestowed on me an apologetic look. "The lands of the dead."

My brow knitted. I flashed my eyes to the charging hell-horses and their riders. "We're already going there," I argued even as a swirl of ethereal light was beginning to suffuse the surface of the stone.

"I'll lead us," Merilanna assured then added and urged, "We can't escape them here. We have to go."

There really wasn't time to consider another option. Fighting five death-wraiths wasn't one. "This is a bad idea," I muttered.

"Come on," the priestess called, reaching for my hand.

Consigned, I gave in and was immediately pulled into the whirl and through the Veil. Eindrac followed. And the door shut.

Chapter 14: The Spirit Path

Trekking into Twilight is a bit different than riding the Cusp. Along the Veil, both the corporeal and the ethereal worlds are at hand. A step sideways one way or the other delivers the rider into the lands of the living or the lands of the dead. Typically, I don't cross over. I've hunkered down in Twilight before, of course, but to spend an extended time in the lands of ghosts was something new.

Now, my more ardent fans may say, "But, Lyri, you've traipsed into Shard Worlds and Horizon Realms. You've been everywhere!"

That's a bit of an overstatement, though I appreciate the enthusiasm.

Admittedly, I have been to some pretty bizarre places. Some weren't bad. Aeryldar was nice. Some were nightmarish. Assybah's realm comes readily to mind. And, yes, I have flown through the soul-devouring Etherstorm and survived the oblivion of the Nephthylan. I get it. I've been places – lots of places. But, still, there are countless worlds along the Veil and even more beyond Twilight, beyond its outer border: the Verge. So, to be truthful, I've only been to a few of them.

Saving the Bright World from despotic overlords, alien gods, and armies of demons is sort of a second job for me – my first being thumbing my nose at the local administration sitting up there in the Palescia. So, not meaning to disappoint you, but I really haven't been everywhere.

To be honest, Twilight, though close at hand, is mostly a mystery. It's like a dark reflection of the world, an eerie place where sounds and sights are warbled and distorted and surreal. Cast in bluish colors, it mirrors Narianna, but not completely. True, there are trees and rocks and water – everything you would normally see here is mirrored darkly there. But there is one big exception: there's nothing alive. Not even a gnat.

Twilight is the realm of the dead, so what it does have in abundance are ghosts. Sometimes, I call them spirits; but, as Rhasha Khan would be quick as a cat to point out, spirits and ghosts are not the same thing. I won't bore you with a long, metaphysical treatise. However, basically, spirits are bound to their worlds and souls are not. What happens to a spirit's world happens to it. They can't escape. They change as it changes – for better or worse.

Fey, for instance, are spirits. They're beautiful, but also susceptible to taint and corruption. A powerful will or trauma can warp them. Don't believe me. Ask Eindrac.

Ghosts are something quite different. Ghosts are souls and souls are like worlds unto themselves. They aren't bound the way spirits are. Thus, they can move between worlds, carrying with them their life-force and adapting as they do. In a way, then, they are more resilient; and, as such, more valuable to creatures that draw their power from the energy they possess.

Demons, for instance, harvest souls, but not spirits. The more they acquire, the more power they have.

As for Twilight, you can think of it as the slimy stuff that surrounds the yoke of an egg. Narianna is the golden yoke and the shell is what we call the Verge. I know that's a rather elementary simile, but it will suffice.

Back to ghosts…

When someone dies, their body quits working. Whether that's from old age, disease, getting beheaded, or whatever, their body has run its course. The soul, though, lives on – just without all the breathing, eating, sleeping, shitting and etcetera. For many, death is quite a traumatic shock. I'm getting used to it, but most won't.

Often, death leaves the suddenly evicted soul bewildered and confused. "What do you mean, I'm dead? I'm too pretty to be dead! Where's my stuff!"

Some habits – like living – are hard to break, so some ghosts go about their old routines stubbornly, unable to accept their new condition.

If there happens to be a priest or priestess around, the soul of the dearly departed can be pointed in a direction and ushered off to their proper afterlife in the halls of whatever deity has dibs on them. Gods and demons aren't much different in this regard, if you think about it. The currency of the soul is big business.

If no helpful funerary rites are available, the ghost is left to figure out its afterlife on their own. Some will be fetched to heaven; some will be dragged to hell; some will haunt their old reality; some will wander off into Twilight to who knows where.

That's how it's supposed to work.

As for Twilight, the deeper you go into it, the farther away you get from the rules of the gods and the weirder the place becomes. Once you're past the Verge, all bets are off. The gods of Narianna no longer have much sway outside their Tapestry. At that point, you've entered the Maelstrom and reality is pretty screwed up. Farther out lie the Doldrums and the Nephthylan, the dead space beyond the reach of the gods and the nothingness that is everything that may or may not be.

I'm going to stop there on that subject. Reconciling the paradox of possibilities makes my head hurt. The last thing I will add is that there are worlds scattered throughout the nothingness that are just as real as Narianna. They're just different. Apparently, there are lots of them, and they have their own gods!

Hmm, I wonder if there are lots of Lyri's out there, too.

Nevermind.

Horizon Realms and Shard Worlds?

Well, let's see.

Horizon Realms lie at the edge of Twilight. They are bubbles – some call them cysts – within the Cusp and are created, strangely enough, by the wills of their creators. The Palescia, if you want to get technical, is a Horizon Realm created by the combined wills of the Aesyr. It's a place they made to dwell within that is connected to but set apart from the Bright World. Other powerful beings like the Arcanalestri, T'Ethranir, and various demons, for example, also make Horizon Realms to call home.

Shard Worlds are somewhat similar, but they occur beyond the Verge. When the Destroyer, Dyerbazog, shattered Elyarsa Altairas and blasted bits and pieces of the Tapestry through Twilight and out across the Doldrums, Shard Worlds appeared. Upon these fragments of Narianna, survivors reconstituted reality and made islands in the Etherstorm Sea. Ephemeral, umbilical threads bound them back to the Bright World and kept them alive.

I've been to a few of each, as I conceded; but, despite my disagreements with the gods of Narianna, I prefer here to anywhere else. Here – for better or for worse – is home.

Twilight, the albumen of reality – that's egg white to most of you – can be a useful place because, as I mentioned, the rules of the gods don't hold fast. I, who habitually defy the gods anyway, find it especially useful, especially when running away from death-wraiths that want to devour my soul. Which is precisely where we left off before I got sidetracked trying to explain the cosmology that the gods follow.

Oh, that's another point: the gods follow the cosmology. They didn't invent it. Some other greater, mysterious power did. He wrote it all down somewhere and they are obliged to follow it.

One last thing before I get off *this* sidetrack: Morthalin.

I really haven't gone into the subject of the Dark World much so far, but I would be remiss if I didn't at least touch on it. After all, the entire history of Narianna is intertwined with its shadowy antithesis.

To begin, we have to start with The Balance, the underlying foundation for everything. According to people with big brains, for everything there is an opposite, a matching counterpoint: good, evil; light, dark; Narianna, Morthalin. I'm not really sure what all the pairs are. What's the opposite of a potato? A demonic potato?

Anyway, if you go with this nonsense, everything has an anti-everything. In the case of Narianna, there is its shadow, Morthalin, and the two of them don't get along.

Some famous elf – Shanalestian, I think his name was – wrote up an explanation for Morthalin that basically said that Trillanta Xorconum – that's his Turanian name – my people call him Xorcos – it's simpler – the top god of the Aesyr, shined his magnificent light on Narianna and her shadow was cast on the swirling chaos of the Etherstorm, the Maelstrom. In so doing, the order her shadow imposed brought forth Morthalin. But, twisted by the never ending turbulence, the Dark World spawns only facsimiles and aberrations of life – demons, if you like.

Where is Morthalin?

A lot of people say it is underground. "You descend into hell," after all. Others say it is in the sky and that it blots out the sun, turning day into night ever so often. Fanciful notions, but neither are quite correct.

Morthalin and Narianna share the same space. Don't ask me how, but they do. You couldn't have light without darkness. There has to be something there to compare to. Contrast is important.

Now, you may recall that I talked a little about demons earlier. I said there were Shadow Demons and Shades and true demon – the big nasty kind – and that they rise from Morthalin during Shadowfalls to cause us trouble. All of that is true, but how does this work when it comes to Morthalin?

I guess the easiest way to explain it is to think of Morthalin as a coexistent realm, a black layer onto which a white layer, Narianna, is laid. Here and there, holes are poked allowing the black to seep into the white and the white to seep into the black. We don't really think much about the latter holes; but, undoubtedly, they do exist.

I wonder if the people of Morthalin ever say, "Ah, heaven, we're being invaded by angels again!"

Anyway, as you may have deduced, the Waygates are these holes. When a Shadowfall occurs, the blackness spills in and the demons incarnate. Wars are waged and the process repeats. Etcetera and etcetera. In the end, you have the messed up history of our little world.

Twilight surrounds it all. It contains both the Bright World and the Dark; but, actually, it is neither. It's more like an aura or corona around them.

Beyond Twilight, maybe there are an infinite number of worlds of light and shadow. I think there are. Recent troubles with that Mordûn fellow invading Narianna seem to bear that out. Other worlds, other gods, bigger scale, same Balance.

At the moment, the little scale was troubling enough.

Merilanna, Eindrac, and I had ducked into Twilight through a magical doorway located at a Sentinel Stone overlooking where Tyresvrad, my future birthplace, would stand. Behind us, five death-wraiths sent by the Shadowlord, Darkyr, were hot on our heels. Before us, the phantasmal lands of the dead spread forth. Around us, the priestess' song made a shield of dim light, protecting our life-forces from the deathly chill of the place.

Generally speaking, when mortal folks go on spiritual walkabouts, their bodies were extraneous and left behind. A sort of silver cord stretches out between the corporeal flesh and the incorporeal soul, binding and anchoring one to the other. Severing it means instant death for the body, and the soul, like a kite that's string had been cut, sails away on the ethereal winds. That's how most sojourns into Twilight are usually done.

I, being immortal – and defiant – transcend this method and carry my incarnate self along. Well, sort of. To be honest, I think I disintegrate whenever I cross over and reintegrate when I cross back. I'm not really sure. I was burned to ashes once, but I got better. I think it's something like that. My stubborn will puts me back together.

Regardless, Merilanna's song seemed to have the necessary effect, which is very good. We didn't have to leave our bodies laying in the dirt for the death-wraiths to destroy while we were in Twilight, which would have been very bad.

The priestess, I noted, appeared at ease in the blue-white haze. I guess she had walked in Twilight before. In retrospect, Death-Maidens probably do that a lot, I guess.

Eindrac, on the other hand, was having a harder time.

Remember, he is an elf in a dragon's body; and, as an elf, he is a spirit of Narianna. While Twilight is not another world – which would have been a real problem for him – it is diluted. Being here was like being on a mountain top for him. The air, figuratively speaking, was very, very thin. I could see his spirit flickering like a suffocating candle from the moment we entered the Veil. If we stayed in here long, he would be snuffed out.

"Where do we go?" Merilanna asked urgently.

I glanced back at the approaching undead. The Sentinel Stone's magic would keep them at bay, but we couldn't go back the way we came. They would be waiting.

"Leading the dead to somewhere nice is your job," I replied curtly. "Find us a path and let's get moving."

Merilanna frowned, frustrated. "A soul's path of destiny is different than this," she argued. "There is no soul-song to follow to heaven."

By that, she meant the gods were no help. None of them had dibs on my soul. None of them wanted it. As for Eindrac, spirits don't go to heaven. They return to the mystical pool that brings life to their world. That's their paradise.

"Listen to your own song then," I called to her. "Follow it." She still looked stumped. "Ask your damned Lady!"

The priestess' stumped look became a scowl, but I guess irritation is a good motivator as she turned her aggravation towards the vast blue landscape, closed her eyes, and prayed.

"Show me your path, My Lady," she sued. "Guide me by your gentle hands."

Icy claws, you mean.

When Merilanna's eyes opened, a divine glow filled them and shined forth.

"This way," she said serenely.

"Sure," I replied and shrugged, "that way's as good as any. Let's go."

And, so, we started walking.

Brave Eindrac didn't complain a bit even though his spirit shivered and shriveled in the deathly ether. He was a creature of life. He needed Narianna's touch to survive, and Pri's hand did not reach him here.

"Can they follow us?" he asked.

"Maybe," I answered honestly.

Looking back, I could see that the death-wraiths were circling the monolith on their nightmarish steeds. They didn't seem happy. Good. At least for now, they had lost our trail. The Oröm magic that guarded these lands had hid us from their view.

"They can't enter Twilight through the Sentinel," I assured my worried companion, but then added, "But their souls were torn from these lands. Once we're beyond the protection of the Stone – I don't know. They may be on us again."

Eindrac acknowledged with a grim nod.

Merilanna offered no comment. She was intensely focused upon our course.

Weaving through the eerie forest, in short order, we reached a shimmering river of light. As it came into view, I recognized it immediately.

"We're back at the Grymryl," I cheered.

"Yes," Merilanna confirmed calmly. "It's still the way My Lady shows us we must go."

There were no death-wraiths galloping down it towards us, so I had no objections.

Satisfied, the priestess stepped out of the forest and onto the spectral cobblestones. As she did, instantly, her figure blurred and shot forward like an arrow leaving a bowstring. Eindrac and I barely had time to blink before we were hauled into her wake by the magic of her song and carried after her.

Two blinks of an eye later and we reached one of the trilithons that stood along the causeway. There, we paused.

"What happened?" Eindrac begged.

"It's a damned ley line," I groused as the three of us faded back through the Veil to stand once again on the solid ground.

"Yes, I think so – in a way," Merilanna concurred readily. "But I think it's more like a relay, a fast highway stretching from stone to stone."

"Nice," I added, thumbing the trilithon, "And this is an exit back to the world."

"Or an entranceway from it," the priestess suggested. "Instead of going to a specific spot like a Circlestone, travelers can simply ride the road wherever they find it."

"Wish we had known earlier," I grumbled. "Let's keep riding."

So, we did, but only to the next fallen and desecrated stones. At that point, we were back on foot in the normal manner. Upon reaching the next trilithon, though, we went riding again, this time for several more jumps until we encountered another broken segment.

Asteranoth's army had done great damage to the magical road, but they had not destroyed it.

Unfortunately, our quickened pace ended shortly thereafter, not because we ran out of road or one of the terminals was broken, but because we reached a trilithon with a ward upon it. It's magic had been restrained; the ley line, disconnected.

"I know this place, too," I announced as the shimmering road faded. We were on the banks of another, even wide river. The trilithon marked the bridge, this one with a series of ten arches that spanned the waters and carried the Grymryl onward. "We're near Olde Asgevan." I pointed northeast. "It's there." I angled again and pointed northwest. "And the Clangrym Stones are that way. I remember coming here when I was little. It was spring and there was a festival with jugglers and music and colored ribbons hanging in every tree."

Merilanna was smiling at me.

I checked my grin instantly and stiffened my spine.

"It won't be Olde Asgevan yet," Merilanna reminded me gently.

"Right," I said, snorting away my silly enthusiasm. "But we know where we are, at least."

"There's nothing wrong with happy memories, Lyri."

"The happier they are, the more they hurt when they're torn away," I answered bitterly.

"The more it hurts, the more you need to hold onto them. They're what will see you through. In the dark, sometimes just the memory of light is enough."

I didn't scowl. I didn't snarl. I didn't curse – either her or myself. I just looked away and stared back into my memories of those happier times. It did hurt, but the laughter was still there, waiting to be remembered. In a way, it was what I was fighting for.

After a moment, I swallowed the pain like a pill and returned my focus to the road again. The bridge was waiting also.

The priestess' hand settled upon my shoulder. I looked at it then up to her radiant eyes.

"We have work to do," I said.

"*We* do," she affirmed then simply smiled and nodded once.

"How far to where we're going?" Eindrac inquired.

I gave him a quick glance then reset my gaze towards our future to puzzle out the answer. I wasn't sure. We stood on the southern banks of a river that one day would be called the Thaegrimar, a cousin of the Thaedrimar we had crossed earlier. I knew it fed from the mighty Astraelon somewhere to the east. The town of Gyveth would stand and fall at that fork eventually. Fhaed, Sir Iaom, and I had passed through its ruins in pursuit of Dyards and demons what seemed a lifetime ago. The Circlestone that had booted me into Merilanna's company lay a couple days ride north of there, near where the Aesdana – or whatever they called it now, was flowing out of the foothills of Caerith Orömdyr to join its waters with those of the Astraelon. It was the Aesdana that I had crossed chasing ghosts at the start of this strange odyssey.

"Three days more," I answered. "Maybe less. But first we have to get across this bridge."

Tentatively, I stepped forward with my hand extended, testing the air. The instant my fingertips crossed the plane between the trilithon's uprights, a searing surge of elemental energy bit them. It was not unlike the sensation I sometimes felt when quickly pulling off my woolen cloak on some dry, cold, winter's day. There was a loud pop and a little flash. I had expected something, but I wasn't really ready for my hand to go completely numb and for lightning to shoot through my flesh and bones. I startled and jolted back, grabbing at my rebuked limb.

"Lyri!" Merilanna cried. "Are you alright?"

"No!" I snapped. "Our way is blocked."

Indeed, magic coursed through every stone that formed the bridge. Ephemeral tentacles, like misty vortexes, swirled through Twilight, rising from the water itself. The river had become a wall.

"Blocked how?"

"Magic," I snarled, shaking and rubbing some sensation back into my hand. I didn't like the feeling when it returned. Pins and needles pricked every pore.

I glared at the bridge indignantly.

"Dragon magic," Eindrac added, his voice a rumbling, low growl.

He was right. Even as he identified the spell, I began to feel the drake's primal energy moving through the earth. The sensation quickened my cursed blood.

"Orömgundr," I said flatly.

"Yes, of course," Merilanna chimed, "the earth dragon of Asgevardír, the guardian of Olde Asgevan. This is his spell!"

"Orömgundr?" Eindrac mused. "Why do I know that name?"

I scoffed and snorted. "You don't even know your own name. How would you know this one? Besides, it's an Asgev name. Your people called him something prettier, I'm sure."

A long paused followed, waiting for an explanation to fill the void. Unexpectedly, one did.

"Because that's the name the vampire used," Eindrac replied, his reptilian eyes narrowing as he squeezed the thought from his tortured mind. "He spoke of the dragon when talking to the Shadowlord. He told of some scheme to poison the T'Ethranir, to weaken him. It had something to do with the dragon's attendant."

My eyes rolled and I sighed. "The *Naeryni*," I said, naming the attendant. "That's who he is talking about. She's a priestess and the keeper of the holy spring that flows from the dragon's lair."

"The spring is called the *Aesyriath Naedrom*," Merilanna added. "It is described in some detail in Shanalestian's *The Chronicles of Eidrinor*."

"You read too much," I quipped at her, shaking my head.

The priestess smiled. "I had a lot of time on my hands at My Lady's temple."

"What does this *Naeryni* have to do with the necromancer?" Eindrac probed.

I sighed again. "Normally, I would have said its history repeating itself; but, since that scheme won't happen for a thousand years, I guess it's more like the future dictating history." Neither of my companions had any idea what I was babbling about, and I wasn't sure I did either. Lots of things had happened before I ended up here. It was Iaom that had told me some of that story: about the poisoning of the dragon through his keeper, the *Naeryni*, a girl named Amberlyss.

"Vespirak was talking about an old scheme," I explained. "Back in the future, a witch was trying to poison the dragon through the *Naeryni*. I don't know all the details; but, apparently, the vampire had something similar in mind. I suppose he and Darkyr chatted about it."

"Yes," Eindrac agreed, "that's what they were discussing. I remember. They were trying to find a way to break the dragon and conquer these lands."

"But they haven't been conquered yet!" Merilanna realized. "Your people may still be here, Eindrac."

The dragon-man's countenance slumped rather than soared. "What am I to them now," he said bleakly, looking down at his scaly hands.

"Whatever you decide to be," Merilanna replied strongly. There was a challenge in her words.

"Won't matter if we don't get across this bridge," I interjected, bringing the predicament back to the fore.

My two companions shouldered up beside me and considered the invisible barrier.

"It can't keep everything out," Merilanna reasoned. "If it did, elves seeking sanctuary would be lost. There must be a way through it."

I scanned up and down the trilithon that marked the foot of the bridge. "But how?"

A notion flared across the priestess' face. "It's the same as the Sentinel Stone!" she realized, her smile spreading wide. "We're not meant to walk between the uprights and tread the space between. Orömgundr is a dragon of the earth." Her hands flew to the surface of the stone leg of the monument and traced the symbols. "His magic is in here."

I slid my gaze up the towering structure then dropped it back to the exuberant priestess and nodded.

Eagerly, her fingers moved, following the chiseled glyphs, feeling the flow of their magic. "There has to be a key," she exhaled.

Eindrac joined her, searching for the right arcane mark.

I stood and watched, still puzzling as their frustration mount. Minutes past. "We're missing something," I said under my breath. My preternaturally sharp ears, though, perked. They didn't miss the sound of doom approaching.

I whipped about.

"They're here!" I exclaimed, whirling to face the first of the death-wraiths as it materialized on the Grymryl behind us. "They're riding the road!"

"Eindrac, help her!" Merilanna yelled. "Buy me time. I've almost got this."

The dragon-man appeared at my side, barbed spear in hand.

I gritted my teeth. "Keep them off of her," I snarled then sprang into the Cusp.

Wind-Song sang as I reappeared upon the path of the first dark rider. She bit hard into his steed's legs. So sprawled the first hell-horse. Hard, it fell, rolling calamitously.

There was no time to gloat. The next rider was upon me.

His sword, too, was made of Shadowsteel. I could feel its evil emenation, draining my lifeforce even as he bore down.

Desperately, I parried. The impact of his great blade, though, overwhelmed my defenses and would have split my skull in two if not for those feeble efforts. As it was, his sword slammed me to my knees like a carpenter flattens a nail. I heard and felt the hiss of his weapon as it skidded by my left shoulder. Icy fire seared my skin.

Reflexively, I rolled with the blow, something I had learned while training with the Argrym, the fearsome fire giants of Ardra. I had no hope of matching the creature's strength, but I could deflect it and use its power to propel me. That's exactly what I did.

Unfortunately, the next rider was ready and waiting. The cut of his stroke came before I even finished tumbling. The impact caught me and slit my right shoulder from joint to spine. Had his weapon been slightly longer, his swing slightly more extended, or my body slightly larger, I would have been gutted. As it were, I rolled to my feet, flinging blood and stunned by shock. The pain had not even registered yet and already I was staggering. My black fire gasped, powerless to resist the wicked aura of his weapon as it drank my soul.

The third rider drew back to smite me, to end my pathetic struggles. My eyes flew wide and my jaw dropped, overcome by disbelief, overwhelmed by horror.

The blade swept, hungering to end me, but a friend's spear intervened.

I only saw the dragon-man's weapon in the instant after it pierced the blackness within the death-wraith's hood. The missile lodged, half in and half out of the cowl. The creature's head marked the center point with the shaft protruding grossly fore and aft.

The death-wraith jerked backwards as it toppled from its saddle across its mount's hindquarters.

Three had passed me. Two more were coming. But I was fevered by the Shadowsteel's cut. I could barely stand, barely see. Wind-Song hung in my trembling hand limply. My own blood was flowing down my arm and over her.

That's when the arrows came and death was rebuked.

Chapter 15: Shadows of the Light

A rain of light fell upon Darkyr's minions. Their black forms hissed like white-hot steel drawn from the forge and plunged into water. Where the arrows struck, molten swirls appeared; divine wrath bore into the riders' shadowy essences. Their undead mounts shrieked, a sound so terrible that it chilled my veins. They reared; they wheeled; they cried out; and they burned.

I was in the midst of it all: three riders, afore; two, arear. All about me, vengeful flames spread. White light pierced the deepest dark. A different sort of terror took hold of me. The blackness in my soul recoiled and cried out. The magic of the *Shi* ignited my horror.

"Lyri, run!" Merilanna screamed.

I could not. I was on fire, inside and out. What the Shadowsteel had not burned, the aura of the elven arrows set to flame.

I threw up my arms before my eyes, desperate to shield some part of me from the conflagration.

Something struck. Something lifted me from the fire. I clung to it, not realizing for an eternity of seconds that I was being carried by a dragon's claws.

"Hurry!" the priestess cried. Upon her voice, I fought to focus. "They're still coming!"

The fire in my eyes which blinded me stuck some wall of wind. I gasped, unable to breathe. Then there was silence, brief but complete, before my senses exploded again.

"She's not your enemy! Don't hurt her, I beg you!"

My consciousness collided hard with the unmoving earth. The ring of steel against steel tore a tiny window through the white light briefly. Beyond it, I spied the black scales of Eindrac, his claws bared, his feet set. A circle of shining folk, like avenging angels, held swords of light leveled at his heart.

I shook my head hard, fighting to see more even as the blackened embers of my soul burned out.

Vaguely, I sensed Merilanna's presence.

"The demon must die," a perfect voice decreed.

"No!" shouted Death's maiden. "She is a child of shadows, not a demon, not a monster – Damn you! – Not everything in the dark is evil!"

"Leave her be!" the dragon-man roared.

Within, I thrashed and gnarled. Without, I simply convulsed. Four arrows had found me in the darkness, though I could not count them at the time.

"Surrender!" a new voice, deep and immensely powerful, commanded.

Even my seizures obeyed. I froze, succumbing to the godly light. Yielding, my defiance dying, I whispered my last rebuke. "Never."

Fhaed's face formed in the glow that filled the air around me. His golden eyes looked down. His damned, smug smirk taunted my return to sentience.

I blinked hard, uncrossed my eyes, and stammered an unintelligible curse.

I looked again and the face before me refocused.

It wasn't Fhaed.

His features were similar, but not the same. They defined him as a man, an elven man, with silvery hair and aureate eyes. He regarded me with an intense glare. Neither sympathy nor pity lived in it.

To someone behind, "She's awake," he said, then stood and withdrew.

Movement, barely the rustling of silk, brought my captors into view. Neither Merilanna nor Eindrac were to be seen.

A new face attended me: silvery hair, silvery skin, eyes the color of amethyst.

"I am Palantel Ar'Ronin, High Minister of Syralliador," the stately elven lord proclaimed. "You and your companions are safe, Lyri Shadow-Child. This is the court of Tarlandraxas. You are under the protection of our lord, Prince Syrath Sil-Yarithyr."

"Long names," I muttered. "I hope you don't expect me to remember them."

A thin smile graced the elven minister's lips. "Perhaps, in time, you will. For now, you need remember only that you are a guest in this noble house of Eriandor and compose yourself accordingly."

"Behave, you mean." I looked around the strange chamber at the faces that watched over me: two guards in scaled armor, holding fine spears and dressed in the colors of the Silverwood; a young woman with straight, white hair that flowed like silk and blended with a long, light-blue dress of the same ephemeral hue; and the man who I mistook as Fhaed in the moment of my awakening. All were watching me. The girl's eyes were hazel and gentle – those of a healer. The guards' were alert but impassive. The High Minister's, stern and discerning. And my herald's countenance, curious but cautious. "Where are my friends?" I asked.

"Safe," the High Minister assured. "I have sent word of your recovery. They will be here in a moment."

I glanced down and realized that I was dressed in a white gown. There was neither dirt nor blood on me. It felt weird. I was on a bed with clean, soft linens. The chamber was circular and ribbed by alabaster arches that domed the ceiling above. Between these supports, the walls were like translucent milk-glass. Soft light diffused from beyond them. I could see dim shadows as they passed outside, their forms vague but colorful. A single door, also pale, was the only egress. Its surface wore the texture of a woven basket as hundreds of viny tendrils entwined to make it solid. Too, then, I realized that the whole of this place was of a living nature. The arches were the splaying members of some great tree's roots. The walls were membranes spanning between them. Even the bed on which I sat grew from the earth and cupped me. Only the floor was distinct. It was tiled with smooth stones set in a radiating pattern, like the spokes of a painted wagon wheel – shades of white and gray.

"What do you want with me?" I demanded, flicking glances at the soldiers then back to the High Minister.

His thin smile widened a hair's breadth, then he answered, "All will be discussed in good time. For now, my prince requests only that you rest and recover. There will be opportunities to talk soon."

Of course, I was suspicious. When am I not? The last thing I remembered with any clarity involved me taking arrows from my new hosts.

Footfalls in soft leather. Someone was coming.

The door opened and Merilanna rushed in. She looked unblemished, sporting a fresh, new dress but wearing the same, radiant smile.

"Lyri," she called happily, moving quickly – if unceremoniously – to my side.

I was glad to see her, but I still groaned as she sat upon the edge of the bed and pulled me into her arms.

"Stop," I protested mildly, "I'm trying to be petulant."

She laughed with her eyes and her sweet voice. "It's good to see you well."

"I only had to recover become someone shot me full of holes," I grumbled accusingly.

"I'm sorry for that," came an apology from the doorway. Another elf stood there, his hands folded quietly within the long-sleeves of his regal robes.

"I don't see a bow," a quipped back at him.

His handsome face smiled. "I have one," he replied, "but so, too, do the archers I command. For them, then, I offer the apology."

I shrugged and said incredulously, "It's easy to mistake me for a monster."

"Especially when your dark fires blaze," he concurred.

By the suppliant bending of my attendants – except for the straight-backed guards – I discerned easily enough that the new elf was someone of great importance.

"My Prince," the High Minister said reverently as he bent.

He was acknowledged with a nod.

"I am Syrath," the prince said simply as he stepped to within a few paces of me. He did not bow, but he did grace me with a polite nod also. A delicate circlet of small, silver leaves rode his handsome brow. A similar, brocade patterning adorned his mantle and trimmed the cuffs and hem of his long tunic. Breeches and high boots completed his attire. All were in the colors of the sky: white and blue with hints of silver and gold. His hair was wound and secured behind his ears into a long, circling braid that conjoined to flow down his back. Great artistry went into it. "Welcome to Syralliador, Lyri. Lady Meri has shared with us the nature of your visit and the purpose of your cause."

"'Lady Meri' is it?" One of my eyebrows arched at his cordial familiarity. I looked at the priestess squarely. "She talks too much."

Merilanna's lips held firmly to her smile, though it did purse a bit playfully. "Prince Syrath has been very kind."

"Thank you for the arrows," I said snarkily.

Before more barbs could shoot from my tongue, at the door, a new shadow appeared. Eindrac had arrived. I sensed his spirit approach but was startled by his appearance. The dragon-man was gone; and, in its place, a young elven man remained. His hair and eyes alone retained the dark semblance that his frightful form had held. Both were a shimmering, almost iridescent, raven black.

"Hello, Lyri," he said from the doorway.

Reflexively, I glanced to Merilanna – her smile had not faded – then back to him. "Eindrac?"

He, too, smiled, though somewhat abashedly. "Yes, forever will I be," he began, "but my true name is Tir'Synd. Thanks to you, I am he once more."

"You're…welcome?" I stammered, confused and barely able to babble the words. To all gathered, I then asked more determinately, "What's going on here?" I didn't like all of this effusive attention. My eyes circled that gathering, looking for the duplicity I knew was present.

It was my friend, Merilanna, that answered – as if right on cue. "Prince Syrath has offered to arrange a meeting for us with Tarlandraxas." The prince nodded. "He is aware of our plight and the urgency that propels us to Tal Dalme. We were simply waiting for word from the physician of your recovery." The Fhaed-like elf that had first appeared to me gave a slight bow. "Now that you are, our journey can continue."

"I see. Simple as that? A pat on the head and off we go then?"

"Simple as that," the prince assuaged. "You'll be back home very soon."

There were too many agreeable faces in this crowd. All of them seemed intent upon waylaying my fears. Even the guards wore the hint of a wan smile. They all did...except for –

My gaze rounded the circle then shot to the quiescent figure standing farthest from me: the young attendant, the silent girl nearest the door. My eyes narrowed upon her as I focused. Everything else around me muzzed and hazed. She alone remained crisp and clear.

"Will I?" I asked, my question darkening and directed solely to her. "Will I be back home soon? Back to my own place in time?"

Her chin rose as our eyes met. "If the gods are willing," she said, "and if time is on our side."

The other figures in the room seemed to freeze in place as if the time the girl mentioned had released its hold upon me.

"I don't like magic," I said severely. "Who are you?"

The girl drew a measured breath and released it slowly, steadying herself. She knew she had been caught. "My name is Esmë Anii. I am a member of the First Circle of House Syralliador and the keeper of the sacred waters."

I tasted her words and knew them true. "You're the *Naeryni*, the dragon's priestess."

She nodded but did not loosen her gaze from mine. She watched me like someone would watch a hungry wolf, waiting for it to attack.

I revisited the illusion surrounding me and gave her the snarl she had undoubtedly expected. "Stop all this," I commanded. "I've no time for your games."

"It is by these games that I buy my people's future, Shadow-Child," she countered sharply. "Time may have lost its hold on you, but it is not our ally." Nevertheless, abruptly, the priestess dismissed the spell and a darker world engulfed me.

In form, the chamber was the same, though its becalming glow became instantly somber and wrapped in gloom. Fire had devoured this place. Black soot marred the walls. Too, in spots, these had been breached allowing the darkness without to claw its way within. I could smell and taste the acrid air now. There was blood in it. Syralliador had not escaped war. The Shadow Lord's army had already been here.

Merilanna, Eindrac, and even the prince evaporated. Along with the girl, only the two guards remained; but they, also, were marred with black stains and grim faces.

At least, I noted, my grimy, bloody clothes had rematerialized. I was feeling myself again.

"Talk," I growled.

Uncowed, the priestess laced her fingers before her, forcing an air of calm she clearly did not feel.

"Asteranoth's army will slaughter my people," she began matter-of-factly. "His forces, lead by the Shadowlord, Darkyr, stands at our borders even now. All efforts to repel him have failed – even mine. Soon, he will claim *Aesyriath Naedrom*, our sacred spring and our lives will be his. My people are about to die and I cannot stop him." She paused briefly to let the dire statement sink in, then she continued. "Many – those that could – have already fled: some went to Andraelyspa. Nothing has been heard from them. I fear they are lost. Others are trying to escape into the golden mountains to the east, but the lich's monsters are on their heels. I can only pray for them."

"But some of you are still here," I stated the obvious.

She nodded gravely. "Yes, a few, we are buying what time we can for the rest."

"So, why the spell? Why were you lying to me?" A thought flashed into my mind even as I asked the questions. I guessed the answer, and anger cinched my brow. "I'm what you intend to buy that time with. Is that it?"

"Yes. The Shadowlord wants you very badly," she explained. "Five horsemen were on your trail! There can be no mistaking his desire."

"So I am to be the fox for his hounds while you run away."

The allusion escaped her. I guess elves didn't chase foxes with hounds. Still, my meaning was taken.

She hesitated, confronted with the truth.

"Where are my friends?" I demanded. "I want to see them...now!" The black fire inside of me hissed and tried to surge, but there was no strength in it. More fey magic checked my flames. I snarled.

"I can't do that."

"Why?" I wanted to gut her with my bare hands, but fought back the urge.

"They're already dead."

I gnashed my teeth. "Tell me what happened…carefully."

The priestess' countenance became more subdued. She released me from her stare and, either as a gesture of submission or as a suicidal wish, dropped the spell that bound my fire. Then she dismissed her guards. The two warriors exchanged uncertain glances, but obeyed, albeit hesitantly. Then, it was just her and me in the burned out shell of the room.

Her tale began. "My sentries called me to the Oröm gate at the river bridge. Your companion, Merilanna, had almost succeeded in opening its wards. You and Tir'Synd, Eindrac, as you call him, were fighting to hold back the riders."

"To buy her time," I spat coldly.

The *Naeryni* nodded then continued. "Time that would cost us many lives."

A fragment of the tale unspoken snapped into focus. "Merilanna succeeded. She broke your line."

"Yes."

Thinking black thoughts, I moved to a singed gash in the wall and peered outside. All was carnage. The charred remains of an Alurishi village filled my view. Homes and other communal structures that had been woven within and about the great silver trees stood in ruin, gutted by fire. Many were still burning. The earth itself had been slashed open in places as if by enormous claws. A few, forlorn spirits – soldiers mostly – moved through the horrific scene. Their faces were ashen and haunted; their eyes seared by smoke and tears. I wanted to pity them, but I was too angry. I wheeled back to the young priestess, my fists clenched. "Where was your damned dragon when all of this happened?" Incredulity, frustration, and rage spilled into my words.

With unexpected strength and composure, Esmë lifted her chin and answered directly, "Fighting to help those that could be saved." Graciously, she did not return my fire and turned away before continuing. "Tarlandraxas drove back the darkness. He almost succeeded. But its master was too near. Darkyr appeared on the road, his hell-sword in hand, and rallied his riders. He raised his blade; and, like a black wind, an army of shadows assailed."

"If Darkyr's army took this place, why are any of us still alive?"

The priestess returned her troubled, tormented gaze to me. There was almost an apology in her eyes when she said, "It was not demon fire that burned this place. It was dragon's fire." She looked away, back out through the tear in the wall. Her shoulders slumped from the burden she bore. "Tarlandraxas did what he had to do: he struck back; he cauterized the wound. I could neither save your friends nor my own. I could only watch as the fire spread; I could only gather their spirits to me. That is how I came to learn part of your story."

"You've bound their souls to you?"

"Yes. Our defenses had fallen. An army of demons was upon us. Somehow, you endured even Tarlandraxas' elemental fire. It is no wonder that the Shadowlord wants your power."

"I don't understand. You brought me here from the road – Merilanna and Eindrac, also. Darkyr's forces attacked – using the breach that Meri had made – and the dragon burned everything to stop his army?"

"To buy us time," Esmë reiterated. "But Darkyr's army yet remains."

"Where is it now?"

Without words, the *Naeryni* led me from the charred shell beneath the now dead, ancient, silver oak. I followed her through the ashes of the burned out village. Her weary soldiers watched us silently. Blackened corpses littered our path. Some where fey. Some were monstrous. Evidence of violence was everywhere.

She brought me to an overlook. There, the outpost crowned a hilltop above the river. When the world was still green, it would have been concealed quite well. Now, it was laid bare. Through the smoke and the husks of the still smoldering trees, I could see and be seen. A curtain of fire, blue and violet hued, blazed upon the water's surface and traced a meandering line. The river was boiling and burning. A strange scent, the sickly sweet breath of the earth, touched my nose. Fissures – the rips I had seen – were open within the ground all around. Intermittently, wisps of gas rose from them and flashed with fire. My eyes ached and I coughed as I beheld the world they blackened. Aghast, I could not help but marvel at the earth-dragon's power.

Beyond the frenetic flames, on the far shore, a horde of shadowy demons and beastly men waited with clutching claws and weapons bared, eager to advance.

"The fire won't hold them much longer," the priestess said. "Tarlandraxas is pouring his spirit into that wall, but his spirit is not infinite. The waters he blesses yet flow, but his blessings will not flow through them forever. The Shadowlord will come again, and, this time, we won't be able to repel him."

I turned and faced her, but she did not meet my fierce gaze. Her eyes stayed downrange, watching the evil at her gate. "Darkyr won't follow me," I declared, "no matter how important you think I am."

"You were mistaken about what I intended, Lyri," the *Naeryni* said solemnly. "You were not to be a fox for his hounds." She regarded me askance from the corner of her eye. "You were to be our dagger in his heart."

"What do you mean?"

Her eyes lowered into the darkness of her desperate scheme. Almost mechanically, she explained. "His attack would come; and, when it did, you would strike back. I've watched your dreams –" she shuddered "– I know what kind of weapon you are: sharp, sure, quick, and terrible. You appear as a child, but your blood and his are the same. He senses that just as do I. He would let you close to him, his heart thundering, eager for the thrill your challenge brings. He would let you close enough to be his undoing."

Defiantly, I seethed. "Why would I do that? Why would I fight him to save you?"

"You wouldn't – not to save me or even to save my people." She faced my judgment: her eyes, wet with remorse; her words, whispers that roared like thunder. There was no pleasure in what she said next, only pain. "But you would see what I crafted for you to see. You would watch as he claimed your friends. You would fight. You would avenge them and, in so doing, save those you would not save otherwise."

She was right. I probably would. I couldn't deny it. If I watched Merilanna and Eindrac fall, my wrath would be terrible. But I had caught her in her deception. Her illusion would not compel me now. Instead, I faced a grim choice: Which monster was I going to be?

The *Naeryni*'s finger pointed to a place within the jostling horde. I followed it and spied the Shadowlord, riding on an unholy steed, moving up and down his lines, stoking their fury. When I looked back to her, she held a crystal vial in her hand. Golden light scintillated within it.

"Behold the holy water of *Aesyriath Naedrom*, distilled from the blood of the dragon, the elixir of creation and, in these dreadful times, perhaps, the last hope for its salvation."

I stared at the thing as if it were a viper. I had seen its like before: once, in the Etherstorm, in another of my living nightmares. It was the essence of all things, the quintessential first element, the beginning of all possibilities. "Aurium?" My tone rose with amazement.

The word seemed strange to her. "By whatever name, it is our only chance now."

"What do you want me to do with that?"

"Hold tight to it, then release it when your end is near. Darkyr *will* take you; and, when he does, it will be his undoing."

Horror crossed my face. There was irony also. "You want me to be his poison?"

"I want you to save my people. And, perhaps, if you succeed, save your friends, as well."

"You're mad."

"No, I'm desperate. I need time: time that only you can buy, time to reach the spring, and, maybe, time to save us all."

"So, why are you wasting it? Why are you still here?"

Her gaze guided me back towards the blue flames blazing on the river. "Because the spirit of the dragon is still here. Because, if this gambit is to succeed, it must be played out."

I looked down at the spectral fire burning on the waters of the river and tried to understand. I didn't.

"I am only a vessel, Lyri. When Tarlandraxas falls, I must bear his spirit back also." He voice softened. "I'm sorry I lied to you. I was afraid. All of this happened so fast. All I could see was that you burned with his black fire. How could I chance what you would do with it? I did not know you. So I did what I thought I needed to."

I did not hide my bitterness. "What's changed? You still don't know me or what I will do. It was your dragon that killed my friends. It was you that spun the illusion with which you meant to bait me, to show me their deaths, and to set me against the demons. I was to be your sacrificial pawn!"

"You're right, I still don't know you, but I'm starting to believe the voices inside me. They tell me you are a good person. In truth, Merilanna is very stubborn in pressing that point." The priestess lifted the vial towards me once again. "You can still save her and Tir'Synd. The sacred waters of the holy spring can do many things – even restore lives lost. Please, buy me the time I need."

Fuming, I glared at her but I shot my open palm towards her anyway. Into it, she placed the crystalline vial.

"Where's my damned sword?"

Chapter 16: Curse of the Blood

Inside, I raged. I hated magic and I hated being used. Always, people want to use me. Usually, it's the bad people. That's bad enough. The *Naeryni* wasn't a bad person. That just made it worse.

Of course, she gave me back my sword and my Whisperer. Her soldiers obeyed and brought them, albeit, reticently. She also gave me something unexpected: Merilanna's horn. I examined its scorched surface somberly, tracing its lines as my memories of the priestess drifted behind my eyes. I didn't cry. I refused to. Instead, I set my glare towards the future and I vowed to make it bloody.

From the crest overlooking the flaming river, I surveyed from where that blood would come. There were – as I had noted at Skullborough – a lot of demons: thousands; some seen, some awash in shadows. And, with them, a lot of undead and brutish beast-men stood.

Spotting Darkyr amidst the horde again wasn't difficult. He was still on his horse-corpse in the front of his army, waving his hell-sword around and shouting about all the terrible things they were going to have fun doing. His audience clearly approved. They were so eager for blood, they were practically fight each other, straining at their leashes.

Another stupid idea flashed across my wicked mind.

"How good are you at those illusions?" I asked over my shoulder to the *Naeryni*.

"I know my arts," she answered. Her tone was not smug. She was confident in what she said.

"Good."

As Esmë had presaged, the dragon's spirit waned. Just before midnight, the fire upon the river guttered and was gone.

Behind me, I heard the priestess draw in a long, even breath, steadying herself. I could feel the earth beneath the soft leather soles of my boots begin to tremble. The Veil shimmered as the dragon's spirit retreated to her and rejoined with its vessel.

T'Ethranir, the most ancient of elementals, are like that. They were subdued by the Aesyr long ago, their primal spirits bound to talismans. Some were devices: amulets, rings, jewels, or even common objects, but not all. Some, as in this case, were bound to living hosts. Esmë Anii, the *Naeryni*, was the talisman for Tarlandraxas, Orömgundr as my people called him, just as my friend, Ahlandra Maurel, was host to her *Sii*, the efreet spirit that lived inside her, its *Asati*. In some ways, I was similar, but my soul was the playground of shadows and demons.

"Cast your spell then go," I said. "I'll buy you the time you need. Save my friends; save everyone you can. Despite what you think of me, I would have fought for your people."

Apologetically, Esmë nodded once then turned her focus to the horde. Its front ranks were already across the river. Bloodcurdling war-cries rolled through the pitch-black air. She closed her eyes, said a short, hushed prayer, then snapped back to focus upon her fateful tasks. A spectral glow illumed her irises. Silent words of magic moved across her lips. She was seeing what she wanted to see. The world below her shifted as she did.

Seemingly from everywhere, a vast host of elven warriors erupted from the darkness and swarmed into the onrushing monsters.

For several long moments, the priestess wove her wishes and tied them to the dark army, perfecting her phantasm.

The elven defenders were, of course, merely projections of her will. However, the moment she bound their images to the demons, their Aluri blades were given the force of reality. In the chaos of the melee, the illusions covered some of the monsters. To their comrades, elves appeared everywhere in their midst. Every slashing blade and bashing club bloodied the scene further. Almost instantly, Darkyr's forces were cleaving and chopping at themselves, believing that their foes were among them. The ploy spread as fast as ignited vapors burn.

"Go," I commanded sharply, "and don't look back."

I didn't wait to see if she obeyed. I slipped the Veil and dove towards my enemies.

Most of the Shadowlord's army was mundanely gifted. Their eyes could not peer into Twilight. Thus, along with the fact that they were in disarray, preoccupied with slaughtering each other, I was able to weave through them swiftly and advance undetected.

I did say most of his army were mundanely gifted, but not all.

A dozen specters rode at Darkyr's side. They saw me coming. The death-wraiths' mounts clopped across the bridge unhurriedly. Ghostly fire limned their hooded figures within the Veil. Blazing eyes found me the instant I broke like a comet through the lines and closed towards their master.

One rider was bad enough. Five had proven overwhelming. Now, I faced a dozen of the devils – along with Darkyr himself – and knew my charge was hopeless.

Nevertheless, between the army and the Shadowlord's entourage, I stopped and claimed my ground and lifted my little blade to challenge my maker for, ultimately, that's who Darkyr was. It was his curse that filled my hammering heart and flowed through my pulsing veins.

Once I stopped, a dozen riders spurred forward and quickly formed a circle around me. Their steeds stamped the trampled earth with their hooves; they were desperate to devour me. Together, as one, the fiends drew their wicked blades and leveled them my way. Cruelly crafted Shadowsteel surrounded me. I could feel its malevolent aura. I could feel my black fire raging, taunting them, goading them to advance. Their demonic metal readied to extinguish my absurd audacity.

Darkyr joined the circle and reined. Beneath his fearful helmet, he neither smiled nor frowned. He was utterly cold and callous.

"So, you've come to die, have you?" he asked plainly, his gauntlet-clad hands resting calmly upon his saddle's horn. "Is that the wish you beg me to grant?"

"Sure," I sneered, "come kill me. Cut me down if you can." I shifted my stance, sword readied, and refocused my guard, offering an opening in my defenses that any seasoned warrior would recognize.

Without hesitation, the towering giant dismounted and strode into the circle. "As you wish," he said without pretense.

There wasn't any either. The moment his words were uttered, he crossed the distance between us, Riding the Cusp, and slammed my sword aside as if it were a mere twig I was brandishing. So hard fell his sidelong stroke that all sensation was hammered from my arms. The jarring blow nearly tore them from their sockets, but the shockwave rendered them numb. I was stunned and I was in big trouble.

Rolling with the force, using its momentum, was my usual ploy when fighting giants: parry, catch the blow, spin with its power, and counterattack. But I never had a chance to do any of that. Wind-Song flew from my grasp upon impact and I sprawled on my face after her, barely registering the despondent clatter of her steel against the Grymryl's paving stones.

Darkyr gave me no quarter. He neither hesitated nor gloated. He was all business. I felt his wide, serrated blade impale my spine between my shoulders before I could even draw my next breath. My last had been blasted from me. His wide sword nearly cut my small body in two.

And that was that. I was dead before a single barb could leave my tongue. It was a profoundly unsatisfying moment.

Of course, I'm immortal, so I didn't stay dead. My soul reawakened and pried open my eyes a missed heartbeat later. The cold stones beneath my cheek leveled my perspective as I laid there, tasting my own blood. My view rolled into bleary focus. I saw Darkyr turn away to go back to his undead horse, a trail of blood, my blood, dripping from his blade and hissing on its surface. The evil runes that covered it drank it in.

"She's yours," I heard him say dismissively to his deathly minions midstride.

Damn, I muttered in my mind, unable to even cough out the word.

The chill of the approaching Shadowsteel iced my soul, so I bit down upon the only hope I still had: the crystal vial that I had concealed within my cheek.

Aurium is a wondrous thing. It truly is the elixir of creation. Esmë called it the dragon's blood; but, truth be told, it's more like the blood of the gods. Every manifest thing, every living incarnation, has at its core the pure quintessence that is Aurium. All other elements are basic. It is prime, the mystical substance of all else. It is also pure potential, without the taint of any will – an unwoven Thread of Creation that no psyche had imposed itself upon. It was boundless; it was eternal.

As its energy entered me, my black fire was transformed. Once again, I became the fulcrum of The Balance, and all that was light, all that was dark, rested within my small hands. Khazul Mordûn, the Stormlord that had dared to invade Narianna in the future that was my present past, had witnessed a moment such as this and had paid the ultimate price for provoking it. Now, Darkyr and his minions experienced it also.

Like a phoenix, I exploded into flames, but my fire was not mundane. It was celestial; it was divine. And all things wrought of lesser stuff succumbed instantly and were consumed.

A dozen death-wraiths astride their hellish mounts were the first to know their doom. Their shrieks, though brief and terrible, heralded my rise.

All the world vanished as I became a pyre of pure, white, frenetic fire. The puissance of the dragon's blood engulfed my being. By my defiant will I forced it outward. There, it spread and expanded like the birthing of a star. Everything clinging to the light that it touched was restored. Everything wormed with shadows was ignited and burned away.

Through the glare of the fire, I watched as Darkyr's army was swept up by the expanding ring. The death-wraiths were the first. Their shadows became flaming tatters then they were gone, blasted to nothingness, cast to Oblivion. The host of monsters behind them vanished even quicker.

Too, Darkyr was caught. I glimpsed his form as it splayed, a blurred stain suffused against a tidal wave of light. I caught his deathly eye as he looked back at me, awed and – I think – strangely amused. I felt the Veil shudder as the auric blast struck him, lifted him, and carried him to his end.

Then all sound, all motion, all sensation abruptly ceased. Everything became nothing: blank and void.

My next recollections were of warmth on my face and of dappled light sparkling beyond my eyelids. Golden, glowing circles swam through my mind. They interlinked and rejoined my memories, re-forging my consciousness. I awoke in a very different place from that which I had known. From a horrid nightmare, I entered a prosaic dream.

Nearby, the river still flowed. I could hear its waters singing. The chorus of nature was all around me. Above, the boughs of silvery trees entwined, caressing each other in the gentle breeze. Xorcos, Trillanta Xorconum as the Turanians dub him, looked down from his glorious throne set higher still within a clear, blue firmament, his golden gaze fractured by the leaves and limbs. The earthy scents of the forest filled my nose. Gone was the stench of death.

Slowly, I sat up and appraised the scene around me. Nothing remained of my foes. Not a bone, not a scrap, nothing. Ferns and flowers had spread to cover all. Time had passed me by once again.

I looked towards the bridge. It was there, unchanged and unblemished. I looked to the ridge above, towards where the priestess and I had stood. The green of the world had returned and restored it, but no one looked back. Only the forest sounds greeted me as they rode the cool air.

"Damn," I finally muttered the last word my tongue had held.

Slowly, I regained my feet and examined my risen form, realizing to my chagrin an uncomfortable truth. Like any newborn, I needed some clothes. "Just great," I muttered and threw an irritated glare skyward. "Thanks a lot."

Shaking my head, I scanned the overgrowth that had claimed the disused road. A glint rewarded my efforts. A couple of old friends were still waiting for me. Smiling blithely, I retrieved my little sword and two small, shiny orbs. Somehow, they had survived where all else had not. I was grateful they had.

With them, also, lay Merilanna's horn. My disposition grew more melancholy as I brushed away the dirt and retouched the memories that swept through my mind.

"You're still not forgiven," I said to the heavens.

Turning back towards the northeast, I heaved a sigh and set my toes on the road.

"I hope I bought you enough time," I called down my path after a long departed spirit. Partly, I was glad no one answered back. I looked ridiculous: naked with a sword in one hand, two, silver balls in the other, and Ilé's damned horn strung on a vine over my shoulder. The gods do enjoy their little jokes.

Plodding up the hill, I felt very odd inside. Wisps of my black fire and the dragon's white light still danced and twirled, but a strange quiescence had befallen me, an afterglow that filled my soul. I felt...happy.

Yuck!

It had happened before.

Then, the divine, bright half of my sundered soul had reunited with its demonic, dark legacy. Within me, the powers of creation and destruction had vested thus. I held them in my hands and forced a new reality to be, transforming an apocalypse in the process.

Hooray for me. I saved the universe. Not bad for a little barbarian whelp, I suppose.

Well, somebody had to clean it up. The gods had made a mess of things – they're good at that – and, as usual, they had left it for me to fix.

That odd, strange, weird sensation that I was enduring was what some people referred to as "inner peace." Others, those that like fancier words, called it "equilibrium." I didn't care what it's called. For me, it was just annoying – which, in a way, was a good thing. I don't particularly like rainbows and unicorns dancing in my head, and sarcasm is very therapeutic.

Mercifully, the euphoria caught wind of my annoyance and retreated fast. By the time I reached the top of the rise, the unicorns had run off and my storm clouds had returned.

Crisis averted.

Once upon a time, in a future past, the area I was walking into had been dotted with small farmsteads. Where elven ruins had stood, that land had been cleared of dead trees and fields had been planted. Scanning the locale, how all that had come to pass made sense to me. The dead trunks of the trees were still here at the moment and the burned out buildings had not yet been recycled, but I could imagine all of that coming. Once more, the variable in play was time. Some had flowed by – enough for the forest to reclaim the area – but not so much as to see settlers embrace the site. That, I deduced, would happen later.

So, how much time had I lost? How much had I bought for the *Naeryni*?

Looking at the landscape, more had passed than I had figured. Acorns had sprouted into young trees in the open areas. Years had passed.

"Damned unicorns," I grumbled.

I moved on, following the Grymryl.

The shadows of evening were very long by the time I reached the border stones of what would become Olde Asgevan. I could have used the Cusp to travel quicker, of course, but I didn't. I had already spent enough time dallying at the edge of Twilight and found walking in the living world more to my liking. So, just before Xorcos' bright chair bid the day goodbye, I stood with my bare backside looking him in the eye and regarded the outskirts of the settlement – a human settlement!

"Years," I said to the wind that combed my unkempt hair.

Heroes of the Third Age: Merilanna

From the hilltop, I could see the wide lowland along the banks of the Astraelon River. White smoke rose from dozens of longhouses. The smell of cookfires rode the breeze. Families were gathering for their eventide meals. Along the banks of the river, canoes were banked and curtains of fish were strung. Men dressed in deerskin jerkins and breeches were cleaning the last of the day's catch and readying them for the smokehouses, the stacked-stone buildings that stood beyond the high-water line on the shore. Too, there were womenfolk busying about, tending to other mundanities of village life and calling after rambunctious…children. There were children running here and there…playing.

I caught my breath before it escaped me and stared wide-eyed with a sudden revelation. Some of them appeared nearly my immutable age.

"Ten years," I muttered.

Scanning uphill, I cut my eyes from the riverside settlement and spied where the great steading hall, Asgevardír, stood. The only problem: it didn't – not yet. The tor, the great mound of earth, was there, covered in mid-summer grass. White sheep, their wool still short from the spring shearing, dotted the open slopes, grazing between the concentric circles of standing stones that ringed the hill like a crown upon some titan's green head. But the kingly building was not there.

My heart sped my blood, but still I swooned. I stared down at my shadow, watching it grow longer upon the road before me. Anger, fueled by my growing unease, fought back the dread that was darkening the edges of my vision.

I cast a bitter glance back at the setting sun-god. Time was his to command, and I was bound to the capricious game he was playing.

"You there! Girl! What are you doing?"

No, it wasn't Xorcos yelling.

I had stood on the road too long, lost in my dark reverie and hadn't heard or seen the trio of men approach.

My gaze shot to the caller: a hunter, his spear in hand. Two more, their bows slung over their shoulders, eyed me with their leader's same perplexed look. A young stag was trussed on the pole they bore between them. Their hunt had gone well.

Reflexively, I spun and my sword appeared, thrust between us. The trio exchanged quick glances, but it was wonderment, not fear that shot between them.

"No one's going to hurt you," the hunter assuaged, his empty hand patting the air slowly. His voice was calm and deep, his accent and words like unto Asgev; though, were it not for the wonders of Twilight, they would have escaped my comprehension.

"Care, Caedric," one of his men, a redhaired warrior with a spiraling blue design painted into his skin around his left eye, across his left cheek, and over the left half of his forehead cautioned. "These lands are still filled with dark spirits. That one – she be a demon, I say. Don't let her take your soul."

The younger, dark-haired man with him nodded once in agreement. I watched, my glare narrowing, as his hand moved slowly towards the knife sheathed at his hip.

"You're right," I whispered, never taking my eyes off the blade slipping into the crepuscular light. "No one's going to hurt me."

"Sheath your steel, Fengr" the man named Caedric said sternly. His gaze, though, never left me. I was like a serpent before him, and he sensed it keenly.

The knife stilled; then, a considered moment later, it was sheathed.

My attention returned to the golden-haired hunter.

"What's your name, child?" he asked.

Before I could answer, hurried footfalls from down the road reached my ears and a woman's voice, filled with both disbelief and fervent hope, cried, "Lyri. Is it you?"

My face turned to her in an instant, and the storm clouds over my soul parted. Rays of light flooded my eyes. "Meri?"

It was her, Ilé's priestess. The girl I had known, however, was now a woman in the fullness of her bloom. She stopped a few strides away, and the astonishment she wore exploded into her unmistakable, joyous smile. "You're alive. By the goddess' grace, Lyri, you're alive!"

"Mostly," I said brusquely, without thinking.

Merilanna's smile did not fade. She ignored the reflexive barb and rushed to me, threw her arms about me, and wrapped my nakedness in her shawl as she did. She pulled me to her and hugged me tight.

"Stop," I protested feebly, "I was being scary and you're messing it up."

Meri laughed even as tears raced down her cheeks, but she did quit smothering me.

"I thought," she said, beholding me at arm's length as if she expected me to vanish into the wind, "– never mind. I'm so glad to see you."

"So, this is Lyri," Caedric remarked, taking a knee beside the priestess and bringing his face down to my level.

Yes, he was very tall; and, yes, I'm very short. So, what? I bet you've never ridden a dragon!

Merilanna fussed with her shawl, adjusting it upon me. "Yes, Caedric," the priestess affirmed happily, "this is her."

"I thought she would be taller," the lummox jested, a smirk teasing his lips.

I glowered at him. "I am when you're lying on your backside looking up at me down my sword."

Caedric's smirk broke into a full, admiring grin. "She's just as you said," he commented aside to the priestess. Then, to me, he bowed low, humbly and earnestly. "Welcome."

A small gathering of people had come with the priestess and were standing about, gawking and muttering, staring at me like I was some sort of legend. As Caedric bent, I looked past him and watched as the others sank slowly to their own knees and bowed just as low.

Confused, I looked to Meri. She was still smiling warmly. "What did you tell them?" I asked, a hint of accusation in my tone.

"Only the truth," she replied.

Caedric lifted his face then stood. "It was you that freed us," he said. "It was you that drove back the Shadowlord. It was you that broke our chains."

I stared at the hunter, reading his eyes. He was speaking the truth he knew, but I didn't comprehend much of it.

"Darkyr?" I shook my head, still dumbfounded. "What are you talking about?"

"The *Naeryni* told me what you did," Merilanna explained.

"And Meri" – not Merilanna, I noted – "told us," Caedric added.

"Come," the priestess suggested, "we can talk about all that has happened. But, first, let's find you some clothes and let's get you something to eat."

Neither prospect offended me. "Sure," I muttered, surveying the sea of eyes intent upon me. "Something to eat; some clothes." I cut my gaze back to Merilanna. "And a lot of explaining." I remembered something else. "Oh, you dropped this," I said, drawing the instrument from where it hung on a vine in the small of my back."

"My Lady's horn," the priestess gasped, joy shining forth from within her eyes. "I never thought I would see it again."

"Thought the same of me," I commented gruffly, handing it over.

"Thank you, Lyri," Meri said, checking my sour mien with her honest appreciation.

Obliged, "You're welcome," I replied.

Soon, we reached Asgevan – not quite Olde yet – and were surrounded by its people. The afternoon that had started as a routine affair within the village, swiftly became a celebratory occasion. Family meals converged into a grand feast. Everyone gathered. Altogether, there were, perhaps, two-hundred people, and I was at the center of it all, a curious attraction.

I don't mind crowds. Showing off without them is pointless. It's affection I have trouble with, and these people were effusive with it. Once word of who I was had spread, they all felt the need, apparently, to offer their thanks to me. I wanted to say, "For what? Not killing you." But I refrained.

Conversations between them flowed as freely as the strong drink in their cups. They were a hearty, ribald bunch. Admittedly, my kind of people: barbarians.

After a while, the lighthearted chatter worked its way back to more ominous subjects.

"We were monsters, back then," Caedric was saying, his voice, even, his countenance, empty, his emotions separated from his words. He took a deep drink of the dark mead in his clay cup. Merilanna offered him a supportive smile. He continued. "The Shadowlord's evil had nearly devoured our souls, Lyri. Uncountable were the horrors that we had done. Death and destruction were all that we knew.

"We came to the banks of a river, eager for more fey blood. There, a magical wall of blue fire held us back, enraging our desires. But, it, too, fell, and we rushed to claim our spoils. Our enemy, though, was ready and met our charge with swirling steel. Then, there was blood aplenty to be had.

"But, it was not to be so. In the midst of it all, white fire exploded and engulfed us. I remember the heat. It was unlike any other. I remember it purging me of my shadow. I and the vanguard with me were spared the fullness of its wrath. We *were* burned, but we were not vanquished.

"In terror, we fled, following after the S*hi* that we had sought to destroy." Caedric looked about meaningfully, scanning the attentive faces gathered around the campfire. "We came here, broken, near to death, but we did not die, though it would have been just if we had."

His gaze settled upon me and held me firmly before he continued.

"That's when the priestess appeared, the *Naeryni* at her side. Meri embraced us and she freed us from the shadows that had enslaved us. To our disbelief, the elves here did us no harm. They received us. They bound our wounds, and they healed our bodies. They gave us their holy waters, and our black souls were given back some light." Caedric glanced again to Merilanna. Her smile approved.

"Where is the *Naeryni*?" I asked. I had seen nothing of the elves.

Heroes of the Third Age: Merilanna

"She and her people departed," Merilanna explained. "Their time, she said, had come to its end in these lands."

"She entrusted them to us – the destroyers," Caedric said humbly. "We are its keepers now. Orömgundr guides us and gives us strength."

I'm an idiot!

I shot to my feet as if stung by a bee. "You're him!" I cried. "You're Caedric Einhern!"

Perplexed glances ricocheted around the gathering.

Merilanna said nothing, but she was covering a furtive snicker.

"And you're Lyri," Caedric said, shrugging, yet confused by my reaction.

"You're the first king of kings," I blurted, "the lord of the *Einhervaldin*."

To my surprise, the warrior before me chuckled, his blue eyes sparkling as he shook his head. "I'm no king," he said. "I'm just a man – a man whose trying to do the best that he can to lead his people."

I crossed my arms and canted my head to the side. "What do you think a king is?"

Caedric's expression became more somber. I could see in his eyes the workings of his thoughts. The rulers that he and his people had known had been far from benevolent. He reconnected his attention to me and his smile flickered. "I guess I'll have to learn," he replied earnestly.

"You're doing very well," Meri assured, resting her hand gently upon his broad shoulder.

My outburst had brought all eyes to me again. I looked about the circle, somewhat embarrassed – somewhat, because I'm too brash to be easily embarrassed – and nodded, thinking. "You're my people," I said. "Brave. Strong." I looked back to Meri. She was behind all of this. "Caring."

Before I could wax too poetic, a little girl, four years old, perhaps, with auburn locks and bright green eyes, stepped into the firelight. She was clutching a straw doll close to her heart. "Are you a goddess?" she asked innocently.

How to answer? When someone asks you if you are a god…

I moved over to her and squatted down so my eyes were level with hers. Her mother and father were watching very closely. The man's arms encircled his wife standing before him, her own arms cradling another child, the girl's baby brother, I deduced.

"Well, I am a little bit," I answered wryly. "What's your name?"

She giggled and pointed her little finger at my nose. "Yours," she said.

My brow pinched, unsure what she meant. "No," I repeated, "what's *your* name."

Now, she seemed confused – and a bit annoyed. "Mine's *yours*," she declared, also adding emphasis.

"Lyri," her mother called in that unmistakable mother's voice.

Reflexively, I looked up to her and the girl turned quickly as well. "Yes?" we both answered at the same instant.

The girl's mother smiled proudly.

That's when it hit me. I stared back at the little imp. "Your name is Lyri," I said, feeling suddenly small and deeply humbled myself.

She regarded me curiously, a pouty frown on her freckled face. "That's what I said." She stamped her foot, impatiently. "Gods are supposed to listen better!"

My astonishment burst into a barely restrained snort of laughter. "You're right," I agreed wholeheartedly, tears of mirth welling in the corners of my eyes. "Gods should listen better!"

Laughter spread through the gathering.

At that, the girl's father retrieved her. She waved and smiled over her shoulder to me; and I, with no thought of maintaining my dour demeanor before the onlookers, smiled and waved back. Only in the silent pause that followed did I consider my grim façade.

Slowly, I rose and turned to Caedric and Meri. He sat proudly. She was beaming, her face aglow in the firelight. Both were smiling.

My own smile, I hammered back into a false scowl – which only seemed to amuse the priestess more. "Let's talk about war," I said curtly.

Caedric nodded; and, though it pained her to do so, Merilanna concurred.

For the rest of the evening and long after the children and most of the womenfolk had withdrawn to their homes, we did just that. Caedric explained, to my chagrin, that Darkyr had survived the white light that had destroyed much of his army. The Shadowlord had retreated to a boggish lowland west of what they called the South Delving.

"Near Telbren," I muttered to myself.

"What?" Caedric queried.

"Nothing," I answered. "It's a place that isn't there yet. Go on."

"There's not much more to tell," Caedric confessed. "We've managed to make a home for ourselves here and to defend these lands. There are raiders everywhere. Groups of them are scattered throughout these silver woods. We're doing what we must to survive."

"What about Morzog?" I asked, using the name by which my people, the Asgevar, called Darkyr's master, the Arcanalestri, Asteranoth.

"Little has been heard of the lich's army," Caedric explained. "The last we knew, it had stormed the mountains to the east, pursuing the elves, but there has been no word of its fate. Some believe that it was destroyed." He shook his head. "But I dare not hope that to be true. Still, Orömgundr has been quiet of late. He will rumble if shadows enter the lands again."

"Speaking of the earth-dragon," I said, changing the subject, "what became of his sacred spring?"

"The *Aesyriath Naedrom* still flows," Meri assured. "It gives life to these people, just as it did to the *Ayl-Alurishi*."

"And the *Naeryni*?"

"My Lady gave me leave to fulfill that role for a time. Esmë Anii taught me the rites and baptized me with the waters of the sacred spring. Apparently, I have a gift for raising the dead and purifying their essence." Her eyes flared with mock surprise, the corner of her lips turned up.

"In the years since, Tarlandraxas – Orömgundr – has chosen my successor. You met her this evening, in fact."

"The girl?"

"Yes, she was anointed not long ago, at the end of winter."

"But she's only a child. How can she do that? How can she serve the dragon and protect these lands?"

"Children are capable of amazing things," Merilanna said meaningfully.

I could only frown at that, not argue the point.

"We'll protect the land and protect her," Caedric stated. There was no mistaking the conviction.

My expression made it clear that I didn't like the idea of the burden resting on the girl's shoulders. I knew what it meant to be a child carrying the weight of the world. To me, this was no different. "Who made that decision?" I challenged.

"The dragon, of course," Caedric said plainly.

"She is pure of heart," Meri added, "and nearly as willful as her namesake."

I withdrew my complaint and just shook my head. It must have loosened another query. A new, worrisome thought crossed my mind. "What happened to Eindrac?"

Meri offered a fleeting smile and said, "He was reborn from the sacred waters as was I."

"As an elf or as a dragon-man?"

"Thankfully, as an elf. The sacred waters restored him. Tir'Synd is his true name."

"I know."

Meri regarded me quizzically, but did not ask how I knew. 'Still clever, I see' she mouthed before she continued, "He went with Esmë Anii and the others. They set out for Nariandor a year after the Dark Lord withdrew. I pray and believe that they are safe and well."

I hoped the same and nodded.

"We're very glad you are also," the priestess added.

"Thank you," I replied absently. My mind had already shot off into the shadows of another dark path.

Merilanna saw me go down it. "You can stay as long as you wish," she said sincerely.

I turned my gaze to her light, but I still felt dark inside. "You know I have to go, too."

The priestess' lips thinned into a hard-pressed smile and nodded. Then she looked to Caedric solemnly. In words, she said nothing, but in her eyes she said much. He looked into the fire and gave a slow, painful nod, releasing her as his gaze and his heart surrendered to an inevitable truth they had discussed many times before.

Meri looked back to me. "We both do," she said at last.

It took me a moment to understand what was happening. Ten years had passed. She had changed. The teen girl I had known had become a woman, a leader amongst these people, but she was still bound by an oath she had sworn to me.

I started to protest, but the priestess hushed me with her hand and affirmed clearly, saying, "These are not our times, Lyri. We have to return to our own."

Even as she said that, her delicate hands gathered one of Caedric's and held it tightly.

Slowly again, the hunter's face lifted from the firelight. "Tomorrow," was all he said.

Chapter 17: New Tomorrows

I couldn't sleep that night. Caedric and Merilanna had stayed by the fire the longest, keeping me company, but our conversation had done nothing to ease my restive heart. Before they left, I was offered a warm bed – more than once – but, respectfully, I declined, choosing instead to remain by the campfire, alone with my thoughts. Reluctantly, near midnight, Ilé's priestess and the forefather of my people withdrew, her hands in his, her head leaning upon his shoulder as they walked away to say their goodbyes privately.

The song of the night soon surrounded me: the crackle of the fire, the fiddling of crickets, and the steady ambience of the river.

Tomorrow. Tomorrow, north towards where Gyrnvenan would one day be built. Tomorrow, to the circle of stones, to Tal Dalme, the place where this strange journey had begun. Tonight, all of my past played through my waking dreams. Would there be new tomorrows, or would there be only the darkness of my past revisited upon me again and again? Where would this tangled skein lead at last? Could the snares in the Threads be unwound? I didn't know. And, even if they could be, what would that mean?

Amidst my solitude, I looked about the village and wondered what the people in their beds were dreaming. Were they happy? Were they filled with nightmares? Always, mine seemed the latter. I had vanquished countless demons; my black fire had consumed them. But I never forgot a single evil thing they did. Every sin, every wicked act was branded upon soul. Thick were the scars that remained. They hardened my heart and left me cold inside, no matter how close to the fire I edged.

Still, I looked about the village and was glad for it. I did not know if the people's dreams were black or filled with joy, but they had survived a Shadowfall – perhaps the darkest one that ever was – and they still held to each other. They still hoped for bright tomorrows. They still dared to bring forth children and love them – even if they named them "Lyri." Maybe my world would rise also. Maybe, the shadows wouldn't last forever. With people like Merilanna in the world to show the way, perhaps there was hope.

It was with that thought that the predawn glow was received. I watched as the sky turned from pitch to the color of blood, then of fire, then swelled with the aureate splendor of morning. In those moments, the eternal promise of the heavens was reaffirmed: Every night ends. Every night has its dawn.

Soon, life emerged from its resting places. The cock crowed and the songbirds sang. The people of Asgevan rose from their beds, and the last days for me in the past, the beginning of my new tomorrows, was at hand. I wasn't sure I was ready for them. I wasn't sure if they would even come to pass. My path always seems to twist.

Within an hour of dawn, Meri and Caedric returned to the fire that I had stoked all night. I offered a sullen welcome, still picking at the embers.

The priestess knelt beside me and placed her hand on my shoulder. I was too numb to flinch. "We can leave whenever you wish," she said gently.

I tossed the stick I had been using into the coals and watched it kindle. Then, I rose and met her kind eyes. Mine were dead. "Let's go," I replied.

Merilanna glanced to her friend for his assent and he gave it. I could feel his pain, his loss, but I could also see in him his strength. He loved her enough to let her go, knowing that she must, if not to save his world – for that, in no small measure, she had already done – but to save her own.

A small entourage of warriors emerged from the village and joined our circle at the communal campfire. Their families watched from their doorways. All wore their finest armor and bore their proudest arms. Each man and woman was painted with the blue, spiraling marks of what would one day be called the *Kaelvrot*, the magical, holy script of my people. When all were assembled, without ceremony, Caedric took the lead and we departed Asgevan. Death's priestess walked at my side.

The way to Tal Dalme followed an ancient, elven path along the Astraelon River. Ten years had seen much of it overgrown and reclaimed by the Silverwood. By noon, the length tread by human hunters came to an end. There, the *Einhervaldin*, Caedric's mighty warriors, had erected a Sentinel Stone of their own to ward against any evils that might dare come their way. Orömgundr had blessed it. I stopped only briefly to examine the runes chiseled into the menhir's surface. The pigments that filled these marks: gold and crimson, blue and white – were distinct and dramatic. Time had not yet worn them away, but I knew that it would. Only the wisest among the clans in my own age even remembered what the symbols meant.

"*Ban'Naerdyr*," Meri called it, "the place where tears begin."

I suppose its meaning was two-fold. It was a border and a warning. For those that trespassed, death would bring them sorrow. For those that ventured beyond, a world filled with darkness would inflict it upon them.

On the banks of the river nearby, we rested and ate a light meal. There was still a day or so of travel ahead, so we did not weigh down our bellies. Conversations were brief as well. All knew that we were walking into danger. Wariness, though, suffocated neither the camaraderie nor the morale of the group. Little was said, but spirits were high. These people were not afraid to die; they only feared dying badly. That sense of honor, of courage, of heroism filled Asgev lore. I was walking among legends that would never know all that they meant to the people they beget.

As late afternoon arrived, we came to where a tributary joined the Astraelon. Its fertile waters flowed from the east, rich with the scent of the moors and highlands. A wide wetland spread along the far shore, pushing back the trees. Plants grew in great abundance in this space. Sun and nutrients were plentiful. Where we stood, the land's elevation forced the merging waters to turn sharply to the west. We were at a divide where the forest and the hills, spreading from the unseen mountains to the east, collided. I noted the higher land beyond the floodplain also. It was the perfect spot for a town to crown.

"Gyrnvenan," I said aside to the priestess. "That's where it will be built. These lands will someday grow crops.

Merilanna nodded, trusting in my memories of the future.

Caedric came over and shared our view. "The river will turn back north, following the land before it rounds west and makes for the sea. There's a bridge a few hours from here. We could be there before midnight; or, if we chose, we could camp here and scout ahead. Once we cross, we will be challenged. Others claim the places we must go."

"Other clans?" I asked.

"Yes – remnants of Morzog's army. They call themselves the Aesdana. Their chieftain, a man named Aesgyrn, is grym-blooded. He suffers none to enter his lands."

"Will he parley?" Merilanna asked, seeking a peaceful answer.

"Perhaps," Caedric replied but without conviction. "Shadows claw deep into him and his people."

"Maybe I should talk to him," I snorted, "and give him a chance to repent."

My companions exchanged dubious glances.

"Hopefully, it won't come to that," Caedric said. "If we're clever, we can cross the river and head north before we're noticed."

I smirked. "I don't think so. We're already being watched." My preternaturally sharp eyes had spied others looking back at us from the wood line atop the distant hills.

Caedric and Merilanna scanned the shadows, but could not see what I could see.

"What do we do?" Meri asked, looking up at the mighty laird.

Caedric's eyes were still narrowed, searching for our foes. Bloody thoughts were flowing in his mind behind his eyes.

"We'll make a friend," I answered before the fire growing inside the warrior reached his tongue. Then, without another word, I vanished, slipping the Veil.

I was across the river before the rest of our band even noticed I was gone. Meri and Caedric shared troubled looks as they searched the panorama, seeking after me. Through the bluish blur of Twilight, they looked like ghosts, their ethereal souls tattered by a spectral headwind. I felt it, too, the moment I crossed the damned river. There was magic in the air. I could smell its sulfurous emanation.

Nevertheless, I pressed on, trying to be as subtle as possible. My movements, though, sent ripples through the Veil. Even a small stone disturbs still waters. Someone, I knew, was watching them spread.

The sentry on the hill, however, was not that watcher. No, the eyes that watched us were dark and red, the eyes of a youngish troll with greenish skin and dark, grey hair. I found him hiding in the woods easily. The bow he carried was stout and his arrows were sharp and envenomed. Still, he could not shoot what he could not see.

The tip of my sword touched the back of his muscular neck.

"Don't be a fool," I warned in a whisper, Twilight carrying my words into his mind. "I will kill you before you scream." He didn't, so, apparently, he wasn't. "Smart boy. Now, turn around slowly." He obeyed, his hands holding his bow and its arrow wide apart.

When he saw me, his fear was startled into disbelief. A little girl wasn't the nemesis he had expected, of course. His hanging jaw, filled with sharp, black teeth gave clear evidence of that.

I smiled devilishly. "We're going to go for a little walk," I instructed. Before he could reply, I vanished again and reappeared behind him once more. He wheeled to find my sword still leveled at his neck. "You won't see me, but you'll know I'm behind you. Do you understand?" He nodded once, slowly. "Good. You're going to take me to your chieftain, Aesgyrn. I want to talk to him."

His red eyes narrowed. "No betray him," he vowed in a coarse, gravelly voice. "Die for him."

My eyebrow raised. *Honor?* His conviction surprised me. "I believe you would," I said to the troll. "But it is neither your life nor his that I wish to take. I just want to talk."

To say that he was suspicious would be a grand understatement. But we were at an impasse with only one way for him to survive: do my bidding. Nonetheless, he suggested. an alternative. "Me carry your words. No take you."

I considered his offer. "I could follow you, you know? You'd never even see me." I could, he realized, and confusion raced across his angular face. He wasn't thinking that far ahead, I guess. Noble, but still naïve. "So what are we to do?" I prompted musingly. Of course, he had no answer. He had no good options. After a moment, I sighed and said, "Alright, you've convinced me. You go and you tell Aesgyrn that a demon wants to talk to him. I'll just wait here –" I glanced aside "– beside this nice tree."

Suspicion narrowed his eyes further. I watched as his jaw clenched with frustration that was quickly turning into anger. "Don't mock, demon," he warned.

Have I mentioned that diplomacy is not my strongest suit? I promise that I try, but I'm just not very good at it. I get bored or impatient after a while, that's all. It's not my fault that people are boring or stupid. I didn't make them that way. Blame the gods.

"I'm not," I protested, my voice rising in pitch to impart just how hurt I felt by his cruel accusation. Of course, I *was* mocking him. "But it's either that or I kill you and follow your trail back to your village anyway and introduce myself. Really, this is your best option – well, it's your only option." I canted my head cannily. "So what's it going to be?" I tapped my foot, counting down the seconds as he struggled with his alternatives. "Come on, I don't have all night."

The young troll growled. I smiled as innocently as I could. He really, really wanted to kill me.

Finally, "Me take words," he said, snarling. "Who your master?"

I wanted to laugh and say, "What makes you think I have a master?" But I didn't. Instead – again, I don't know why I do these things – I said flatly, "Darkyr. He's my father." It wasn't entirely a lie, just a stretched truth – not that I really cared.

I think the green-skinned troll blanched, and he may also have pissed himself a little. His dark, red eyes certainly flew wide with alarm. "Sh-Sh-Shadowlord," he sputtered.

"Ye-ye-yes," I said back. "We're in a hurry to conquer the world. So, run along now and tell your chieftain to come say hello." I pointed to the tree with my sword. "I'll be here, I promise. It's a nice tree."

Haltingly, at first, the sentry departed. I guess he was still expecting me to kill him or something. Within a few strides, though, he broke into a dead run and vanished into the darkness.

Again, I sighed and shook my head. It was a nice enough tree, but I wasn't keen on the idea of parleying with a bunch of trolls.

Trolls? Sorry, I guess I should have explained.

Trolls, like demons, come in all sorts of varieties. Some even have wings. In most ways, though, they are like men: two arms, two legs, one head – usually – and, generally, a bad disposition. I'm not sure where they come from exactly, but I think they were made by sorcerers or perhaps by evil priests, blending together human stock with some nasty, toad-like creature, perhaps. Regardless, they're part of the monstrous bunch I call beast-men. They have sharp senses; sharp claws and teeth; gangly limbs; they heal very quickly; and they prefer to stalk during the night. I don't really know that much more about them. We don't hang out together.

I returned to the waiting *Einhervaldin*.

Merilanna spun my way as I materialized. I guess she, too, could feel the disturbance in the Veil as I slipped the Cusp.

"We have to move," I declared.

Caedric and a few of his warriors reacted to the tone of my voice and regarded me anxiously.

"What's happening?" Merilanna asked.

"Nothing much," I said, "but the hill on the far shore is about to be overrun with trolls and whatever else Aesgyrn commands." To Caedric directly, "You need to get to that bridge you were talking about. I'll give you the distraction you need, but you need to move now."

"What about you?" Meri pressed. "This whole thing is about getting *you* back to that Circlestone."

"No," I countered more sharply than I had intended, "it's about getting *us* back; and, right now, that means getting you and Caedric and the others safely past the Aesdana." I smirked, trying to be reassuring. "Don't worry. I don't plan to chat long with the trolls. Get moving. I'll catch up." The priestess and the warlord exchanged worried looks. "Go!" I urged.

The bizarre screech of war horns sounded in the distance. Apparently, the sentry had reached his master with my words.

"That's a lot of horns," one of the Asgev warriors commented.

Caedric looked at me questioningly. "What did you do?"

I shrugged. "Well," I hedged, "I may have told the sentry that I was Darkyr's daughter."

A small cough covered Merilanna's chuckle. Apparently she'd outgrown her snorts. Not sure I liked that.

Caedric's expression flipped from dumbfounded to amazement. He grinned evilly. "You're right," he laughed, "we'd better get going."

Merilanna started after him then paused to look back at me. "Be careful," she said seriously.

I sighed and nodded. *Just like Fhaed.*

Once the party had moved off into the shadows towards the bridge, I returned to the spot where I had chatted with the sentry and settled myself comfortably at the base of the nice tree. It was there that the warband found me, idly fussing with my fingernails. I pretended not to notice them until they were nearly upon me. It was a large group, perhaps fifty warriors. A few were trolls, each with their own particularly gruesome features, a couple were Urgrym, hulking brutes with big muscles and small brains – unlike my friend Urrdo in Morgaradar, who was large but also exceptionally smart, a sorcerer even – the rest, to my surprise, were men. At the center of their gaggle strode an impressive figure who could only have been Aesgyrn.

Clad in studded leather and mail, he wore a mantle of black fur, bear hide, I think, and carried a massive sword, its fuller filled with twisting symbols that seemed to have a life of their own. That air of magic that I had sensed when first I crossed the river to this hill buffeted me again as he approached, radiating from his weapon.

Aesgyrn was a large man as you might expect, on par with Caedric in height and athletic build. His hair, restrained by a thick, iron band that rode his heavy brow and sported the same sort of writhing knots as his sword, was shoulder length and black as night. His eyes were dark, fierce and intelligent. His jaw was square and covered by a kingly, black beard. A trace of grey, though, trimmed his temples and crept across his chin, adding to his distinguished, if ominous, appearance.

"*This* is your demon?" he asked incredulously of the young troll following close behind him as he came to stand before me. Despite his cavalier tone, the rest of his troupe, I noted, spread quickly to encircle me.

"Yes, king," came the sentry's uneasy reply.

Aesgyrn took another step my way and squatted down to my level, eyeing me as he would any curiosity. He leaned upon his massive sword as he balanced on the balls of his feet and cocked his head, unsure what to make of me.

I finished picking the last of the dirt from my fingernail and looked over to him finally. "You must be Aesgyrn," I said casually. My gaze, however, was anything but casual. Our dark eyes locked; we were two predators sizing each other up. His mirth, his disarming façade, settled into a thin, knowing smile. There were demons riding his soul, shrieking madly, raging behind his stare, warning him of danger.

"I am," he said simply in a cavernous voice. "And who are you, child of Darkyr?"

A half-smirk hooked the corner of my lip. "Me? I'm just passing through," I said.

Aesgyrn chanced a glance back at his sentry. "Out to conquer the world," he added, repeating the report he had received.

I shrugged. "That's my father's hobby. I'm more…more a collector of things."

The warlord rose back to his towering height. "And what have you come to my lands to collect, little demon?"

"Time, mostly," I answered wryly, looking up at him through the hanging strands of my black hair, my stare piercing deeply into his soul. Thus far, I had kept my black fire checked, but I could see it reflecting in his eyes now. He could sense its hunger. He knew his peril.

"We immortals have a great deal of time to collect, don't we?" he said.

"Um-hmm, we do," I said with a slow nod. "If we're smart about it."

Aesgyrn took a deep breath, closed his eyes, and released it. "There aren't many of us, you know," he said, his voice low and sonorous. Slowly, he lifted his great sword and admired it, his dark thoughts reflecting on its wicked blade. "The lords of Armadar only bestowed their blessings upon a chosen few: me, Darkyr, Einhern, Verrek, Sarven, a few others." He looked past his sword and down at me. "I did not conceive that the dark gifts would pass to our childer, but I see now that I was mistaken." His lowered and settled his weapon back at his side. "So, what it is that Darkyr wants of me? Our master, the lich is dead, entombed by the mountains he dared try cross. The *Shi* have powerful allies within the earth. I am done with his war. But I will not yield if it comes for me again. So, tell me child of shadows, what time have I left before my sword shall feed again?"

I liked this man. His soul was filled with demons, but – like Caedric Einhern – he was fighting against them. The tide of the Shadowfall had turned, indeed. The Balance was in motion, its scales tipping back towards the light. From the ranks of darkness, leaders were emerging, trying to forge a future. I scanned the warband around me. Aesgryn was their blacksmith. They rang with the sound of his hammer. Tempered steel would be needed in the centuries to come.

"Not long," I replied to the warlord's question. "Darkyr is rallying his army in the west. He means to claim these lands even if Morzog cannot. I have spoken with Einhern and have told him the same."

Aesgyrn's stare narrowed. "Why? Why would you call upon your father's foes thus? Is it a trap you wish to lay? Are you the spider in the web?"

I shook my head. "No, I am of his blood, but not his mind. My reasons are my own. That must suffice."

Without turning, Aesgryn spoke over his shoulder to the sentry. "How many?" he asked.

"Fourteen, king," came the quick answer.

It was received with a nod. I knew well-enough the count and what the report had delivered.

"I have sent a hundred warriors to the bridge over the wide river," Aesgyrn said evenly. He gestured to one of his men. "If that horn," hanging at the hip of the indicated man, "does not sound, they will kill those you led." His deep voice darkened even more. "These are my lands. None shall enter them except as I bid or allow."

"I have no quarrel with you," I said, my voice nowhere near as ominous as his, but the warning in my tone was just as clear. "So, I suggest that you sound that horn before I do."

Aesgyrn's countenance remained unreadable. "Why are you really here?" came his stoic reply.

I lifted my chin defiantly and held his glare, matching it with my own. "I told you. I'm just passing through. Those that I protect are doing so as well. Sound your horn and let us be on our way and the lands you claim will remain yours. Do anything other, and the few that remain to honor you may bury you beneath this nice tree."

Aesgyrn did not move, save for the small muscles in his jaw and in his broad neck. They clenched and released, pulsing with restrained fury. That same tension swept through all his warriors. I could hear their breath hissing through their teeth. The thrumming of their hearts beat like drums of war. The writhing runes on his sword and his crown began to glow, heated by hellfire from within.

I did not move either. I just stood there – on his ground. The slightest of curves edging the corner of my lips.

Are you that good? His dark eyes asked.

You're about to find out, mine replied back, a single eyebrow raising to taunt him. The Veil shimmered around us both, invisible to mortal senses save for the chill that was running through the veins of those that encircled us. Death's winds were beginning to howl. He, too, knew the Cusp. We soon would ride it together.

And then…

Aesgyrn laughed. No, it was much more than that. He threw back his head and bellowed uproariously. "Ha," he yelled, startling the warriors nearest, "a thousand demons have I slain! My sword is over-full from those feasts. Monsters fall and quake with fear at my very name; and, yet, here, a girl-child, barely even a waif, would dare my wrath!" His broad, toothy grin leaned my way. "You're either the damnedest fool I've ever met or the most dangerous foe I'll ever know." He leaned back and scratched his bearded chin, thinking. "What's your name, girl?" he asked.

"Lyri." My glare softened, but it did not fade.

A few of his men shot glances to each other. A few retreated a step. They'd heard my name before.

Aesgyrn's grin faded a bit, too. "Now, I understand," he said. "I guessed as much. Who else could you be, Little Death."

I jutted my chin towards the trumpeter. "The horn," I prompted.

Aesgryn smiled and nodded without turning from me and gestured with his free hand.

Three long blasts were sounded.

"Come," Aesgyrn said amicably, waving his massive paw in the direction from which he and his warriors had appeared. "One of us has just earned a little more time in this world. Let's share a fire and talk. I will send a herald to speak to your friends and ask them to join us."

I assented with a slight nod.

"You're not really Darkyr's daughter, are you?" the warlord asked as we began the stroll. Amusement and respect were playing in his voice.

"No," I confessed, "but we are related."

Aesgyrn let the question drop there. He dispatched the troll sentry to find Caedric and the rest of my band.

"Don't get lost," I quipped at him as he started away.

The troll paused, befuddled, then shook off the comment and raced on. I gave a little snort as he did.

Chapter 18: Shadow Pact

Aesgyrn's stronghold was grander than I had imagined. It wasn't palatial – I don't mean that – but it was formidable and built by skillful hands. At its center, there stood a stone and timber keep that, though not as elaborate as those of my own time, already bore the hallmarks of my people's steading halls. Heavy beams formed its pitched roof. The tails of its eaves were carven into draconic figures that looked out in all directions. A pair of great, arched doors, twice the warlord's height lead inside. Their surfaces were graved as well with frightful, entwining figures: dragons and fell-beasts. Torches blazed therein and a firepit ran most of the main room's length.

All around the hall, which dominated the highest hill, were three concentric palisades. Between these, the Aesdana had built their settlement. Closest in were the communal structures: smitheries, storehouses, tanneries, livestock yards, and the like. In the middle, homes and hovels grew like mushrooms. A thousand wisps of smoke rose from their cookfires and hearths. Farthest out was the widest ring. Therein were implements of war. Abatis, stone redoubts, timber towers, and trench lines spread throughout this maze of death. Gruesome totems marked the walls. The tattered corpses of their enemies dangled everywhere, their bones rattling and their remains shivering in the idle breeze. Too, there was powerful necromancy here. To cross this ring would mean overcoming far more than what the mortal eye could behold. The Veil was rifted, and hungry wraiths lurked in every shadow. Far worse than death awaited the Aesdana's foes.

Accompanying Aesgryn and his warriors, I wound my way through the labyrinth and climbed the high hill. Beyond the second palisade, I was met with another surprise. It was early, but was still night, yet there was no lack of activity about. Hundreds of people, all told, perhaps a thousand, many of them women and children of various races, greeted their king as he strode among them, calling out accolades as he passed. These he acknowledged with quick glances, nods or gestures. This laird, despite his fearsome mien, was well-loved and not the brutal tyrant that I had assumed. He, too, like me, had learned to marshal his demons and draw upon their power. To his kindred, he was more than just a king: He was their protector and their greatest champion. The young troll had not lied. He – and these gathered, I reckoned – would gladly have died for this man. Such was the depth of the fealty that he had earned.

"Gyrnvardír," Aesgyrn said, naming his hall proudly as we approached.

I studied the structure and nodded, acknowledging his acclaim.

With a vast entourage, we entered the steading hall's gilded and sculpted doors and stepped into the orange glow of the fires therein. At the far end, as was expected and proper, stood his dais and upon it his throne. Trophies: the weapons and armor of his enemies, much of it elven – surrounded the sovereign chair, mounted on the walls to create a grand, if grim, display.

"Come," Aesgyrn beckoned. "Sit near to me and take your fill of drink and food, Little Death. We will have time to talk more when your friends arrive."

"Unharmed," I added pointedly.

Aesgyrn grinned. "Unharmed," he agreed as he took his honored seat.

Soon, the hall was filled with raucous clamor. I wasn't really sure what they were celebrating. I was equally unsure that they needed a reason. The Aesdana seemed to enjoy bombast for its own sake. Voices were loud. Laughter came easy and often. And there was no lacking in food nor strong brew to add to the volume. There was so much of it, in fact, that even this great hall could not contain it, and it spilled out into the night air, surrounding the building and spreading to the bonfires that were built all about. Thick were the shadows and many were the demons that cavorted within the souls of Aesgyrn's people, and I – I sat among them, still and wary, quiet and watchful. I could feel the fiends' eyes upon me. My black fire was irresistible. It called to them, incensing their dark passions, drawing them to the fore. I could hear the hissing of their wicked thoughts. I was sitting in a room full of serpents.

Food was passed my way. It was a carnivore's feast. Impassively, I declined and let the seared haunches and fowl carcasses go by. Ale and mead, too, was offered in great abundance. I accepted a flagon of the latter and sipped of the bittersweet drink, letting it effervesce upon my tongue.

Within a couple of hours, a herald approached his king and whispered in his ear. My own discerned the report easily enough, despite the persistent roar of the revelers. Caedric and Meri, along with the *Einhervaldin*, had reached the bridge into Aesgyrn's demesne and had been hailed by his messenger, the troll. The encounter had been tense, but no blood had been spilled.

Aesgyrn cut a glance to me. I was already staring back. Casually, he raised his drinking horn and toasted me wordlessly. Promise kept. I returned the gesture with my oversized mug and nodded once, acknowledging, that I, also, had heard the report from my place beyond mortal earshot.

"So, tell us, Little Death," Aesgyrn boomed, hushing the rumbling crowd as all eyes and ears attended him. "What king do you serve? From where do you come?"

Always, that assumption: I must have a master to whom I bend my knee! Was it because I was a girl or a child? Maybe, in part, but probably more so because mighty warlords couldn't wrap their thick heads around the idea that I was no one's servant. For that matter, the gods hadn't seemed to figure that out either.

"No one," I answered, lifting my voice to be clearly heard. "I serve only myself. As for from whence do I come, I come from your tomorrows, where your future is my yesterday."

Aesgyrn scratched at his black beard, pondering. "Many here," he said, fanning his hand across the chamber, "served no one either. Their shackles had shattered when the lich-king was crushed. But, now, they serve me for all men need a strong leader and kinsmen with whom to stand when darkness comes. Alone is a dangerous place to be in this world of sorrows. To serve no one is an unnatural state."

I smiled coyly. "You're welcome to serve me, if you like."

Aesgyrn's expression flushed blank then quickly erupted with hall-shaking laughter. "Ha," he shouted, jumping to his feet, his horn sloshing, "that I may! That may we all!"

His explosion tore through the ranks of his people. In its wake, they joined him with their roar. Moderation was clearly not in their blood.

Aesgyrn's grin was broad; his eyes, wild as he seated himself once more. "My tomorrows are your yesterdays, you say." Tears of mirth tinged his eyes. "Then tell me, how drunk will I be by then?" Again, he burst with laughter, stoking it throughout the hall.

I didn't bother with a reply. I just smirked and shook my head, letting him have his fun.

At length, reclining in his throne, he looked back at me, his expression, a mixture of amusement and amazement. "By the gods, your mother must have been a wild-cat to birth one such as you!" he opined. "And you're father was a demon, no doubt. Such seed alone could have sired you. He must have been a king in hell, Little Death. If your past is my future, then, I'll be damned if I'm going to let this night pass me by without drowning your words in my cup. Here, now, I am lord. But if children are like you tomorrow, my crown won't stay mine for long."

"I don't want your crown, Aesgyrn," I replied. "Like I said, I'm just passing through."

The Aesdana king made no further comment. He just stroked his beard and mused, letting the hall's thunder return to fill the silence.

It was well after midnight when Caedric's band arrived and were escorted into Gyrnvardír.

Aesgyrn stood as they entered and greeted them, throwing his arms open wide and calling out, "Hail, Einhern! Son of Cordric! Dragon-master of the Asgevar! Welcome to my hall – one and all. Come. Sit. Join me at my fire. Let us burn away the past and drink to tomorrows that may come." He winked to me and grinned.

Caedric with his warriors, Merilanna at his side, surveyed the gathering and replied, "We are honored, Aesgyrn, Son of Rornar. King of the Aesdana. And accept your fire and your drink to warm us without and within. We thank you."

People shifted and places were opened for all to sit. Merilanna moved to my side, bringing with her a host of amorous eyes. I don't think a man in the room failed to watch her. Even the old, blind bull in the corner lifted his face her way, scenting the fragrance of her beauty.

Aesgyrn, too, grinned wolfishly and followed her steps. "We are deeply honored," he exhaled, his words for Caedric, though spoken towards the priestess.

Merilanna simply smiled politely and settled in beside me.

"Are you alright?" she whispered, knowing that I would hear even if her question was barely more than a thought.

I nodded in reply and flashed her a quick glance before returning my gaze to the enthroned lord.

Caedric took a seat cross-legged on a mat as was the typical custom across the firepit from me. His warriors split into two groups. Half sat beside their laird. Half sat next to Meri.

Quickly, more food and drink were brought. Everyone was tired, it seemed, but their appetites were not. When one round was done, Caedric turned his face towards Aesgyrn expectantly.

The cue was proper. Hospitality had been shown. Now it was time to talk.

Aesgyrn began and minced no words. "Warriors come to your lands unannounced and unbidden. What do you do, Einhern?"

Caedric finished drinking from his flagon, wiped his mouth upon his sleeve, and regarded our host. "No less than you have done," he answered.

"Good," Aesgyrn responded, his voice even, his expression unreadable. "We can speak in peace." His tone darkened. "Why are you here?"

"Our errand takes us to Tal Dalme," Caedric explained. There was no point in lying about it. Aesgyrn would not leave us unattended anyway. We wouldn't be allowed to go anywhere without his release. "There, we will see Merilanna and Lyri –" he nodded to us "– away through the spirit's door, returning them to their own lands."

"And their own time," Aesgyrn interrupted. "To where our tomorrows are their yesterdays."

Caedric paused and looked to me. I nodded and he said, "Yes."

"And why should I allow this, Einhern? The Circlestones are quiet. They have been so for many years. But I do not believe that the demons are gone. They wait and they watch, ready to invade our lands when the gateway opens. You guard a child of shadows, my brother. How may I be assured that she is not a harbinger of our doom? Shadows lift from this world, but their darkness lingers. What would you do?"

Caedric understood Aesgyrn's concern very well. He had already considered these questions. I could see that clearly in his countenance. No doubt, our furtive venture had been conceived precisely to avoid them. Nonetheless, Caedric was ready with his answer. "As you have," he stated evenly, "and as I trust you will do when the full tale is heard."

Aesgyrn accepted these words and gave his consent to hear more.

Caedric extended his hand across the firepit and Merilanna spoke. Her voice rolled with the ebb and flow of a master skald. She told of our meeting, mine and hers, of how it came to be, and of what had come to pass. She explained the twisted Threads and the snarl in the Tapestry of Creation that had occurred. She expressed her fears and conceded that the outcome remained unknown. But she held to her belief that unless the knot was untied, the Bright World would be rent apart. Such, she confessed, was the outcome her mistresses had foreseen as well and the reason for the urgency of our quest.

All this, Aesgyrn absorbed, his fist at his chin, his eyes affixed upon Ilé's priestess. At times, he posed questions, clarifying some detail or another. Ever, though, did he maintain his stoic expression.

"Our future – your future – depends on the steps we take now," Merilanna concluded.

"Will you help us?" Caedric asked, punctuating the matter.

Aesgyrn's hand left his chin and settled upon the arm of his throne, gripping it, knowing that his decision carried the authority his seat bestowed. "I will consider your words," he said evenly. "Tomorrow, when Xorcos' chair sits highest, you will know whether I will gamble with your past or our future. One or the other will weigh my decree. Until then, rest within my hall and be at peace."

With those words, the king of the Aesdana rose and took his leave. Few hours remained until dawn and his head was heavy with thoughts.

Many of the Aesdana, those that could still walk, at least, had departed during the night and returned to their homes. Those that remained were primarily the king's guards and retinue, including the young troll that I had tormented. I could see his red eyes watching me from the shadows. I guess he never considered that I could see into the darkness far better than others of my race could. Not that it mattered, his stupefied expression remained the same throughout the night.

Caedric moved over to where we sat after Aesgyrn left.

"What do you think?" Meri ventured. "Will he help us?"

"Hard to say," Caedric replied. "Aesgyrn is a survivor, but how real this danger may be to him is impossible to know. It's hard to imagine that something happening a thousand years from now could be more dangerous than opening a gateway behind which demons may wait here and now."

Merilanna drew a deep breath and exhaled it slowly, calm settling across her features. Rather than a mask, they remained warm. Alive. The stillness of the frozen north had lost its chill upon her flesh. What Caedric said made a lot of sense. In truth, she could not even argue the point. None of us knew for certain what the twist in time in the world from whence we came could mean – then or now.

I felt especially grumpy after all this – like I was locked in a cage. My options were limited. Certainly, I could defy Aesgyrn and go to Tal Dalme; but, without Merilanna, doing so was useless. Further, people were likely to die if I did that. Irrationally, I blamed the troll. If he had not been doing his job, we might have slipped through Aesgyrn's lands undetected. That, of course, was just my immaturity squawking.

If I actually told you half of the stupid things I think about doing, you would call me an impulsive halfwit at best. But, I'm telling this story, so I don't have to. Thus, you may continue to regard me as the amazing strategist that I am. Oh, wait, I already said I'm not that earlier. Oh, well…

I mentioned that I was grumpy which also meant that I was bored and restless. "I'm going outside for some fresh air," I announced. It was true. The steading hall was smoky and smelled like sour ale and sweaty leather.

"Don't go far," Merilanna's gaze beseeched, though she held her tongue.

I wasn't going to, but sometimes things change.

For instance, when you step outside in the middle of the night and you see the glow and smoke of something burning on the horizon in the direction from which you came, that's one of those moments when things change.

"Asgevan's under attack!" I shouted as I burst back into the steading hall, rousing even those in the deepest stupor.

I knew no one else could intervene. We were a day's travel north of the settlement. For me, Riding the Cusp, it would only take minutes. I was gone before Caedric and the others had even reached the great doors. But, though it would not please Merilanna how it happened, I didn't go far.

I slipped the Veil and had dashed only, by mortal measures, a few steps before the Aesdana's guardians surrounded me. The necromancy I had sensed in the outer circle of the palisade rings snared me like a fly. The Cusp had become a spider's web of Aesgyrn's spinning. My flight ended instantly. Nearly as quick, a host of specters, the fallen kinsmen of Aesgyrn's army, whipped towards me with spears and swords, axes and bows – all cast in the watery, blue illumination of Twilight. They gave me no quarter and the icy chill of death shot through my veins even before the first weapon struck. I almost had time to gasp, but not quite.

"Stop!"

Everything did. Then I blinked and realized that I was not yet frozen.

Whirling, contorted faces all around me, their expressions bloody and cruel, I pivoted to the one voice the ghosts all heeded.

"Meri," I finished my gasp.

The Death-Maiden stood in the open doorway of Aesgyrn's hall aglow with divine light, a wintry-white nimbus of pure power. Her outstretched hand held the wicked souls around me as if time itself had submitted to her. I was awestruck, but I didn't have the luxury to marvel.

"Go," the priestess commanded me. "Save them."

My eyes cut to the hungry specters. Left. Right. They did not advance. My gaping mouth slammed shut. My jaw set and my teeth gritted as my snarl returned. I gave Meri a determined nod, then I spun and vanished, swirling the shimmering ether as I took flight again.

Most of the way, the Twilight-lit forest surrounded me, a surreal blur that engulfed my passing. Only when I reached Asgevan's sentinel stone did my otherworldly speed abate. The magic that filled the menhir flared at my approach, limning me with a silvery radiance like moonlight shining on fresh snow. A moment later, I felt my feet upon the earth again and was running down the hunters' trail towards the village. The blue of the lands of the dead evaporated and the black and orange of this world's deadly night swallowed me. The screams of dying impaled my ears and drove pain deep into my heart.

The scene was as I expected. Homes were aflame. People were running for their lives. In their frenetic shadows, images of horror played out. Inhuman raiders roared with bloodlust and fury. Armored silhouettes slashed at everything that moved. Butchery was everywhere. I had seen these images before. I had lived them, and I had absorbed them into my soul, drowning in the blood. A thousand sins had I consumed in my short life. So many were just like this. The cruelty of war; it gave me no respite. It gripped me and twisted me apart, wringing from me any noble thoughts. All I could do was join the hellish scream and add my voice to the cacophony. I threw my fire into the flames and let it burn blacker than this pit of night had before.

Faster than thought, I added to the dying. The exhilaration devoured any light left in me. Soon, it was the wails of demons that overtook the struggle. The people – the Asgevar – staggered and stood, staring in shock as my rage raged and the slaughterers were slaughtered.

Panting like a mad beast, I stopped in the center of their burning world and dropped to one knee, leaning on Wind-Song to brace me lest I fall. My hair hung before my face like prison bars, thick with blood dripping. I was covered with it, a sanguine mantle that oozed across my skin: hot, burning, and foul. I could taste it with every pore. It hissed as my black fire seethed.

Through the blood-haze, I cut my glare, staring into the souls of the wide-eyed people watching me, their faces either aghast with horror or ashen with terror. I could see their sins, too. Few among them, the children only, were without such taint. The demons I had devoured, the demons that were still burning inside the hell to which I had cast them, cried out for their blood. They beseeched me to kill them all, to bring my fire to them also. The madness, the hunger, was almost too much.

I drove Wind-Song deeper into the earth, holding onto her, anchoring myself against the storm exploding inside of me. Wicked winds whipped me, driving my frenzy. I held on. Both hands now. My brow creased. My eyes slammed. My teeth ground to the point of shattering. I shook and trembled the earth.

"Kill them all!" the demons screeched.

Then, a hand touched me. My eyes flew wide. A small hand lay upon my gore-matted head. It was as if a thunderbolt had struck me, though there was no pain, there was no sound, no clap to deafen the world, no flash to blind it. All my fury flushed into the earth, drawn away from me as if all my fire had been doused. The dragon, Orömgundr, inhaled my black smoke and took it away.

"You're alright now," a little voice said, reaching through the darkness.

I lifted my trembling gaze and beheld a tiny, luminous hand. Delirious, exhausted, I reached for it and took hold. So small, but so immensely powerful.

Through the malaise, a smiling face materialized. Her bright eyes shined with kindness. As I met them, all my suffering dissolved and the world slipped back into focus. Other souls drifted my way. I let my gaze drift to them also. Wonderment looked back from all around.

I returned to the little girl still holding my hand. She just smiled innocently.

Slowly, unsteadily, I pushed myself to my feet and straightened by back, letting the last drops of my darkness fall to the earth. As I did, the people all around slowly knelt and bowed their heads. The only sound was the crackle of the fires. My eyes circled the scene and I inhaled, drawing in the cool night air with my next breath, soothing my seared soul.

"You're name is Lyri," I said down to the little girl.

"So is yours," she countered merrily with a giggle.

I nodded and, in that unguarded moment, I smiled back.

Her own dropped to a frown and her little, freckled nose crinkled as if she suddenly smelled something bad. "You need a bath," she chided with an all so maternal tone.

I snorted, fought it, then lost. All that remained of my grim demeanor was gone. I laughed. "I do," I managed through my tears. "I really do."

Looking about me, the Asgevar rose, stood and stared. Reflected in their eyes were the flames that still burned around us. The killing was over, but the healing had not yet begun. My release from darkness, though, gave promise that it could.

Shortly after noon, the thunder of hooves announced the arrival of Caedric, Aesgyrn, Merilanna, and a hundred warriors. I walked forward into the center of the village and looked up at them. The Einhervaldin gave no heed to me. They rushed passed to gather their loved ones into their arms. Many sorts of tears began to fall.

My gaze lit upon the king of the Aesdana. Grimly, he was surveying the destruction.

"Well," I prompted, bringing his eyes to mine. "It's past noon. What did you decide?"

Aesgyrn dismounted and stood towering above me. "Darkyr?"

I nodded. "He will send more," I said dryly.

Aesgyrn glanced back at Caedric and Merilanna as they moved to his side. "I am with you, Little Death. My future, your past: They are the same thread. Your fate is ours."

Merilanna and Caedric shared a solemn look.

"Then our pact is made," I said. "It's time that our people were joined. There's a Shadowlord out there that needs to feel our strength."

Chapter 19: Blood of Kings

"Raiders only," Caedric said to the warriors assembled upon the tor. Some nodded their agreeance.

"A probe then," Aesgyrn stated, echoing the growing consensus. "Light troops – fast and deadly – but nothing more."

"For the moment," Caedric concurred, his voice darkening, "but not for long."

"The coward waited until we were gone," Osvern, one of the Einhervaldin, a red-bearded veteran, noted contemptuously, his face filled with color and his green eyes flashing with hate.

"Yes," Caedric said, his tone held steady and reserved. "Which means he's been watching."

"Are you surprised, Einhern?" Aesgyrn asked. "What better time to strike than when your enemy's best fighters are away."

Caedric bowed his head and nodded, chewing on the obvious. "We were lucky," he said, lifting his gaze and sending it towards me, sitting on a knob of rock just outside the wall of warriors. I said nothing back. I was listening, but chose not to submerge in the irritating discourse. Instead, I was watching Merilanna and the people of Asgevan down below gathering the charred remains of their lives. "But we can't always be here," Caedric concluded.

"No," Aesgyrn agreed, "you cannot. And Darkyr knows this. Any general worth his name would. But, you see, he did not send an army in your absence. That has meaning."

"It means he's testing us, trying to draw us out – away from the dragon."

"Yes. 'Twould be my guess. He has not forgotten Orömgundr's fire."

"It wasn't Orömgundr's fire that broke him then and it's not what saved us now," Caedric noted.

The Aesdana's king nodded gravely and said, "No. But be sure: Darkyr saw that, also. He knows the earth-dragon sleeps."

Caedric exhaled his frustration. "The Shadowlord has been on the move since early spring. More troops flock to his banner every day. Villages have been attacked throughout the west. Those that did not bend their knees to him were burned, their people, killed or enslaved. He means to be the overlord of all these lands."

Aesgryn snorted, "What else can he do? Conquest is all he knows. He cannot return south. The demon-priests of Armadar had no love for the lich, our master. They would destroy him for his failure; and, with

Morzog gone, what other options does he have? He must claim these lands. He's fighting to survive."

"You sound like you admire him," Osvern growled and spat.

Aesgyrn faced the hot words and did not flinch. "No, but I do respect him," he said evenly, restraining his anger. "We all share the same blood."

"*Rial*," I scoffed from the periphery, drawn in once again to their tedious bickering. "The blood of kings: What good is it?" The circle opened my way and its warriors regarded me. I met their fierce eyes. "One day, you may become legends. One day, I may be born from your legacy. But those days will sure as shadows never come if you don't do today what is necessary!" I hopped from my rock and strode into their midst. I probably looked absurd: a child standing amongst giants, lecturing them. But I held their stares and not a one of them dared smirk. I was tired of their endless arguments. They had not ceased throughout the morning and now noon was upon us and we seemed no closer to settling these matters. Each man gathered here was a laird, a chieftain in his own right. Still, not one had stepped forth and dared to lead these people. Squabbling seemed their only skill. "One day, these lands may be called Einhervaldheim, but you've got to earn that honor. Darkyr is a monster! He is your enemy! If he reigns, the shadows will never lift, and your damned blood – my blood – will never be the blood of kings. It will forever be and remain the blood of the Destroyer, of fools, and of cowards. For your sake, for your people's sake, you cannot let that happen!"

Pride was stung. Egos were pierced. The huddle around me shifted uneasily and seethed. Blood was in their eyes. The demons that yet dwelled within their souls howled for mine. But none dared draw his blade, for each knew that I would feed its steel into his guts by the most direct of routes.

Finally, Caedric spoke. "Lyri's right," he said after the long pause, somehow still maintaining his tense but steady tone. "For ten years, all we've done is fight amongst ourselves. Our companies became our clans. We carved up the elven lands and made our claims, killing each other for patches of dirt. But we are all just pretenders here, sitting on fragile thrones."

"We swore never to wear chains again, to never bow to an overlord," Helroth, one of the eldest Einher said, his words dark and bearing a warning that all understood.

"Yes. We did," Caedric agreed firmly. "Every man here is a king and his clan is his kingdom. That is what we said. And that has not changed.

We are all brothers –" he looked to me and offered a thin smile "– and sisters born of war. Peace has not been easy for any of us. We have known too little of it; that is certain. But, for what little we have known, we have all fought, we have all bled, and, many of us, have died. In these ways, at least, we are united in blood as one people. If we are to remain free, that unity must endure."

"I will follow you, Caedric," Helroth assured. But then he cast his firm gaze to the king of the Aesdana and said, "But I will not follow a Dark Blade, a demon no better than the one we dare to challenge!"

That sentiment, that very vow, had coursed through the men atop this hill for hours. Not-so-old hatreds flared with the slightest spark. Aesgyrn's supporters called for the Asgevar to bow to the crown that adorned his head. Caedric's cried for the Aesdana to do the same for his. Neither side would yield. The day had already been very, very long, though but half of it had passed.

"If we do not unite," Caedric said, his voice low, his frustration threatening to overtake his composure once again, "we will all – one by one – return to those chains! We cannot undo what is past. But we can choose our future."

Aesgyrn folded his arms across his chest. "What say you, Little Death?" he asked, drawing from me my counsel. "Darkyr's army is very powerful. I'm not sure that, even if we rally every clan, we will be strong enough against his beasts, his demons, his host of restless fallen."

"We have to try!" Osvern growled through gritted teeth, his voice shaking once more with anger, threatening to re-spark the rancor that had been raging. "Every day that goes by, he grows stronger. We have to do something or all of us are dead!" He looked at me. "Or slaves."

"Let the girl choose," someone said.

"Yea," another voice concurred. "Of us all, only she has defeated him."

"Yes, let her decide," more called. "Let her choose the chieftain of war."

I felt my zeal waver as those words rose and gathered strength around me. I could feel their weight, heavy upon me. I also remembered well my encounter with Darkyr. It had not been as glorious or decisive as these people's myths had made it to be. Truth be told, had it not been for the *Naeryni*'s gift, the crystal vial of Aurium, my fall would have been certain. Darkyr had no problem swatting me away before I drank of that divine elixir.

"You said you were with me," I reminded Aesgyrn, reading his resolve, judging the demeanor of his warriors.

He nodded. "Here I am," he said simply, opening his arms as if to embrace whatever I might say next.

I scanned the faces of the Einhervaldin standing with Caedric. They were hard, expectant, but brave.

Again, I was the fulcrum, but this time I was weighing the fate of my ancestors and desperately trying to remember the sagas told of them. However the past might have been, all that changed at the moment Merilanna and I were cast back into the tangle of time. I had to decide what happened next not knowing what the ripples would upset. There would be no calling back the storm once it was unleashed.

According to our legends, it was Caedric Einhern who united our people and who led them from the darkness of the Shadowfall. Aesgyrn was remembered well and honored for his part also, but he was not our first High King. So, in a way, the choice was already made for me. I needed only to follow that which my past had decreed. Still, I struggled. Still, I had my doubts about them both.

In the old stories, it was Orömgundr that chose Caedric, bestowing upon him his might: his golden shield, his golden spear, his golden sword. Now, it seemed, it was given to me to play that part – a role I did not want, and I had no golden shield, no golden spear, no golden sword to give.

Changing what is by changing what was: that's thinking far beyond the limits of my simple mind. I had no patience for it. I just hoped that I hadn't messed things up already. In my recollections, there weren't any tales of Lyri, the Child of Shadows. Though, given my complicated history, maybe the skalds did have verses to sing about me, they just didn't know it yet. Or, maybe, I simply never heard them. The gods are a bit vague sometimes when it comes to the details of the lives they weave. Would there be some after today? I didn't really care. Would this jaunt into the past, no matter how it occurred, only add to the snarled skein. Probably. Remember, I'm not the optimistic sort. Slaying demons isn't cheery work.

"Caedric," I said with finality. "He will lead you. He will be your war-chief, the High King."

Expectedly, my terse decision wasn't well-like by half those assembled. The growls started instantly.

I ignored them and stepped in front of Aesgyrn. "Are you with me?" I asked again, my eyes burning into him.

It was clear that the king of the Aesdana would rather wear the figurative crown of all kings himself, but he kept his word. "I am," he declared and drew forth his eldritch sword, silencing all contemptuous voices. With a slow, steady motion, he turned to Caedric and offered the weapon, hilt first. "I and all those pledged to me are yours to wield in this, Einhern. Wield us well!"

Caedric stepped forward and took hold of the demon-sword. He thrust it up, its blade stabbing towards the heavens, and cried loudly, "Aesgyrn, King of the Aesdana, you will know glory; and, when peace is won at last, I will honor you and your people."

With that, all the warriors drew their blades and held them to the sky. I looked up from the center of their circle and glared at Xorcos on his throne. "So be it," I said.

Lowering the fell weapon, Caedric returned it to its master, hilt first as well. All drawn were then sheathed.

"Let us make ready," Caedric said. "I will speak with the dragon."

The circle dispersed, but I stayed on the tor, watching them go, each to their own. Only in the heat of battle would their metal be truly forged. There, were blood is molten, the dross would be burned away and a new people would emerge.

Merilanna climbed the hill, stopping to share a few words with Caedric as he made is way towards the entrance to Orömgundr's lair within the mound. "Well, that took long enough," she joked mildly.

"It's only a beginning," I replied mirthlessly, my frown affixed upon my face again. I eyed her, sighed, and added, "Not much changes with men. The lairds still argue in our time just as much. It's how the wolves find the strongest amongst them when the need is greatest."

Meri smiled at me, proudly. That look always presaged trouble. Apparently, she knew my thoughts and laughed. Then, tipping her head towards Caedric and Aesgyrn down below, she said, "I could have saved them a lot of time. I already knew who the strongest on this hill was, and it's not either of those two."

My color reddened just a touch.

"Don't worry," the priestess chuckled and promised, "I won't hug you. I remember how much you hate that."

I shrugged. "I don't hate it all the time."

Her smile brightened. "Just when you're growling, eh?"

"I'm always growling."

"Not always," she countered. "Come on. There's a lot to do."

Merilanna had started to turn, but stopped as I delayed.

"We may not make it back," I said, my voice no longer ringing of steel.

She looked at me gently. "We will, Lyri," she assured. "We'll do it together."

Reticently, I nodded, accepting her promise. Faith was not easy for me, even when given by a priestess.

Merilanna led and I followed down the hill. We entered the ruins of the village and were quickly lost in the preparations. Aesgyrn, along with the mightiest of the warriors – Asgevar and Aesdana side by side – were gathered again, discussing their plans. None, I noted, stood with their arms crossed in defiance. Maybe there was hope for this bunch. But, against Darkyr, it would take more than just an alliance to win. How much more or even what more, I didn't know. Something, though, was missing.

"Meri," I said, stopping abruptly on the path.

"Hmm?"

"Darkyr's power: It comes from his sword, from the demons held within."

She looked at me quizzically, but nodded.

I lifted my face to her, my thoughts still coalescing behind my eyes. "I think I know how to beat him."

Before she could ask, I dashed by her and raced after Caedric. He had already disappeared between the three great stones set into the hillside that marked the entrance to the dragon's nest. "Have your horn ready," I called back to her over my shoulder.

At first, she had started to follow, but reined where she was and watched me go, acknowledging my direction with a quick nod.

Reaching the trilithon, I paused for only an instant and looked upon the flowing water that followed the swale of stones that emerged from within. Even with my extraordinary senses, barely a sound lifted from its smooth, silvery course. I could feel the elemental's power moving through the earth. I could see the shimmer of magic gleaming in the spring's stream. A cool breath exhaled from the darkness of the hole. The air was pure, like that which follows a springtime rain.

I drew it in then dove between the standing stones and into the darkness after the Asgev hero.

By my time, the interior of the tor was filled with the buried bones of my kinsmen. A maze of tunnels had been dug and hundreds, perhaps thousands, were interred within, guarding and guarded by the dragon. Now, however, there was but a straight tunnel plunging into the depths. Elven script and elaborate symbols adorned the stone walls and arched ceiling. I didn't recognize them, but I knew that they were wards, magical words and signs that protected this holy place.

Admittedly, I didn't like being inside. The demons burning upon my soul hid their fires and left me nearly frozen. Nevertheless, I pushed deeper, padding alongside the steady stream until, at last, I emerged into a vast chamber.

At its center, water welled up from within the earth. A stone basin had been built around it, containing the pool. The fountainhead was here, beneath a vaulted sky of stone held aloft by stone arches. It glowed with a sublime, auric light that filled the chamber. A single spillway gave release to the blessed water.

At the basin's edge, Caedric stood, his back towards me, his head bowed prayerfully, his body divested of all carnal things. He was nude, his arms held forth, suppliant and obeisant.

Gods were something new to him, I supposed. A decade ago, only the dark deities, Mithcran, the Silent One, and Urrel, Lord of the Dead, were his to worship. Now, the host of the Aesyr reached for his heart and for the hearts of his people. Caedric, though, I knew, was here for another purpose. He had come to speak with the dragon.

From afar, I listened, waiting at the threshold.

"Hear me, o' great one. I call upon you, Orömgundr, Lord of the Earth," he was saying. "I am Caedric, Son of Cordric, called Einhern, the Chosen, and I beseech you and ask for your blessings. Soon, I will face the Shadowlord, Darkyr, and fight him to protect these lands just as you do. I pray that you will be with me, that you will make me strong so that I may defend my people from this demon's fire. Accept me now into your embrace, mighty Orömgundr. Gird me. Give me some sign of your favor. Purify me that I may do your will."

Those words said, Caedric waded into the water and submerged therein. As he did, I felt the Veil shiver. I watched as the darkness within his soul fled, rising like wisps of black smoke as he surrendered himself and was baptized. His demons shrieked as their fires were extinguished. Moments later, the man was gone and a demigod resurfaced clad in gold, bearing a shining spear, shield, and sword forged from auric light. A legend was born before my wondering eyes.

Stunned, having said nothing, I staggered a few steps, retreating into the darkness of the passageway before turning to race for the world beyond.

As I burst into the sunlight, Meri was waiting nearby. Her gentle mien told me that what I had seen, she had already beheld through visions her goddess had given.

"My horn is ready," she said, smiling.

I stared at her blankly. I had forgotten my own exhortation.

Before I could regather my composure, a powerful tremblor rolled through the earth, lifting every eye about the settlement and focusing them towards where we stood. All heeded Orömgundr's call.

"The dragon awakes," a woman's voice cried.

"A sign," someone else muttered.

Aesgyrn and the warriors broke from their planning and quickly joined the throng converging at the *Aesyriath Naedrom*.

Meri's attention lifted from me to look behind me. I could feel the elemental's presence drawing near and turned.

Light, like that of a new dawn, spilled from within the passage. Its glow ignited the flowing waters, paving the path down which the avatar of the dragon came. The sea of mumbling voices behind me fell silent as gasps of awe extinguished every idle word. Dawn broke as the golden knight stepped forth into the early afternoon sun. I shielded my eyes with my hand as did most others beholding the spectacle. A moment later, the glare eased and Caedric Einhern, his appearance befitting the sagas as they had been told to me, looked out upon us.

Briefly, another audacious knight crossed my mind: He, I called "Shiny Pants." The memory gave me back my smirk and restored my snarky disposition.

Caedric surveyed the assembled slowly before his gaze lit upon me where I stood in the vanguard.

I cocked my head to the side. "You look different," I mused wryly. "Did you bathe?"

The comment drew a broad grin from the mighty hero. He chuckled and shook his head, marveling. "I was hoping to look impressive," he quipped back to me warmly.

I shrugged. "It takes practice. I'm sure you'll get better at it."

Our jesting aside, Caedric strode forth and laid his hand on my shoulder. I turned to the gathered. Merilanna was in the fore, eyes proud upon the new risen king. The people spread alongside her, wide-eyed.

"Hear me, brothers and sisters, sons and daughters of destiny: We have risen from the darkest night, from the pit of despair. We have shattered our chains and thrown off the bonds of evil. Morzog is gone. Only Darkyr remains. The Shadowlord means to claim us, to blot out the sun and cast us again into slavery, but we will not go gently into that black abyss. We will not surrender. We will not bow or bend or break.

"I have entered the halls of the dragon. I have listened to his voice. I have heeded his counsel. And he has bestowed his favor upon me – not for my sake – but for all our sakes. Orömgundr is with us! His fire yet burns. It has purged from me the dross of selfish desire and made of me a servant-king. The light I bear, I bear for you. This day, we are forged together as one people, kinsmen all. Tomorrow, we march to where the sun sets and where darkness dwells. There, our enemies will know us and will learn again why it is they fear the shadows of the light!"

As one, Asgevar and Aesdana, fealty was roared. Shields were clapped. Steel rang.

My heart thundered inside me. It drove my voice forth and I joined my people's shout. Our storm was about to be unleashed.

Caedric marched into the masses and was well-received.

I stayed as I was and watched it all unfold. Meri came to me and shared my reflections, standing silent but resolute beside me.

"We know how this story ends," I said to her.

She nodded. "It's their glory now to claim."

"Is your horn ready?" I asked, the two of us, shoulder to shoulder – well my shoulder to her midriff anyway – watching the world spin into place as it should.

The priestess raised the instrument, cupped in both hands before her like an offering.

"There are thousands of lost souls in this world," I said. "No gods have claimed them. They served – willingly or not – the Silent One. Narianna is their purgatory. She is the sword that holds them. They wait to be wielded." I faced the Death-Maiden. "Do you understand what I'm saying?"

Meri met my gaze. Her eyes were bright with an odd hunger – a blizzard of blue fire. "Yes, I do. I haved longed deeply to guide them, but the Lady bade me wait." Her eyes turned and surveyed beyond the mortal into Twilight and all it held. "The wait is over."

"Good." I retook my place beside her. "I'll do the rest."

Two armies met on the banks of the Eidremere in the South Delving of the Silverwood Forest. One, its ranks filled with hateful creatures and wicked men, was led by a fiend crafted in the bowels of darkness by servants of shadows, priests of the Dark One. The other had risen from that past as well, but it was led by a champion suffused by divine light and joined by a people whose hearts had learned to glow, heroes all, anointed by the gods of the Palescia.

Meri and I fought alongside. It was, I will not lie, a bloody and terrible affair. The armies were not evenly matched – at least not at first.

Through the blood haze, I found Darkyr. I could hear the frenzied screams of his demons and moved to the sound. Around him, the hewn corpses of dozens lay, cut down like grain by the scything of his sword.

Heroes of the Third Age: Merilanna

As before, his countenance was cold, his expression frozen with contempt.

"Shadowlord!" I shouted above the din. There was really no reason to. He felt my presence as well and was already turning to face me. Our eyes locked across the battlefield, the field of slaughter.

Darkyr raised his blade. It was a salute. We had met before and he remember what it had cost him. Nevertheless, though sincere, his moment of tribute was brief. He moved into motion in the instant thereafter and stomped my way. The space between us parted like some red sea. I glared through the bars of my blood-drenched hair and watched him come, my little Wind-Song gripped tightly.

Demons ignited the air around him and formed a blazing inferno of shadows, a dark nimbus that hungered to claim me. Tenebrous tendrils stretched out ahead of him. They reached across the span and began to swirl into my aura. I welcomed them. I did not fight back. I opened my soul wide and engulfed every black essence. I fought back the rage. I restrained my fire, keeping it in check though more and more fuel flowed into me. I strained to compose.

Hold on...not yet...

My breathing became chuffs of desperation and dark ecstasy. My eyelids fluttered. My teeth ground.

Wait...almost there...

Darkyr charged; but, a wary foe, he sensed my strange resolve. By then, it was too late. The demons within him, within his sword were already committed. He was caught in their storm and swept into the outflow. He could not withhold his fury. His stroke was upon me, and I was beyond all salvation...almost.

"Now!" I cried.

The horn sounded even as I shouted.

Darkyr's eyes narrowed then flew wide.

Ten thousand souls – more – exploded into the struggle, answering a call they had held no hope of ever hearing. In that clarion instant, all those that had died in the service of darkness were given the offer of deliverance, a path to redemption, a chance to know some heaven rather than the endless hell they had known. Ilé's priestess opened the doorway to Urrel's Hall upon that battlefield and sang to the dead. As the notes filled the air, the stormwinds changed and the Shadowlord's grip on his power was ripped away. The souls he had enslaved were given absolution and liberty.

Darkyr's momentum ended. He stopped, stunned, and watched as his storm becalmed. Confusion, even terror, alit in his eyes. He looked back at me, his dark fire gone, and beheld his doom for, in that instant, as the shadows around me swarmed, drawn out by Ilé's horn, and now drawn away by Meri's divinely voice, I ignited my snarl and flew like a dragon falling from heaven, my scream, my fury, unimaginable.

The hell-sword was cast into the sky as I struck. It tumbled towards the stars as I sent the monster that had wielded it careening backwards to skid through the bloody mud.

I stood where he had advanced, ablaze with screeching demons, and brought my little blade in front of my fury-filled face. Darkyr's blood ran down her length, across her hilt, and over my hands. *That* was my salute to him.

Between us, the dark blade fell, piercing the earth and trembling where it stood.

This day, this dark night, was ours.

Through the melee, I found Meri's eyes. She was not smiling. Her lips were a thin line, chiseled with defiance and determination. She gave me a firm and resolute nod.

It was done.

As Darkyr fell, his hold upon the souls of his minions was severed. A shockwave shot through them, jarring them, and flinging them free from his dominion. The chaos of battle shifted instantly and the rout began. Caedric and Aesgyrn led the charge and earned their places in history.

I moved to stand above my nemesis. His blood – my blood – covered the muddy ground. Like me, he was cursed with immortality. His body, now broken, would soon heal and he would rise once again. Or so it had been.

But, this time, as I closed my eyes and let my senses slip beyond the Cusp, I knew that his resurrection would be forestalled. Within Twilight, the souls of the Asgevar surrounded him, the phantom spears and blades encircling him as if he were a dire boar. I could see his rage and his desperation.

Darkyr glared at his captors; he glared then at me. The coldness of his visage was gone, replaced by fury and hate and…fear.

The ghosts of the Einhervaldin surged upon their former master. They stabbed and they hacked at his damned soul. A cacophony of screams accompanied them as they drove him into the Oblivion of the Etherstorm.

I watched Darkyr's doom through impassive eyes. I knew his fate; and, if the future proved true, I knew also that the Bright World had not seen the last of him.

Heroes of the Third Age: Merilanna

With a deep breath, I closed my eyes and returned my gaze to the mortal world. I looked to find Meri and froze with horror. A jagged spear impaled her from behind, its terrible blade ripping through the front of her priestly robe, instantly bathing her in her own red blood. The expression of shock that seized her beauty was ghastly. Her eyes flew wide; her lips trembled.

"Meri!" I screamed and hurled myself towards her attacker, a brutish giant, a growling grym-folk.

The ogre died, barely tasting his revenge for his dark master's doom. I hacked off his burly arms and skewered his brain through the jowls. I drew my sword and split a line from there down his chest and fat, bulging belly, spilling his guts at my feet.

But Merilanna, my friend, still fell.

I rushed to her and cradled her head in my lap as she had done for me so often. I stared at the cruel spear, helpless to give life for all I knew was how to take it.

"Caedric!" I cried, my voice cracking and feeble within the roar of the fighting. Somehow, he heard and found us, dropping beside us in the blood and in the mud.

"Merilanna – oh god," Caedric said, his mighty hands shaking, not knowing what to do, but knowing there was nothing he could do all the same.

Meri coughed blood, but she found the strength to do what did not seem possible: she tried to comfort us. "It's alright. It's…it's only a day, same as any other day," she said, lifting her hand to touch my face gently, wiping away my tears. To Caedric, her eyes drifted, fluttering as her life flowed into the earth. "I love you."

Caedric laced his fingers with hers and kissed her. "And I you."

I was shaking. *It's not supposed to be like this. Damn all the gods! It's not supposed to be like this!*

Slowly, Merilanna lifted her horn and put it in my blood-drenched hand. "Power always comes at a cost," she whispered. Her eyes were dimming.

"This was a good life. I wonder if I'll get to keep any of it." A rattling breath. Her eyes sharpened for a moment more, her mouth straining for a weak smile. "Don't worry; death is not forever." Then, Ilé's maiden was gone.

"No," I cried. "No, no, no…please, no."

Caedric pulled me to him and let my screams hammer into his heart. He held Meri also, and the three of us were alone though the fighting still raged all around.

Chapter 20: Destiny

I don't remember very much in the days that followed the battle in the Greymere. My heart and mind were numb. I do know that Darkyr's minions were vanquished, but not before they stole his black sword from the victory. It would languish for a millennium, hidden beneath the ruins of one of Asteranoth's keeps, there to be found in a new age, hidden in the shadows of the past, by a creature of darkness that would ascend into the light and walk by my side. I barely recalled the pyre that gave Merilanna's body to the winds. So many had died, their smoke filled the Silverwood with their spirits.

Caedric, the Einhervaldin, Aesgyrn, and the Aesdana, accompanied me to Tal Dalme a few days later. Our goodbyes were bittersweet and filled with melancholy.

"Peace to you, Lyri," Caedric said. Then he and all those with him, bowed on bended knees.

For their sakes, I tried to smile. I'm sure it was a grimace, but they knew my appreciation was sincere.

I turned and was looking back to where I had begun. The circle of stones waited. I could feel, subtly, its power moving, sensing my footsteps as I passed through its mighty rocks. At the center, I paused and, one last time, gazed out upon the faces of my ancestors. Though the pain of loss was still there – it always would be – I felt something else: a pride that now bore more meaning than I ever could have conceived.

I lifted my hand and waved once, acknowledging my gratitude.

"It's time to go home," I said to the wind. From my side, I raised Meri's horn, the Horn of Destiny, put it to my lips, and blew a clarion note that surpassed all veils. Light spiraled and the gate opened. A cold breeze, like that which carries winter's kiss before the snow falls, blew through my hair. Into the whiteness, I stepped.

Through time and through space, I was carried by the whirling helix of starshine until the auroras faded and my eyes revealed the world from which I had come save for two particulars of meritorious note.

First, it was snowing. The circle and the forest were blanked in pure splendor. This is how it should have been, I reflected, when I crossed the river at the beginning. The season was Ilé's. The goddess had laid her claim to the world.

Second, and most blessedly, a voice that I cherished was singing in the wind that swirled gently around me. My heart leapt as, reflexively, my hand slipped to my hip where a horn had hung, but the instrument was gone, returned, as well, to the place from which it had come.

I exhaled its keeper's name, "Meri."

My dreaming mind filled my waking, and I stood there – I know not how long – and listened to the priestess' song. I closed my eyes and imagined her standing before the great crystal, the Tear Stone at Kyrileshar, lifting her voice into the wintry wind. It was that memory that had brought me to this place and wound about me a new destiny.

"Lyri!"

I blinked through my reverie and scanned the forest, looking for the caller whose voice I knew so well.

"Fhaed?" I called, still beguiled by my waking dream.

"Where are you?" came the afterword.

"Here!"

And then I saw him, trudging through the snow, a torch held into the wind to cast its dancing light upon the trail he followed. Its glow lit his golden eyes as they found me, standing in the center of the Circlestone, a faint sapphirine nimbus shimmering around me in the darkness. I realized it was night as an afterthought.

The Armadeshi grinned widely and waved back to the men coming after. "She's here," he yelled. "She's safe."

"Lord Chael's found her," another voice, Sir Iaom's I had no doubt, relayed the demon-hunter's words.

"Where have you been?" Fhaed asked, relief edged with a bit of chiding riding his question. "We've been searching for you for two days."

"Two days," I mused under my breath. "What took you so long?" I yipped back. It was then that I realized that Meri's song had faded, carried away by the breeze.

Fhaed noticed my distraction. "Are you alright? What are you doing in there?" His eyebrow lifted and his grin became wry with bemusement. "Were you singing?"

I looked back at him and scowled. "I don't sing," I grumbled.

"Well, I'm sure I heard someone." He looked about the area, a roguish twinkle in his shining eyes. He started to tease me some more, but his scan caught upon a detail that perplexed him. "How long have you been standing there?"

Drawn by the question, I studied my setting and grasped the cause for it. Several inches of new snow blanketed everything. There were no footprints leading to me. It seemed that I had been frozen in this place long enough for Ilé to cover my trail; though, as I remembered, it had been the summer season when I had entered the circle. Of course, as I also remembered, it had been mid-winter when I crossed the Aesdana River and had entered into this strange twist of time.

Looking down, my feet were buried in a white drift and my dark gear – that which I had worn the night of my crossing – was sprinkled with snow. "For ages," I answered back, leaving the irony of it in my voice to befuddle him all the more.

"There you are," Sir Iaom called, joining Fhaed at the perimeter of the holy ground. His cohort emerged from the forest behind him. The Galeonian greeted me with a happy grin as well.

I returned it – well, a smirk anyway.

"We feared some demon had claimed you when you did not return two 'morrows ago," Iaom explained.

Guardedly, I tested my legs and lifted one foot then the other. The snow released its hold without undue effort. "I'm fine," I called back, reiterating my claim.

"The Dyards are beaten. We'll finish them in the moors by spring," Fhaed said. "For now, they've broken to the east again and will try to lose us in the foothills before turning south."

My neck itched. I scratched at it and felt a tug on the rough edge of my nail. A pale braid of silver white looped around my finger.

"South?"

Fhaed's expression and his tone became concerned. "Are you sure you're alright? Do I need to come in there and get you?"

"What? No. I'm fine." I hesitated, my thoughts flying away like a flock of birds roiled by a pouncing cat. Suddenly, my focus reset. "I'm going north."

Fhaed's arms folded across his broad chest. "North?" he chirped, cutting a curious glance to the knight beside him.

"Yes," I answered, beginning my trudge towards the circle's edge. As I reached my companions, I paused and looked up at them and added, "I'm going to see a friend." Then I continued past with no further explanation.

Behind me, I heard Fhaed and Iaom turn together then, "What friend?" they called in unison after me. I grinned mischievously to myself but kept walking for a few more paces before shouting towards the path ahead, "Someone I haven't seen in a very long time."

A few more steps and, "What about the Dyards?" Iaom asked.

I waved my hand dismissing the matter. "Chase the cowards, if you want. I've had enough of them."

"What friend?" Fhaed sued again.

I stopped, turned, and regarded him. I'm sure my grin caught him off-guard. "Someone beautiful," I said. That answer astonished him even more. Fully baited, my hook dangled. "Are you coming?"

The two men shared a brief unspoken counsel before the Galeonian said, "Go ahead. She's right. We can handle the Dyards from here."

"You're sure?"

Sir Iaom looked to the east where the predawn was beginning to brighten the sky with a suffused glow through the wintry clouds. He nodded. "Brighter days are coming. I'm sure."

Fhaed smiled and clasped the knight's arm. "Take care," he said then marched to me.

I waved goodbye to Sir Iaom and turned in step with my long-striding companion. I grinned up at him when, not a few steps more, he bit my hook, "Tell me more about this beautiful friend of yours."

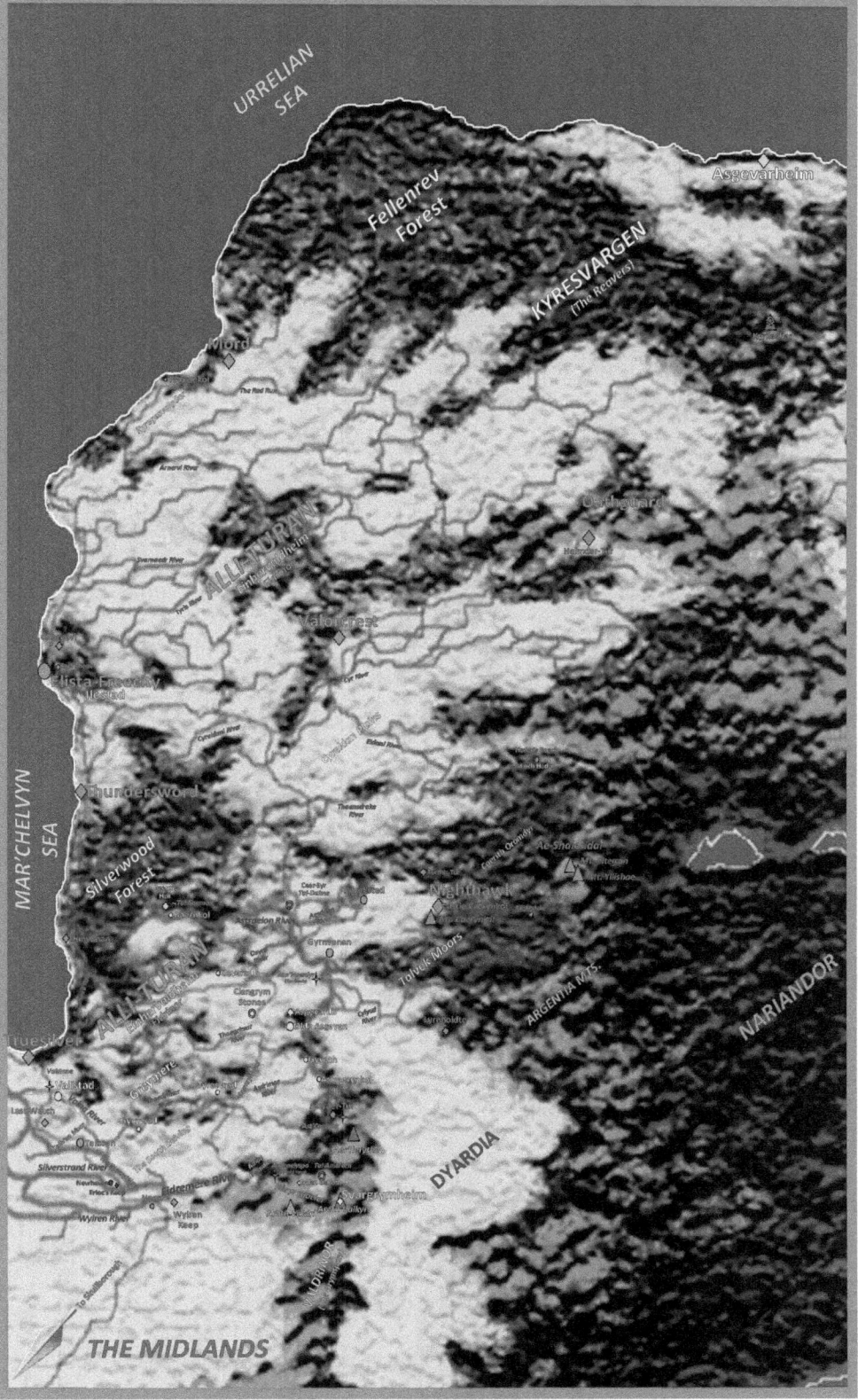

ABOUT THE AUTHOR

Born in 1967 in the quaint, southern town of Social Circle, Georgia, Shane Alford spent his childhood embarking on one imaginary adventure after another. A graduate of Young Harris College and LaGrange College, he holds a Bachelor of Arts degree in Religion.

Currently, Shane resides with his wife, Cheri, their two children, Brendan and Kara, along with a lovable dog, two devilish cats, and one flamboyant box turtle in Columbia, South Carolina. He has two daughters, Chelsea and Alexandra, from a previous marriage.

When not typing some daydream into his laptop, Shane spends his time developing real estate.

The adventure continues with…

Shadows of the Past
The Waystone Saga: Book One

Dawn of Shadows
The Waystone Saga: Book Two

Lightbringer
The Waystone Saga: Book Three

Child of Shadows
Heroes of the Third Age: Lyri

www.mysticmerlins.com
www.worldofnarianna.com